THE WAR WAS OVER...

Rhineman looked up. A man had come in the door, a tall, powerfully-built man. He held a thin cheroot between his front teeth and a thin curl of smoke rose from the tip of it. Memories of officers Rhineman had seen years before in Germany stirred in his mind—the rarely seen but well-remembered elite Prussians. The mustache was thick and black, and the tan cheeks were smoothly shaven, with a silvery line of a scar from the right cheekbone to the point of the jaw. Everything indicated an overweening pride, pride which passed over the line of pride into arrogance.

It came as a shock to Rhineman when he suddenly realized he was looking at his son Karl.

RENDER UNTO CAESAR

Nancy Fairweather

LEISURE BOOKS • NEW YORK CITY

A LEISURE BOOK

Published by

Nordon Publications, Inc.
Two Park Avenue
New York, N.Y. 10016

Chapter 1

The trail was a narrow tunnel through the thick foliage, a path made by deer and bear which had been widened and turned into a shallow gulley by years of spring runoff from the thawing of snow on the lofty peaks above. Rhineman walked along it at a steady pace which rationed his energy for the remaining hours of daylight. His eyes searched a few yards ahead for the best footholds to avoid stumbling under the heavy pack and to prevent undue wear on his boots. The trail curved, then it widened and the foliage on each side began to thin out. Rhineman lifted the musket as he began walking more slowly, and peered cautiously ahead. The five mules plodding along behind him bunched up as he changed his pace, their hoofs clattering against the stones as they broke their steady rhythm; then they spread out again to the length of the ropes between the heavily-laden pack saddles and the bridles. The dense scrub oak and stunted pine on each side of the trail thinned out into wiry brush, and the trail opened out onto a slope covered with long, sun-dried grass and clumps of brush. The gleaming blue ribbon of the Rio Grande stretched out at the foot of the slope. Rhineman stopped at the edge of the foliage, his eyes moving over the slope and toward the open slope on the other side of the river. The mules bunched up again as they stopped.

It was a dangerous place. The previous spring, when he'd had only two mules, he had almost lost one while crossing the river during the spring flood. But a more immediate and deadly danger lay in his memory. He had almost been ambushed while crossing the river on his last trip. It had been a white man, but there were also hostile Indians in the area. His eyes moved slowly over the slope, searching every shadow and clump of brush as he fingered the hammer on the musket. The straps on the pack bit into his shoulders, and the mules behind him moved restively, edging to the side of the trail to nibble at clumps of grass. He finished scanning the slope below him, then began methodically searching the slope on the other side of the river, his eyes moving from one clump of brush to the next.

Several minutes passed, and the mules hung their heads and cocked a hoof on edge as they rested as well as they could under the heavy packs. There were jays flying about on the other slope, and there were stealthy movements in the long grass which weren't made by the breeze. The jays would be shrieking in alarm if there was any activity or anyone else in the vicinity, and the rabbits and other small animals wouldn't be moving about so freely if there had been any disturbance within the past hour. Until the year before, he hadn't seen a jay and the only rabbits he had seen had been hanging in a butcher

6

shop. But he had a lifetime of practice in searching for everything around him which might represent a defense or a warning of danger, so he had quickly found out about the rowdy jays and the timidity of small animals.

He tugged on the rope tied to the bridle on the first mule as he stepped out of the foliage and started down the slope; the mules began plodding along behind him. His boots crushed the grass down solidly as he walked through it. Because he was a large man, he walked easily under the heavy bale of compacted wool on his back. He wore a dark, baggy wool suit with the vest and coat buttoned and the trousers stuffed down into the tops of his high boots, and a wrinkled, collarless linen shirt of a nondescript grey color. His hat was a black felt with a wide, flat brim and a low, round crown, and his mustache and beard were matted together into a thick, black bush which was flecked with grey and hung far down his chest.

The slopes on each side of the river were its spring floodplain, and the deep grass concealed stumps and logs which had been washed down from upstream. He picked his way down the slope, leading the mules around obstacles, but still searching the slopes with his eyes. The mules saw and smelled the water, and they began crowding together and trying to push around him. He held them back and snapped the end of the rope to drive them back into line. As he neared the river, the jays swooped down from the other slope to circle over him as they uttered their penetrating cries. The water had receded until it was a shallow band a few yards across between wide stretches of sand and rocks. He stopped the mules at the edge of the bank and looked at the sand bar. Among other dangers, there were spots of quicksand along the river, and rattlesnakes frequently basked in the sun on sand bars. He scanned it, then stepped over the

7

edge of the bank and dug in his heels, sliding down it. The mules slid down it behind him and followed him across the sand bar, their hoofs thudding in the sand and clattering on the stretches of smooth, flat stones.

The third mule in the line carried two wicker crates of live chickens, tied to the three bales of wool on the packsaddle, and the fourth one had four sheep which were trussed and tied to the packsaddle. Rhineman looked around at the slopes once more as he put his musket down and slipped the pack off his back. He untied the crates of chickens, put them in the edge of the water so they could drink, and untied the sheep and lifted them down. The mules dipped their muzzles into the water, drank deeply, then lifted their heads with water streaming from their lips as they belched hollowly. They licked their lips noisily, lowered their noses into the water, and drank again. Rhineman made sure all the chickens and sheep drank their fill, then he tied the crates and sheep back on the mules and drank himself.

The river crossing was a danger spot, but it was also near the end of his journey. The trek began in Santa Fe, where he left with packs of trade goods and went north to Taos, west to Tierra Amarilla, south to Jemez, then across the Rio Grande near Santo Domingo before turning north to return to Santa Fe. It took an average of a month to make the circuit, and he traded with trappers, miners, and isolated sheep ranchers and farmers. The trappers and miners traded gold dust and furs for foodstuffs, whiskey, gunpowder and shot, tobacco, salt, and other necessities. The sheep ranchers and farmers traded hand woven rugs, handmade jewelry, wool, livestock, and foodstuffs for whiskey, beads, mirrors, needles, patent medicines, bolts of bright cloth, and other sundries. Before he had come, they had done without and stretched their supplies to last between their infrequent trips to a settlement. During the past months, they had come to depend upon him to provide what they needed between their trips to trading posts. The trek through the wilderness was arduous and dangerous, but each trip produced a substantial profit which was multiplied even while the trek was in progress because the miners and trappers traded with him for the foodstuffs he obtained from ranchers and farmers only a few miles away.

The jays continued screeching as they flew up and down the slope and circled overhead. The mules finished drinking and rested, hanging their heads and cocking a foot on edge as the swift water swirled around their legs. Rhineman hoisted the pack onto his back, settled it, then picked up his musket and tugged on the rope on the lead mule. The mules lifted their heads and followed him up the bank, planting their feet solidly and struggling up the steep incline as their packs swayed from side to side.

The trail began again at the edge of the foliage at the top of the slope, a narrow, rocky gulley with walls of thick growth on each side. It gave a feeling of isolation and protection, and Rhineman's caution relaxed from its feverish pitch to his usual state of wary alertness. The sound of the jays faded behind him, and there was only the hoofbeats of the mules, the squeak of the packsaddles and panniers, an occasional squawk and flutter of a chicken in the crates, and an infrequent bleat of protest from one of the sheep. The chickens and sheep had been noisy for the first couple of days, as they usually were. It had been irritating and dangerous to a degree, announcing his presence over a much wider range than the noises made by the mules. But it was a danger he accepted, because it was temporary and there was up to a thousand percent profit between the value given and received for them. And after two or three days their noises diminished and then stopped when they became inured to their hardship. Just as his shoulders always ached from the pack for the first two or three days of a trek and then became numb.

The trail continued upward, a tiny line stretching up the massive bulk of the towering mountains which spread for a vast distance in all directions. The trees on each side of the trail gradually became taller, their branches spreading across the trail and forming a shady roof through which the bright sunlight filtered as a dim, green twilight. It was broken by occasional dappled spots of brilliance where the searching, penetrating rays pierced through openings in the foliage and shone on the filmy shadows of hovering clouds of gnats dancing in delirious ecstasy at having found light in the dark forest. The mules began panting hoarsely with the effort of the climb in the thin, high air, and sweat began beading Rhineman's forehead and temples and running down to form shiny streaks in his mustache and beard as his breathing became more labored. He continued on at the same pace, putting one foot in front of the other, his mind removed from the weight of the heavy bale of wool on his back.

There was a wide spot in the trail where a narrow, dim path turned off to the right between two stumps of large trees which had been hacked down. He turned onto the path and the mules followed him, their panniers and packs brushing against the foliage on each side. The foliage thinned out and the sunlight broke through in blinding, sudden intensity as the path went around the base of a bulging outcropping of rock. The excited barking of a dog became audible over the sounds made by the mules following him, then the barking was drowned in the rushing babble of water as the path crossed a small stream. The mules hesitated and started to take a drink, but Rhineman tugged on the rope and pulled them on as he splashed through the water. The path curved upward on the other side of the water, becoming precipitous as it wound between the massive, greyish boulders studded with pebbles. The barking of the dog became audible again, a louder, frantic yammer.

A gnarled, stunted pine at the edge of the plateau above moved slightly, then a man stepped into view. He was a tall, bearded man in a dark hat, baggy trousers, and the stained, worn top of long underwear for a shirt. He was holding a musket, ready to shoulder it. He lowered the musket as he looked down the path at Rhineman, then he turned and shouted.

"Hank!"

"Who is it?" another man's voice replied faintly.

"It's the Jew!"

The man stepped back out of sight. Rhineman slowed slightly as he went around another curve between two large boulders, allowing some slack in the ropes between the mules so they wouldn't scrape their packs and panniers against the boulders on the tight turn. He glanced back and resumed his usual pace as the last mule came around the turn. The man's tone had been casually disparaging, telegraphing an attitude which was nonchalantly insulting, but which lacked the focus and intensity of the prejudice Rhineman had known in Germany. New Mexico Territory was a frontier and the unsettled conditions produced a certain tolerance between its people. The Mexicans had origins in those who had conducted the Inquisition, but they were meek and unsure of themselves in the presence of the influx from the United States since the acquisition of the Territory, and the wilderness was far removed from Madrid in both distance and attitudes. The Indians judged everyone solely on the basis of what they might possess of value and how their scalp would look dangling from a lodge pole. The white people retained remnants of protocols and attitudes from other places, but for the most part a man was judged on the basis of what was needed from him—how well he might be able to use a knife or gun, and how much weight he could put behind a fist.

It was more than he had expected. In Germany, others had told him that there was opportunity and freedom in the United States, and letters from his father-in-law in South Carolina had been outpourings of such things. And to his surprise, he had found it to be true. In the face of a lifetime of experience with prejudice and the expectation of nothing less, he had found it largely absent here. There had been none of the physical threats which had always seemed to hang just beyond the grasp of perception in Germany; a feeling of impending disaster hovering like the sultry atmosphere preceding a storm; the constant intimidation which had been generated by the whispers among elders about past pogroms and by the beatings when he was a child; the constant apprehension which was fueled by the glares on the street and the occasional shout, shaken fist, or stone clattering across the cobblestones and smacking into a wall near him as he hurried along the street.

There had been derogatory comments directed at him in the New Mexico Territory, but in at least most instances they hadn't seemed markedly different in character from the insults the gentiles hurled at each other in respect to their bewildering multiplicity of religions. The people on his circuit were always pleased to see him, even though the way some of them chose to express pleasure took different forms. His strong German accent and his difficulty in understanding English accented with Spanish made communication difficult with the farmers and ranchers. He was by nature a man of few words, but the farmers and ranchers were eager to gather up what they had to trade and pore over his goods. His brevity in speech was an advantage with many solitary trappers and miners, who were either terse in conversation themselves or were those who accumulated a store of talk to spill out in a steady stream upon the first human ears which came by. He carried plenty of whiskey, which was always in demand, and he broke the deadly monotony of their days by a contact with the outside world. Many of them were illiterate, but he had found that they all liked newspapers, so he always carried a bundle of outdated newspapers from St. Louis, Chicago, and New York and left a couple or three pages of them at each stop. Those who could read did, and those who couldn't looked at the woodcuts and fingered the tattered, yellowed pages which evidenced that the outside world still functioned. Presumably all of them used the newspapers for toilet paper after their intellectual or psychic needs had been satisfied.

The hatred directed at him from childhood had caused thick and sturdy walls of defense to be erected, and it was difficult to perceive nuances of feeling and reaction through those walls. But the months of traveling the circuit had occasioned more of a personal contact with people at large than had his previous forty-six years of life, and it had been an education of sorts. One old miner had broken into tears of despair because Rhineman had once run out of coffee before reaching him, which seemed strangely exaggerated and irrational behavior to Rhineman. But after that he had always made sure he would have coffee for the old man even though it was a poor business practice to transport goods any further than

13

necessary. One miner had injured himself with an axe and died between two trips, and on one trip a trapper had announced his intention of moving further west to the Sierra Nevada. On both occasions, Rhineman had felt a loss and sense of depression. It had nothing to do with the loss of potential profits, because he was accomodating the maximum number of people he could. Finding other customers was simply a matter of searching among the side trails branching off the trail he used, which he had done as his string of mules had grown and which he would do again when he had a few more mules. It seemed that at some deep, remote level within him, meeting the people and providing for their needs was beginning to satisfy some urge within him as much as his presence fulfilled them in areas which had nothing to do with their physical sustenance.

The path went between a couple of scrubby, wind-blasted pines, then opened onto a rocky plateau which had been scoured free of soil and vegetation by the winter winds which tore through the high mountain passes. The mountain loomed above the plateau, looking even more ponderously towering and somehow threatening from the unobstructed view on the plateau, its peak capped with snow and enshrouded in a filmy, fleecy cloud. On the far end of the plateau there was a rude cabin built of logs and sod and roofed with thin, flat slabs of rock. A couple of thin mules stood with their heads drooping in a small corral built of spindly poles by the cabin. A few yards to the left of the cabin, the brook Rhineman had crossed at the base of the rock outcropping gushed down a shallow arroyo which cut into the mountain at the side of the plateau and continued far up the mountain. The walls of the arroyo were spotted with dark holes with raw gashes of turned earth below them, and there were broken remains of several sluice boxes in the stream of water. The stream had been freshly dammed and a new sluice box had been placed in it somewhat above the rest of the holes, and there was a fresh hole with a long streak of earth tailing below it on the edge of the arroyo above the new box. The other miner was coming out of the hole, and the one who had looked down the path at Rhineman was tying the dog at the corner of the cabin.

The mules were panting breathlessly from the steep climb, and their steps were weak and faltering as they crossed the rock and shale toward the cabin. Rhineman breathed deeply, sweat streaming down his forehead and temples into his beard. The wool suit coat and vest felt uncomfortably hot in the direct sunlight on the plateau. The man finished tying the dog and walked to a crude bench made of a split log which was propped against the front of the cabin adjacent to the sagging door. He sat down, grinning at Rhineman as he crossed the plateau with the mules. The other man walked toward the cabin with long strides, dropped a shovel at the corner of the cabin, and sat down on the bench, also grinning. They were both large men, in their late twenties or early thirties, their baggy trousers heavy with mud tucked into their boots, their winter underwear tops stained with mud and sweat, and their sleeves pulled above their brawny forearms. There was a vicious edge to their grins. Their dog and mules were terrified of them. On one of his trips, there had been a couple of fire-blackened and multilated bodies at the foot of the stone outcropping—Indians who had tried to attack the miners and had been captured and tortured to death. It appeared that they had stopped going to a settlement for supplies since he had included them in his circuit, which had happened with several miners, but he wasn't positive that their need for what he brought would always restrain their seemingly innate and instinctive impulses to be cruel.

"Well, well, here's the Jew again," the one who had come from the mine chuckled as Rhineman neared them. "How do, Jew?"

Rhineman stopped a few feet from them, wiped the sweat from his brow with his palm and wiped his palm on his coat. He looked at them silently.

"He ain't saying much, is he?" the one who had spoken laughed, glancing at the other one and looking back at Rhineman.

"He never does," the other one replied. "You got any likker on one of them mules?"

Rhineman lowered his pack to the ground, propped his musket against a rock, walked back to the second mule, and opened the top of one of the wicker panniers hanging across the packsaddle. Whiskey was a commodity he always carried in abundance, with the bottles nested in wool wrappings to protect them against breakage. He took out a bottle, unwrapping the wool and dropping it back into the pannier.

"You better make that a bottle apiece."

"No, you better make that about three bottles apiece."

They both laughed. Rhineman looked at them, then turned back to the pannier and began taking out more bottles. They occasionally joked, and sometimes it was difficult for him to tell if they were joking or serious. But they always took all the whiskey they could afford. Asking for six bottles indicated that their diggings had been producing well. Or that they didn't intend to pay for it. He unwrapped the six bottles, walked back around the mules, and put the bottles in a row on the bench between them. They both took out pocket knives, picked up a bottle, and began prying the corks from them.

16

"You got any tobaccer on one of them mules?"

Rhineman untied a canvas bundle between the two bales of wool on the packsaddle on the first mule. He took it down and opened it on the ground, displaying twists of chewing tobacco and bags of smoking tobacco.

"Give me about five plugs and three bags. And some papers."

"I'll take about the same."

Rhineman separated the twists of chewing tobacco and bags of smoking tobacco, gathered up a couple of folders of tobacco papers, and put them on the bench. He went back to the canvas, rolled it up again, and put it back on the mule.

"You got any salted sow belly with you this time?"

The other one lowered the whiskey bottle from his lips, swallowing and looking at the one who had spoken with feigned astonishment. "Sow belly? What would a Jew be doing with sow belly? He might have some dried beef from somebody's cow that died of old age, but he ain't got no sow belly! What's wrong with you, Hank?"

They both laughed uproariously and took deep drinks from the bottles. Rhineman went to the last mule in the line, opened a pannier, and took out a side of bacon. They both exclaimed with exaggerated, mock surprise as he carried it to the bench and put it with the other things. Rhineman went back to the last mule again, untied the canvas bags of potatoes, onions, and vegetables, and carried them to the bench to open them and display their contents. The two men wanted all of the potatoes, a large portion of the turnips, carrots, and onions, as well as ten pounds of dried beans, a pound of peppers, twenty pounds of flour, and twenty pounds of meal. He took the scales out of the pannier on the second mule, weighed out the beans, peppers, flour, and meal, and tied them in cloth

17

bags and put them with the other things. The two men got up from the bench and walked back along the line of mules as he was putting the scales and bags away. They looked at the chickens and sheep. Then picked out four of the chickens and one sheep. Rhineman untied the sheep and lifted it down and took the chickens out of the crate, tying their feet together with twine from his pocket and putting them with the other things.

It was an extraordinarily large purchase, and he began to seriously wonder about their intention to pay. There could be an argument or a fight over the price, then the wasted time and effort of simply loading all the things back onto the mules. If he were lucky. Another possibility was that his bones would be scattered among those remaining of the Indians at the bottom of the rocks, picked clean by animals and insects and bleaching in the sun. They walked back to the bench and sat down again, taking drinks from their bottles.

"I'd make all this at about three ounces, I guess."

Rhineman looked at the one who had spoken and shook his head, then looked at the things on the bench and on the ground, mentally counting up the value. He looked back at the two men. "Six," he said in his deep voice, his flat tone indicating he wouldn't bargain.

Their smiles faded. "Six?" one of them snarled belligerently. "By God, you're trying to rob us! That little daub of shit ain't worth six ounces!"

"Six," Rhineman repeated quietly.

They grumbled, glaring at him, glancing at each other, then looking away. "'Bout what you could expect out of one of them that crucified Jesus," one of them growled.

Resentment and anger flared within Rhineman, his eyes narrowed, and he looked at the man coldly. "That is little compared to what will happen to you if you do not pay me my *geld*," he said gruffly in his heavy German accent.

There was a long, dragging instant of silence as they both looked at him, then they both exploded into laughter. The bottles on the bench teetered precariously as they whooped and slapped their thighs, swaying back and forth. Both men laughed until they were gasping. The atmosphere had been tense and strained, now it was suddenly relaxed again. One of them rose and went around behind the cabin, and the other one offered Rhineman a drink from his bottle, still chuckling. Rhineman shook his head, opening a pannier on the second mule to take out the gold scales.

Their diggings had been producing well, because the doeskin bag the man brought back around the cabin weighed over twenty ounces. It was also full to the top, indicating there was at least one other bag in their cache which would be partially full and used for their daily take from their sluice box. That was borne out when the other man looked at the bag, started to say something, and thought better of it. He took a drink from his bottle without speaking. Rhineman set up the scales on a flat rock and centered the arms, then put a five and a one ounce counter in one of the dishes and carefully loosened the drawstring at the top of the bag. The two men knelt on the other side of the rock, watching intently.

It was placer mine, yielding small, reddish-yellow flakes with no admixture of nuggets. They had hit a good vein. The expressions on their faces was what Rhineman had frequently seen on the faces of those viewing a transaction with gold, even on the faces of by-standers who had nothing to do with the transaction. It was the utter fascination with the substance which drove them and others to endure any hardship and exert any effort to secure it, the fascination which mountains of gold would fail to satisfy. Rhineman dribbled the gold into the empty dish until the dishes began to even, then he added tiny pinches until the pointer between the arms covered the center mark. He pulled the drawstring and closed the bag, and handed it to one of the men. The men continued watching closely as Rhineman proofed the weight. He carefully poured the gold out of the dish onto a square of paper, put the weights in the dish where the gold had been, then poured the gold into the other dish. The pointer swung back to center. The men grunted and nodded in satisfaction, moving back to the bench and taking drinks from their bottles. Rhineman took a doeskin bag from his inside coat pocket and poured the gold into it. There were a couple of ounces of gold already in the bag, just enough for it to appear that he had taken in a small amount of gold. When he was well away from the cabin he would pour most of the six ounces into one of the pockets of the doeskin belt around his waist under his shirt.

Rhineman put the scales away, took out a couple of sheets of newspaper and put them with the other things, then prepared to leave, walking along both sides of the mules, checking the ropes, packs and panniers. He went back to his pack, picked it up, and hoisted it.

"Hey, wait a minute," one of the men said. "Bring me a shovel when you come back. One like that one over there. And a new pickaxe. One of them big, heavy pickaxes."

"And I need me some new boots," the other man said.

Rhineman dropped the pack again, glancing at the shovel the man had indicated and nodding slightly as he walked toward the bench. He took a ball of twine from his coat pocket. The one who wanted the boots pulled one of his worn, tattered boots off and lifted his leg, holding his bare foot up toward Rhineman. Rhineman measured from the tip of his large toe to the back of his heel with the twine and broke it off, then measured the width of his foot at the base of his toes and broke it off. He tied the two pieces of twine together and put them in his pocket with the ball of twine as he turned back toward his mules.

"So long, then."

Rhineman silently nodded in reply as he picked up the pack and shrugged into the straps, settling it on his shoulders. He picked up his musket and cradled it across his forearm, took the lead rope on the first mule, and turned the line of mules toward the path on the other side of the plateau.

"He sure ain't got much to say," one of the men chuckled.

"No, he ain't," the other one laughed. "He ain't, and that's a fact."

Rhineman continued walking across the plateau with the mules following along behind him.

Chapter 2

The dark and threatening clouds warning of the impending storm of revolution gathered over Restoration Europe through the 1840s, gradually becoming more menacing and ominous. In 1843, Yehuda Bauer, a resident of Bingen am Rhein in Westphalia, began considering immigration to the United States. His roots went deep, because he was the fourth generation of Bauers to own the old building on the corner of Schmetterlingstrasse with the bakery shop on the ground floor and the living quarters above, and he was a man of substantial age. He had seen and heard much during his years, and he was wary of political and social unrest. When mobs gathered and had no readily accessible adversary on which to wreak their wrath, it was all too frequent that the Jewish section suffered their vengeance. He had a cousin in South Carolina who was a prosperous merchant in the shipping trade, and after an exchange of correspondence with his cousin, he began to make preparations.

Bauer had four sons ranging in age from forty to twenty-three, all of whom were married and had children. They were all well situated men, and they were initially reluctant when he approached them about accompanying him to the United States. But they were also respectful and obedient, and all of them eventually began selling off their possessions and disposing of their businesses to accompany their father.

Bauer also had a daughter who was married to Jacob Rhineman, the owner of a small drayage business. Rhineman wasn't the match he would have picked for his daughter. He had been reared as an orphan and had no immediate family, and his background had made him an unusually quiet, withdrawn, and self sufficient man with a disregard for the full spectrum of family attachments. Bauer also saw in Rhineman a disinclination to participate in community undertakings, as well as what he considered an extremely casual attitude toward religious matters. But Bauer's daughter had been attracted to the tall, burly, and admittedly handsome Rhineman to a degree which would be alarming to any father who wished to avoid the possibility of disgrace. Bauer's wife had nagged him about it and he had given permission. The marriage hadn't turned out as badly as it could have. Rhineman was a hard worker if nothing else. They had a fourteen year old son who was a healthy and energetic boy if somewhat too much like his father, and they had a twelve year old daughter who was the image of her mother at that age.

But Rhineman's less desirable characteristics were evidenced when Bauer approached him about accompanying the rest of the family to the United States.

23

Rhineman demurred, and when Bauer persisted Rhineman bluntly told him he was being alarmist. Bauer shrugged the matter off and ignored his wife's tears. He had done what he could. The preparations were completed, and in 1844 Bauer and his family left to go to South Carolina.

Since the 1830's, a crisis had gradually been developing because of the impact of industrialization on the structure of German society. Progressive owners of small-scale industries had gradually been expanding and developing urban factories, and less progressive craftsmen had been gradually forced out of business because of their inability to compete with the prices at which factory-produced wares could be sold. The process had been delayed to an extent through the guilds, then the braking action collapsed when Prussia and Hanover passed laws terminating compulsory membership in guilds for journeymen and apprentices. The immediate result was a rapid expansion of existing factories through a massive influx of farm workers seeking the higher wages paid by factories, and the widespread unemployment of craftsmen.

During the same period, political pressures had been developing on several fronts. There was a growth of national consciousness and a desire for a united Germany, as well as widespread agitation for governmental reforms in the areas of universal suffrage, administration of justice, and abolition of feudal privileges of nobility. The unemployed craftsmen, a substantial portion of the population, added their demands for government action.

The potato harvests of 1845 and 1846 were destroyed by a blight which spread across Europe, depriving the bulk of the European population of their staple food, and a major famine began to develop. Government reserves were opened for distribution, but prices began to rise rapidly because of the widespread hoarding and speculation in foodstuffs. At the same time, communications were poor between the various German governments, producing rapidly fluctuating surpluses and scarcity in various areas. In 1847, a drought destroyed the grain harvest. Food prices became astronomical, and at the same time cholera epidemics developed in various parts of the German states.

Farmers began leaving the countryside and drifting to the towns and cities, where they joined the armies of unemployed craftsmen. As food prices rose, the demand for manufactured goods rapidly declined. The factories which had recently expanded began closing because of the diminishing market, and the numbers of unemployed mushroomed. The food shortages in the towns and cities developed into a famine.

In late 1847, Jacob Rhineman had reason to reconsider the conversation concerning immigration with his father-in-law. His wife had received several letters from her mother and father, and what they wrote about the conditions in South Carolina seemed too good to be true. While many other places had legal restrictions on the activities of Jews, the United States had none and the constitution in South Carolina had long contained a specific statement about the freedom of worship and the conduct of business affairs by Jews. There was a large Jewish population in Charleston, where Rhineman's father-in-law had settled with his family. The old man and his sons had invested their monies in the cotton and shipping trades, and they were prospering.

But in Bingen, things had rapidly deteriorated. The shortage of food was an extreme hardship, and the inflation in prices had produced a situation in which the drayage business was only marginally profitable. Farm workers had flooded into Bingen from the farming districts west of the Rhine and south of the Mosel. They had no money for food or lodging, and the streets were filled with beggars, women selling themselves for a few pfennigs, and large, restless crowds looking for someone or something on which to blame their plight. And while the typical city dweller was a more or less sophisticated individual, the peasants were uneducated, darkly suspicious of anyone different from them, and inclined to violence.

Through the latter months of 1847, there were a few incidents of mobs invading the Jewish section. The community assumed a defensive posture, ready at a moment's notice to shutter windows and block doors on the lower floors and retreat to the upper floors, where barrels of water were stored to empty out of upper windows and dump down staircases if the lower floors were set on fire. A few shops were broken into and looted and there were scattered beatings and rapes, but no one was killed. Rumors that large hoards of food were being kept in the Jewish section spread through the mobs of unemployed, and several large gangs of men armed with clubs prowled through the streets of the Jewish section for a time, occasionally battering their way into a house or shop, searching it, and terrorizing the occupants. Then Rhineman was caught by a mob while hauling a wagonload of grain. He was severely beaten, but he managed to get away during the fight over the grain in the wagon. He hid in a mews in an adjacent street while the mob fought over the grain, killed the team of horses, and fought over the horseflesh. By that time the men were sufficiently battered and bloody that Rhineman managed to slip away unnoticed.

The loss of the wagon and team was a hard blow, leaving him with a single wagon and two teams remaining, and he had to make reparation for the load of grain from the savings he had managed to keep during the difficult times. A couple of weeks later, the weather began turning cold and the mobs on the streets diminished as the weaker ones sickened and died and others found shelter and stayed in it. Rhineman began making plans to emigrate to the United States.

In February of 1848, Louis Philippe fled from Paris and a republic was proclaimed in France. The spark spread to Baden, where political activists met in Mannheim on 27 February and presented the grand duke with their demands for freedom of the press, formation of a people's militia, reorganization of the courts, and the summoning of a German parliament. The grand duke agreed to the demands, and Baden established a pattern for the rest of the German states as the revolutionary tide swept north.

The economic turmoil made it difficult for Rhineman to dispose of his belongings at anything approaching a reasonable price, and the political and governmental turmoil made obtaining travel permits ar.d documentation a maddening nightmare. But there were those among the Jewish community who had weathered other times of trouble and who intended to stay on through the difficult period. Among them there were those who needed housewares and the means of making a livelihood for sons approaching adulthood, so they borrowed and dug into their savings to buy Rhineman's property. The money made it possible to find government clerks who would assume the responsibility for processing and authenticating travel permits and documentation, and the preparations were finalized. By April the German population at large had made the discovery that political rhetoric

27

produced a heat which wouldn't warm the body and that words didn't fill the stomach, a discovery others had made in the past and yet others would make in the future. Mobs were prowling the streets again during the warm spring weather, and rioting citizens were fighting soldiers across barricades in the streets in some of the cities. Rhineman and his wife, son, and daughter were enroute to Le Havre.

The first available passage was on a ship destined for New York rather than Charleston, as Rhineman would have preferred, but the atmosphere in Le Havre was virtually as hostile as Bingen had been. It would be both dangerous and expensive to remain in Le Havre, so they took the passage. Rhineman's daughter became ill and died during the voyage, and was buried at sea. His wife also became ill shortly before they docked. The other passengers warned Rhineman that the immigration authorities would refuse to admit the ill and infirm into the United States. His wife managed to conceal her condition while they were being processed through Ellis Island, then collapsed. A representative of a Jewish relief organization who was meeting immigrants assisted them, finding lodgings for them in a rooming house in the Lower East Side and locating a doctor. People in the rooming house brought food and loaned them bedding and other things; a rabbi visited, and men in the rooming house came to Rhineman and told him about jobs which were available.

With the hardships of the voyage over, and after recovering somewhat from the death of her daughter, Rhineman's wife began to rapidly improve. On the Monday after their arrival, Rhineman found a job on the loading dock of a brewery. On Tuesday, one of his brothers-in-law from Charleston arrived, bringing the money Bauer had sent for Rhineman's wife and son to travel to Charleston.

28

The message was clear. Rhineman could join the extended family group, but it would be on Bauer's terms. At first Rhineman was angered, then the broader implications became clear when he thought about it at greater length. In a way it was simply an offer to care for his family until he could establish himself, which was in implicit recognition of his instinctive desire for independence and self sufficiency. His brother-in-law remained in the city for several days, taking care of family business matters with bankers and shipping factors. Rhineman pondered over the matter at work during the day and discussed Charleston with his brother-in-law during the evenings. And he decided to send his wife and son to Charleston.

His wife was reluctant to be parted from him, but she was an obedient woman and quietly began preparing to leave. Karl, his seventeen year old son, eagerly looked forward to going because of his uncle's glowing accounts of Charleston and because of the opportunity to escape the frequent thrashings from Rhineman for his insolence. Three weeks after arriving in New York, Rhineman saw his wife and son off on the train to Charleston.

Rhineman moved to smaller and more economical lodgings in the home of a widow who agreed to cook for him, and he took on an extra job of driving a delivery wagon as well as working on the loading dock at the brewery. His command of English began to improve rapidly as his wider range of activities placed him into more frequent contact with people outside the Jewish neighborhood, and he began to accustom himself to his surroundings. The widow had an unmarried son living with her, and he helped Rhineman tediously translate the newspapers he gathered up in saloons where he delivered beer. After a few weeks the words in the newspapers and those he heard spoken every day seemed to melt together into a cohesive if less than logical whole, and he began reading without assistance.

Letters from his wife were chatty and informative, telling about her father's and brothers' business activities and always beginning and ending with fervent wishes that they would soon be rejoined. Kark had suffered some difficulty in adjusting to the more disciplined religious atmosphere in his grandfather's house, but it appeared that he had more or less managed to conform. Bauer was having some of Karl's deficiencies in religious education repaired by having him instructed by a rabbi, and as a more or less ultimate testimony to the acceptance of Jews in Charleston, Karl was being tutored for enrollment in a gentile military college called The Citadel.

When Rhineman's brother-in-law had been in New York, he had been dressed in expensive suits and had traveled about the city in hired carriages while conducting his business. The more subtle nuances of attitude and conduct had also evidenced that Bauer and his family had prospered substantially during the time they had been in Charleston. It was clear that Bauer was spending far more money on Rhineman's wife and son than Rhineman could provide, but Rhineman did what he could and deposited money in a bank each week to be paid to his wife's account in a bank at Charleston. He also practiced every economy and took advantage of every opportunity to earn extra money to add to the savings he was accumulating for his own business. Then as he continued to pore over newspapers and became more familiar with New York, the conviction gradually developed that his best opportunities lay elsewhere.

With his two jobs, he was making far more money than the average worker, but working as a laborer was only an interim undertaking. He had always planned on working as a laborer only long enough to accumulate sufficient capital to begin his own business, preferably a drayage or similar company. But it became more and more evident to him that it would take many years of working as a laborer to save enough to start a reasonably profitable business in New York. There were numerous small, independent businessmen in New York, ranging from sidewalk vendors selling shoelaces to tiny shops jammed together along the crowded streets, but their possibilities for profit and rapid expansion were extremely limited because of their multiplicity. The only possibilities lay between negotiating a loan from his father-in-law to enable him to start a larger and hence more profitable business, or to look into other areas where the competition was less severe. He began reading and pondering over newspaper articles on the West.

His decision to go to the New Mexico Territory apparently created a degree of consternation in Charleston. His letter to his wife about it brought an immediate and concerned reply from her and a letter from his father-in-law which described the opportunities in drayage in South Carolina and which offered him a low interest loan to start such a business. Rhineman wrote a reply to his father-in-law, thanking him for the offer and declining it, and he wrote to his wife at greater length, telling her what he had read and heard of New Mexico Territory and reassuring her that he had first hand information that most of the dangers of the West were fabrications of imaginative travelers. Her subsequent letters were no less concerned in tone, but she had accepted his decision. Rhineman began making preparations, and in early 1849 he left for the New Mexico Territory.

During the time Mexico had been under Spanish rule, contacts between the Spanish territories and the United

States had been aggressively limited by the Spanish to diplomatic exchanges, with trespassers being arrested and imprisoned for indefinite duration. In 1822, when Mexico revolted against Spanish rule and gained autonomy, the restrictions were relaxed and the Santa Fe Trail came into being from the caravans of traders traveling west from Missouri. There was a degree of official hostility toward traders from the United States during the brief war in which Texas became independent of Mexico in 1836. It relaxed for a time, then trade with the United States was cut off in 1843 when President Santa Anna closed the customs houses at Taos, El Paso, and Presidio de Norte and ordered the arrest of any United States citizen who trespassed on Mexican territory. The occasion for President Santa Anna's displeasure was a border dispute over the western boundary of the United States, and it was resolved beyond question when the United States established its western boundary at the Pacific Ocean by force of arms. The Santa Fe Trail was opened again by Brigadier General Stephen Watts when he led his army into Santa Fe and raised the flag of the United States over the city plaza.

A more or less formalized pattern for traveling by wagon train had developed during the quarter century they had been crossing the Santa Fe Trail. From St. Louis Rhineman went by boat to Independence, and from there he was directed to Chouteau's Landing, which was becoming more frequently referred to as Westport. There he found a wagon train forming up on the bank of the Missouri, single wagons and groups of three and four wagons destined for Santa Fe and beyond building around a nucleus composed of twenty wagons belonging to a trader going to Santa Fe. In addition to the wagons, there were also some three dozen unaccompanied men without wagons—trappers, prospectors, and a few who looked as though they were escaping family responsibilities or problems with law enforcement agencies, some going to New Mexico Territory but most of them intending to continue on to California.

The trader was the captain of the wagon train, and he told Rhineman that he could sign on as a walker for fifteen dollars, which would pay for his meals with the teamsters and other walkers and would allow him to sleep in a cargo wagon during inclement weather. But he was required to have a musket, shot and powder, a knife, an extra pair of boots, a blanket, and extra clothing for the trip before signing on. Rhineman returned to Independence to buy the things he needed and to mail off a last letter to his wife, then he returned and signed the articles for the trip. After paying the fifteen dollars, he had twelve dollars left.

The religion of all travelers was indicated on the articles in event of their death during the trek, and he experienced a few calculating stares and quiet mutters about him in the three days before the wagon train left. Then it got under way, and some of the wagons became mired down in a boggy, swampy area called Shady Creek on the first day. Several men saw Rhineman break an oak rail with his shoulder while helping lever the wagons out of the mud, and they quietly commented among themselves about it. That night one of the wagon train rowdies picked a fight with Rhineman, and he put everything he had into it, recognizing the value in firmly establishing a reputation. The captain of the wagon train let the fight go to the end, and the rowdy rode in a cargo wagon for the next eight days while he was recuperating. After that, Rhineman was accepted and treated with respect by everyone in the wagon train, and when the meal for the teamsters included pork, the cook silently found him something else to eat.

A few of the wagons were drawn by mules, but the trader's wagons and most of the others were drawn by three and four span of oxen, which set the daily journey at twelve to fifteen miles with their slow pace. The first days were easy and relaxed, following the wide pattern of deep wagon tracks across relatively open, flat country with ample water and shady groves to camp during evenings. It was a new world for Rhineman, accustomed to the more confined spaces of Germany, where boundaries of ownership had been established for centuries and a disagreement over property lines amounting to the width of a man's hand would be the cause of years of litigation in the courts. During the trip to St. Louis and on to Independence and Westport, the spaces had seemed vast to him. For the first time, he saw countless miles of fertile soil without fences or boundaries.

At Council Grove the discipline in the wagon train was tightened, the captain had riders and walkers out on the flanks to watch for Indians, and at night the wagons were formed into a circle, with sentinels posted over the wagons and the grazing animals. A small band of mounted Indians shadowed the wagon trail for a couple of days, then rode into the camp for a conference with the captain of the wagon train when it stopped for the night on the third day. Weapons were held in readiness on both sides, and the conference was short and heated. The Indians demanded two of the oxen for allowing the wagon train to proceed unmolested, and the captain of the wagon train ordered the Indians out of camp. They were outnumbered several times over, but they continued to shadow the wagon train for three more days, apparently watching for stragglers, then disappeared.

There was a choice of routes at Cimmaron Crossing on

the Arkansas, with steep mountain grades on the northern trail and long waterless stretches on the southern. The captain and some of the teamsters conferred after crossing the river. All of the water barrels were filled, the animals were made to drink all they would, and the train set out across the Staked Plains. They crossed the arid stretches in good condition and continued on. The foodstuffs carried in the cargo wagons began to run low, and hunters among the teamsters scouted out on the flanks of the wagon train and brought in buffalo and deer.

The wagon train crossed the border into New Mexico Territory, and went across a wide stretch of prairie where water was plentiful. The mountains became a blue shadow on the horizon, gradually moving closer. When they approched the mountains they stopped for two days to rest the animals and make necessary repairs to the wagons, then they set out again. The trail became a narrow, winding road through the mountains, with everyone struggling and stumbling as they helped the animals pull the wagons up the slopes, and then lashed the wheels together as the leather brakes smoked on the precipitous downgrades.

The first collection of the low, long buildings made of sun-dried mud bricks was at the Gallinas River crossing, and there was another one called El Bado de San Miguel on the Pecos. The small, dark people with their shining teeth and liquid accents brought vegetables and other produce to the wagon train when it camped at night. Rhineman listened and watched, interested to learn what might be of value to him and feeling a kind of wonder that had a value of its own. The wagon train moved slowly on, and it finally arrived at Santa Fe fifty-eight days after leaving Westport.

Chapter 3

The wagon train was the first one of the season, and people swarmed into the city from the outlying farms and ranches to meet it. The trader had been impressed with Rhineman's strength and willingness to work, so he hired him for ten days and paid him a wage of two dollars a day, plus his meals and a space in one of the wagons to sleep at night. The wagons were lined up along one side of the plaza and the trade was brisk, ranchers bringing animals laden with wool and trappers bringing bales of furs to trade for supplies from the wagons. More rarely, miners would bring small bags of gold dust and nuggets to be carefully weighed and exchanged for supplies. Rhineman watched and listened as he worked around the wagons, unloading the supplies and loading the things for which the trader bargained. At night the teamsters would go to the narrow, winding Calle de La Muralla to gamble, drink, and visit the brothels, and guards would watch over the wagons. Rhineman talked with the guards about the bartering, and occasionally the trader would remain with the wagons and Rhineman would talk with him. Within a few days, he had accumulated a substantial store of information on the relative value of the things involved, how to judge the quality of furs and wool, and other things he needed to know.

The retail stores in the city had accumulated bales of wool, furs, handwoven rugs, and other goods during the winter, and on the tenth day the trader began bargaining with the local merchants for the remainder of his wares so he could leave for Missouri to get another load. He offered Rhineman a job on the wagon train, but Rhineman declined the offer and took his wages in an assortment of trade goods, bolts of calico, buttons, needles and thread, beads, knives, bottles of whiskey, and tobacco.

The wagon train left the city on the twelfth day, and on the same day Rhineman set out on foot along the road north of the city toward Taos, with his trade goods in a pack on his back. The people at the first few farms and ranches had been in the city to meet the wagon train and didn't need anything, and he walked on. Then he found a small ranch where the man had been ill and hadn't been able to get to Santa Fe, and he traded part of his goods for vegetables, a couple of chickens, and a bale of wool. He shared a meal of beans and tortillas with the family, then gathered up his things and walked back along the road toward Santa Fe through the darkness. It was almost dawn when he reached Santa Fe, and he waited for the stalls on the plaza to open so he could sell the vegetables and chickens. Then he took the bale of wool to a retail merchant. The merchant exchanged an assortment of trade goods which neared the limit of what Rhineman could carry for the wool, and he set out to the north again. He was stumbling with fatigue by sunset, and he slept in a thicket at the side of the road and continued on at daybreak.

Within a month he had earned enough to buy a mule and packsaddle, and he had learned enough to be able to pick out the dim paths which led to the miners' diggings and the trappers' cabins. The number of wagon trains arriving in Santa Fe diminished with the arrival of autumn, and during winter they stopped. The prices on trade goods rose to the point where people took much less, but his trips were still profitable because the miners and trappers were always ready to trade for whatever foodstuffs he obtained from the ranchers and small farmers along the way.

When spring came, he was among those who were there to meet the first wagon train. All the wool and furs he had traded for had gone to the merchants because he had no safe way of storing them between his trips, but he had all the money, gold, and silver and turquoise jewelry he had collected, as well as a large bundle of hand-woven rugs. He was able to immediately buy another mule and leave on his first trip of the season with both mules heavily-laden and with a heavy pack of goods on his back. By the second trip of the season he was covering the long, circular route to Taos, Tierra Amarilla, Jemez, Santo Domingo, and back to Santa Fe.

On the third trip he bought another mule, and two trips later he bought two more, giving him a string of five mules. He worked on into autumn with the five mules, then the prices went up again and established a limit on the amount of goods those along his route could afford to take. It appeared that he had reached a limit of sorts of what one man could do. If he expanded his route to the point at which it took him much over six weeks to cover, some of the people along the route would begin running out of necessities and making trips to settlements for supplies. But he wasn't making the maximum profit out of his route, because he was buying his goods at retail prices, and the wool and furs he exchanged were being taken at a discounted value so the merchant could make a profit on them when he turned them over to a wagon train trader.

There were several large ranches in the area which dated back to the original Spanish land grants and had been passed through generations of the same Spanish families, the *rico* families. The workers on them were basically in a state of peonage. As he neared Santa Fe on one of his late autumn trips, a crippled old man and his wife approached his campfire one night and asked in broken English if they could spend the night by his fire. Rhineman warily agreed to let them, and he found out in conversing with the old man that they had been ejected from one of the large ranches and were on their way to Santa Fe to see if they could find some means of supporting themselves. Rhineman shared his food with them that night and the next morning before they set out again. The loads on the mules were light enough so that he could combine some of them, and he let the old man ride on one of the mules. He walked beside the mule to talk to the old man as the old woman led the pack train along the road.

Rhineman had spent over a year living in the open and sleeping in camps off the trail, huddling under a piece of canvas when it was raining or snowing and wrapping his blanket around him to keep warm when walking along the trail in the face of the freezing north winds during the winter. During the two or three days he spent in Santa Fe between trips, he usually slept in a stable with the mules or in a field on the edge of the city when the weather was fair and he didn't need to stable the mules. It was bearable, but it was beginning to wear him down and a warm comfortable place to spend the two or three days between trips would be more restful and prepare him better for the exertions of another trip. More importantly, if he had somewhere in Santa Fe to store his trade goods and the wool and fur he received in trade, he could get his goods at a much lower price by buying in quantity from a wagon train. And he could receive full value for his wool and furs by selling them to the wagon train instead of the local stores.

The old man's name was Garcia, and he rambled on about his past experiences and the scarcities and hardships before the traders had started coming from Missouri. The old woman glanced back now and then and rattled comments in Spanish for him to translate. Rhineman nodded absently to the old man, pondering. The old man would obviously work for very little and he was capable of guarding a storeroom of goods, but he would also be in a position to sell the goods and disappear while Rhineman was on one of his trips. He appeared to be honest, but the chance at more money than he had ever seen might be too much of a temptation. On the other hand, Rhineman had only one and a half bales of wool and a few poor quality furs on the mules and he wouldn't acquire too much more until well into the winter. That would give him a period of evaluation of the old man at a time when the loss of the goods would be less than devastating. They stopped to rest for a short time at noon and Rhineman cautiously approached the subject with Garcia. Garcia responded with enthusiasm.

There was a property just off the road a couple of miles

north of Santa Fe which had once been a small farm. It was twenty five acres of stony, scrubby land with a few weathered adobe buildings and sheds on it. The owner of it was a man named Salazar, who owned a livery stable in Santa Fe and had inherited the property from his father. Rhineman had heard Salazar speak of the property, and he had remembered the comment along with countless other bits of information which might prove useful at some time or other.

They arrived in Santa Fe during late afternoon, then went on through the city to the livery stable so Rhineman could talk to Salazar about the property. The price was five hundred dollars, a staggering sum of money but not unreasonable in comparison with prices of other properties in the vicinity of Santa Fe. Salazar was anxious to sell it, and he immediately left one of his employees in charge of the livery stable and accompanied Rhineman as he led his pack train along the road north of the city.

The sum seemed even larger with the late afternoon sun shining down on the scrubby, overgrown hillside and the deteriorated adobe buildings with weathered, pitted walls and collapsed roofs. But it was within reach, and it was by far the most substantial and valuable investment he had ever contemplated. Animals could die and goods could be stolen or lost, but the land endured. In Germany and in other places it was illegal for Jews to own land, and he had always hungered for it. It was the one solid and immutable thing of value. He could envision the time, after he brought his wife and son to New Mexico Territory and when the road between Santa Fe and Taos would be heavily traveled, when people traveling along the road would look up the hill at his warehouses, stock pens, and home. Garcia and his wife uttered muffled sounds of glee when Rhineman and Salazar shook hands on the bargain.

Rhineman left his pack train with Garcia and went back into Santa Fe with Salazar to work out the details of his payments and to go to the land office about the deed.

Rhineman spent four days on the property, helping Garcia and his wife repair the walls and roof on the house, hauling fodder to store in the corral shed, and buying an *olla* and other things the old woman needed. He left money for food with Garcia before he started on his circuit again. During the long nights on the trail, he often lay awake and thought about the property. If he became ill or injured and was unable to keep up with his payments, he would lose all he had invested in it. And the wool and furs he had gathered on the previous trip were in the care of someone else. Gloomy, bothersome worries nagged at him. But as he neared Santa Fe again, a feeling of excited anticipation sprang to life within him. It was a warm, satisfying feeling of homecoming.

It was almost sunset when the place came into sight, and the soft, golden light of the late autumn sun lay over the hill. Garcia had finished the repairs on the house, and it gleamed brightly with its fresh coating of whitewash, with the dark of the eave poles standing out in sharp contrast. The weeds and rubble had been cleared away from the house, and the road up to it had been cleaned off. The corral and corral shed had been repaired. Some of the land behind the house had been dug up where Garcia and his wife were apparently planting some kind of winter crop. Smoke curled lazily into the clear air from the chimney at the side of the house. A cur dog leaped off the porch and looked at Rhineman turning off the road with the train of mules, and began barking. Rhineman could hear the distant sound of the old woman's voice calling her husband. Garcia came around the side of the house and began limping toward the road, waving to Rhineman.

Rhineman returned his wave and led the mules up the hill to meet him, smiling widely.

During the winter the amount of goods his customers could afford went down to the point that three mules were ample to carry it. He had a bad fall while crossing a mountain stream which had frozen over and his back troubled him for weeks afterward. He began riding one of the mules while making the rounds of the circuit. The furs and wool continued piling up in the building Rhineman and Garcia had repaired to use for a storeroom. When it became too full, Rhineman used one of the back rooms in the house for storage. The gold and money he had saved went on his payments on the property and to buy trade goods, and during late winter it began running low. It seemed for a time that he might have to take some of the furs and wool in to exchange for trade goods, but the winter was mild and a wagon train came in earlier than usual.

When Rhineman told the trader what he had to exchange, the trader brought one of his wagons out of Santa Fe to load it. It was tempting to pay off the rest of the money he owed on the property, but he wanted to buy more mules and he wanted a large enough supply of trade goods to make him independent of the retail stores in the city. When he finished his bargaining with the trader, the trade goods filled the storeroom to the ceiling and overflowed into two rooms of the house. Before he left on his next trip, he bought a musket for Garcia to enable him to guard the trade goods, and Garcia found two more stray dogs in the city to bring out and tie on ropes by the storeroom.

The spring was unusually wet, and the extended period of rain made Rhineman stiff and sore most of the time. But he had ten mules, which allowed him to leave a couple of them to rest up between trips and ride one instead of walking. Garcia finished clearing the land and planted beans, chilis, corn, and other crops behind and to one side of the house. He and the old woman carried water in buckets from the creek at the bottom of the hill to water them. The place had a settled, domestic appearance about it which made the three to four days of rest between trips pleasant, with the mules braying in the corral, chickens clucking and scratching in the dirt around the house, and sheep in the pen by the corral making their quiet noises.

During the summer, Rhineman and Garcia began building an addition onto the storeroom to expand it into a warehouse, mixing straw with mud, forming bricks in wooden molds and letting them bake in the sun, then setting them in rows. It was slow work, because Rhineman kept to his schedule on his circuit and Garcia was old and crippled. Rhineman estimated that it would be completed in time to store trade goods the following spring. But when he arrived at the bottom of the hill after making his trip in August, the first thing he noticed was that the addition had been completed and a younger, taller man than Garcia was swabbing on whitewash on the end of the warehouse.

The dogs began barking as Rhineman turned his pack train onto the narrow road up to the house, and the man turned and looked. Garcia limped out from behind the house and into sight. He turned and said something to the man. The man put the swab into the tub of whitewash and he and Garcia walked toward the corral to meet Rhineman. As Rhineman approached, Garcia swept his straw hat off, an invariable courtesy which always made Rhineman feel slightly uncomfortable, and the other man took off his hat.

"Bienvenido, patrón," Garcia said, his smile a trifle

44

unsure. "*Tengo mucho gusto en verlo*. This is my younger sister's son, Pedro Delgado. He has come to speak with you about employment, *patrón*."

Rhineman nodded to Garcia, then looked at Delgado and nodded guardedly as the man murmured a greeting. He was in his middle thirties, tall for a Mexican but still substantially smaller than Rhineman. He looked at Rhineman with a polite, ingratiating smile. Rhineman looked away, sliding down from his mule. "You are tired of working here, then?"

It took an instant for Garcia to digest the question, then he looked alarmed. "No, no *patrón*," he said hastily. "I wish to keep my job, but I thought you might have need of someone else..."

Rhineman nodded, moving toward the gate of the corral with the mules. "We will talk," he said in a noncommital tone.

"Let us take care of the mules, *patrón*," Garcia said limping forward and reaching for the rope. "You are tired, and the house is cool. We will do this while you sit down and rest."

Rhineman nodded and handed the rope to Garcia, then turned toward the house. Garcia murmured to Delgado, and they began loosening the packsaddles and taking them off the mules. The chickens scattered in front of him, spreading their wings and clucking excitedly, and the dog in front of the house looked at him uncertainly, baring his teeth and wagging his tail fractionally. Rhineman passed the dog and walked around the front of the house. He stepped heavily up onto the porch and sat down in one of the homemade chairs on the porch, sighing with relief as he unbuttoned his suit coat and took off his hat and dropped it to the floor by the chair. Garcia's wife came out of the house, smiling and nodding

45

as she offered him a gourd dipper of cool water, and he nodded as he took it from her. Two small children came to the door and peered at him with apprehensive curiosity. Garcia's wife snapped at them and pushed them ahead of her as she went back in. Another woman in the house spoke to the children in the sharp, loving tone of a mother correcting her offspring. Rhineman took a deep drink of the water and frowned with resentment. It appeared that Delgado had already moved his family in.

But it had become obvious to him that he needed someone else. Once he had become independent of the retail stores and had started trading his goods directly to the wagon train traders, he had reached the maximum profit he could make by himself. The only way to expand was to have someone else work his circuit while he developed and worked another one to the south of Santa Fe. But the possibilities of being cheated were endless. He had come to trust Garcia sufficiently to let him do it, but Garcia was far too old and infirm. The only other possibility which had occurred to him was bringing his wife and son to Santa Fe and letting his son work the circuit while he developed another. But he wasn't yet ready to bring his wife to Santa Fe. There was no Jewish community, which was an important consideration in a woman's happiness and a young man's well-being, and he wanted to build a fine house for his wife before he brought her. And nagging doubts had developed about his son. From comments in his wife's letters which reached him, Karl was doing well in college and in the local social life, and it seemed possible that he might not be satisfied to lead a pack train along a trading route and barter with farmers, ranchers, miners, and trappers.

The woman in the house murmured quietly to the children, and their thin, soft voices replied in the liquid

46

syllables of their language. The sounds Garcia and Delgado made unloading the mules and turning them into the corral were barely audible as he sat on the porch. Presently they came around the front of the house and stepped up onto the porch, removing their hats and smiling and nodding to Rhineman. Rhineman emptied the gourd and handed it to Garcia. The old man filled it from the *olla* hanging under the eave on the corner of the porch as Delgado sat down on the bench by the door. Garcia limped back across the porch and sat down by Delgado, and they drank from the dipper. Delgado took the dipper back to the *olla* and started to hang it up, then turned and looked at Rhineman, lifting his eyebrows interrogatively. Rhineman shook his head, and Delgado hung up the dipper and returned to the bench.

The silence stretched out and became uncomfortable. Garcia cleared his throat softly and spoke. "One of the packsaddles is broken, *patrón*.

"The mule slipped and fell on it two days ago. One of the panniers has a hole in it as well.

"It is a matter of small concern, *patrón*. I can repair the saddle, and Pedro's wife Rosa can repair the pannier. She is skilled at working with cane. She makes hats to sell in the marketplace."

Rhineman looked off into the distance, nodding slightly, then turned his head and looked at Delgado. "Do you speak English?"

"A little, *patrón*," he replied in a heavy Spanish accent.

"Where have you worked before?"

"Rancho Santiago, *patrón*."

"Why did you leave there?"

Delgado hesitated, glanced at Garcia, then looked back at Rhineman with a diffident, embarrassed smile. "The *patrón* at Rancho Santiago has a daughter who is . . . not what one would wish to have for a wife, but . . ." His voice faded as he shrugged eloquently.

Rhineman looked back down at the road, stroking his beard and thinking. Delgado was a man who would be attractive to a woman, handsome and rakish-looking, and Rhineman felt somewhat more suspicious of him because of it. But he was Garcia's relative, and Garcia had put himself in the position of vouching for him. He pondered for a long moment, then nodded slightly. "I will give you a job," he said slowly. "You will take a mule train and work as a trader, and I will pay you one dollar each day and one part in ten of the profits you make." He turned his head and looked at Delgado again, his eyes narrowing. "And if you steal from me, I will kill you," he finished bluntly.

Delgado started to reply, but Garcia cut him off. "No, I will kill him if he steals, *patrón*. But he will not steal. You are our *patrón*, and we will not steal from you."

Garcia's tone was as firm and definite as Rhineman's had been, and Delgado nodded in emphatic support of what Garcia had said. There had been numerous indications that Garcia considered their relationship significantly deeper and more meaningful than Rhineman's concept of the affiliation between an employer and employee. Rhineman had interpreted it as gratitude that he had hired him, because his chances of obtaining employment elsewhere were very poor, but it appeared that his interpretation of the word *patrón* as simply a polite honorific might be wrong. Rhineman looked from Garcia to Delgado and back to Garcia, then nodded as he turned his head and looked back down at the road, stroking his beard.

Chapter 4

Rhineman took Delgado on a round of the circuit with
him, then turned it over to him, loaded four mules with
trade goods, and headed south. He worked in a wide
circle, across the Pecos and around through the foothills
and wide basins east of Albuquerque, then ran out of
trade goods and returned to Santa Fe. At the end of the
second trip, Delgado had left the day before on another
circuit, and Garcia had made a record of the transactions
Delgado had told him about. It showed a good profit,
indicating that Delgado had been able to wheedle
somewhat more out of the farmers and ranchers than
Rhineman had. There was a wagon train in the city,
possibly the last one of the season, and Rhineman
exchanged all his wool and furs and spent all of his gold
and money except for a small reserve to buy trade goods
for the winter.

The circuit to the south began to work into an

established pattern of about the same circumference as the one to the north. The trade held up well into the winter months, because Rhineman kept his prices at more or less the same level while the prices in the settlements and in Santa Fe rose sharply during the winter. The profits were still good, and the furs began filling the storeroom during late winter. In early spring, Delgado waited at the house for an extra day for Rhineman to return and he told him about a cousin of his who was looking for employment. Arrangements were made for the cousin to meet Rhineman the next time he returned to the house. Rhineman talked to him, took him on a trip along the circuit to the south, then turned it over to him.

When the first wagon train came and Rhineman sold his furs and wool, there was enough to pay off what he owned on the property, buy fifteen more mules, fill the warehouse with trade goods, and deposit a substantial amount of money in the bank in Santa Fe. Delgado produced another cousin looking for employment, and Rhineman made a couple of trips to the east to work out a circuit, then turned it over to him. It was another wet spring and Rhineman's back bothered him, so he spent several weeks at the house to take care of things which needed his attention. The value of the trade goods stored in the warehouse exceeded the stocks kept by most of the stores in the city, and he had a smith make sets of iron bars for the ventilation windows and a heavy iron gate to go across the door. Keeping inventory of what was in the warehouse was becoming a problem, and Rhineman and Garcia worked out an inventory system. Delgado and one of his cousins had been spending their time between trips in laying the foundations to build small houses for themselves down the hill from the main house, but Rhineman decided to save them the trouble and had workmen come out from the city and build the houses.

During late summer, Rhineman worked out the fourth circuit to the west, and Delgado located another man to take it over after Rhineman made two trips along it. The four circuits began producing an abundance of vegetables, chickens, and sheep as harvest time neared, and Rhineman had Garcia's wife and one of the other women set up a stall in the marketplace to sell the chickens and produce. He bought a pasturage adjacent to his property and had Garcia find an old man to take care of the sheep the traders were bringing in.

Rhineman became ill with a chest congestion during early autumn, making him unable to investigate the possibilities for another circuit to the south and west as he had planned, but he found that there was ample to keep him occupied at home. A cattle dealer decided to return to the East and sold Rhineman his stock and a section of property adjacent to Rhineman's sheep pasturage; a couple of Jewish families arrived in Santa Fe and he helped them situate themselves. One was a tailor named Feldmann, a man of forty with a wife and three small children, and the other was an older, childless couple named Topol who had come to Santa Fe on a doctor's recommendations because of a chronic chest ailment Topol suffered. There was a heavy demand among the Mexican population for highly embroidered men's jackets and sombreros, and the only supply were inferior products from shops in Chihuahua and Mexico City. Feldmann quickly found himself with more work than he could handle in his small shop in the city, and Rhineman gave Topol's wife a job on the marketplace stall in the city and paid her enough for them to manage.

During the winter, Delgado found another man to take over his circuit while he worked out routes to the southwest and northeast and found men to take them over. Rhineman had him stay in Santa Fe when he had finished. The place had become a beehive of activity, and the problems had become far too much for Garcia and Rhineman to handle. Mule trains arrived and left at frequent intervals, there were one or two mules every few days which had gone lame on the trail and needed to be replaced for a time, and there was a constant need for mules to be reshod. The inventory in the warehouse had become much more complicated and fluctuated rapidly, and two or three people from the city and outlying areas called each day to buy a cow or sheep from the pasturage. To add to the confusion, there was a growing daily swarm of people who wanted to buy goods out of the warehouse, because Rhineman had kept his prices at more or less the same level while the prices in the stores in Santa Fe had gone up as usual during winter.

Delgado found a smith who was out of work and had workmen come out from the city to build a shop for him adjacent to the corral. Rhineman found that it was more economical and convenient to have the smith as an employee than to have mules shod in the city. Then Delgado began checking the traders in and out when they arrived and left, going over the goods they had taken in and issuing trade goods to them. He did what he could to help with the warehouse inventory and the people coming to buy, but the problems diminished rapidly when a schoolteacher named Johnson came to Rhineman looking for work. He had come to Santa Fe for his health, a thin and sickly but serious and industrious-looking man of thirty five with a wife and two small children. Most important of all, he had a good knowledge of bookkeeping. Rhineman put him in charge of the warehouse, and kept Delgado receiving incoming goods and issuing to the traders. Then Rhineman had a retail kiosk built at the foot of the hill by the road and hired Johnson's wife to operate it. The steady stream of people coming up from the road to buy from the warehouse stopped.

The smith, Johnson, and two more of the traders wanted houses by the others, and three old men Rhineman had hired to keep a constant armed guard on the warehouse also wanted to live on the place. The corral and stables had been extended and added onto a couple of times but more space was needed, and it had become obvious that a much larger warehouse space would be necessary. The place had been growing rapidly if haphazardly and was larger than many of the small villages to the north, and there was every reason to anticipate more growth. Rhineman discussed it with Johnson, Delgado, and Garcia and worked up a master plan for the hill, then hired workmen from the city to come out and do the construction. Shortly after that, Rhineman began hearing the name the traders and others were using in referring to the hill. They were calling it Rhinaldea, a combination of part of his name and one of the Spanish words for village.

With people and money involved, trouble was inevitable. At rare intervals, one or another of the traders limped about, their faces battered. When they gave embarrassed, evasive replies to his questions, Rhineman assumed that they had become involved in a confrontation along Calle de la Muralla in the city. Then from hints Garcia dropped, Rhineman found that Delgado exercised strict and punitive discipline over the traders. From his experience on the routes, Delgado could tell when the lonely days on the trail had made a man too vulnerable to a winning smile on a pretty face. When a trader turned up short an ounce of gold or part of a bolt of cloth, Delgado dealt with him immediately and severely.

The next trouble was more serious. A delegation from the storekeepers in the city had come to Rhineman when he opened the kiosk on the road, complaining that his low prices were cutting too deeply into their business. By common agreement among themselves, they had been raising the prices during the winter somewhat higher than necessary, and Rhineman's consistent pricing had revealed their practice to the area at large. Rhineman shrugged it off, telling them that he wanted a fair profit and nothing more. Two of them, a man named Haley and one named Phillips, became abusive and darkly threatening. The other four merchants disassociated themselves from Haley and Phillips when they began snarling and cursing, but Rhineman lost his temper and told them all to get off his property. A couple of nights later, riders raced out of the darkness and threw firebrands onto the roof of one of the warehouses, then disappeared into the darkness. The guard's musket firing and the frantic barking of the dogs roused everyone, and the fire was quickly extinguished, but much of the roof had to be replaced, and some furs and wool were damaged. A search party sent out for a missing trader a few days later found his body where he had been shot from ambush. The mules' throats had been slit and the goods had been scattered about in a mute and ghastly message of warning.

Delgado spent a few dollars and a few hours on Calle de la Muralla, and when he returned he told Rhineman that Haley and Phillips were behind it. He wanted to have them killed, but Rhineman was adamantly against it. Rhineman had all the traders armed and warned, and he went to see the captain of the police in Santa Fe. He had a whimsical attitude about it, telling Rhineman that there was no evidence against Haley and Phillips and that he was losing good money and causing trouble by not raising the prices on his goods like everyone else. Rhineman had Delgado bring a skilled sneak thief up from Albuquerque and paid the man to give Haley and Phillips a Mexican warning, a dagger soaked in chicken blood on their pillows while they slept. It cost fifty dollars, but the trouble stopped.

Rhineman wasn't through with them. The next step required changing some plans, because he had intended to buy some wagons and oxen the following spring. Instead, he kept his money and gold in the bank. As Rhineman had started absorbing more of the local trade and the bulk of the furs and wool in the area, some of the merchants in the city who made marginal profits had started taking notes on their stores at the bank to buy their spring stocks and paying off the notes in the autumn, after the harvest. The first wagon trains of the season began coming in and Rhineman shopped at the bank for mortgages. He bought those from Haley and Phillips at a suitable discount, then lowered his prices below those in the city. Virtually all the trade in the city began coming to him. When Haley and Phillips missed an interest payment on their mortgages, he foreclosed on them and raised his prices back to the former level. The captain of the police served the eviction notices, Haley tried to burn his store and was jailed for a couple of weeks, then both of them left for California and it was over. Rhineman had the retail kiosk at Rhinaldea demolished and the stores stocked, one as a general merchandise and the other as a hardware, and picked out a couple of the men and several of the women among the families at Rhinaldea to staff them.

Several more Jewish families arrived in Santa Fe. Among them was a man named Buchner who was experienced in merchandising, an intelligent and resourceful man but one who lacked the confidence and initiative to strike out on his own. Rhineman employed him at the stores in the city for a time to work out some problems which had developed there, then he decided to try something he had been contemplating for a time. He offered Buchner a position in charge of a branch operation at a substantial increase in salary, and Buchner immediately accepted the offer. Rhineman made up a convoy of men and mules to go to Socorro and set up circuits in that area, sending along Delgado to help Buchner get established. Delgado returned in a couple of months, and Rhineman went to Socorro with the next resupply convoy to inspect the operation and make the rounds of a couple of the circuits. The operation was running smoothly, but it took several weeks for him to satisfy himself. The chest congestion returned and the pains in his back became agonizing, and he was bedridden for a week when he returned.

One of Garcia's sisters-in-law came to live with him and his wife, and they moved into one of the houses along the street down the hill from the main house, leaving Rhineman alone in the house. Topol died at about the same time, and Rhineman brought his widow to the house to cook and keep house for him. She was a severely religious woman, and in the face of her stern disapproval Rhineman began observing customs and rites more closely. But it was satisfying rather than bothersome, because his illness and infirmities had brought a growing and more constant awareness of his mortality, and the continued separation from his family had become more difficult to endure. It wasn't unusual for a man to be separated from his family while getting himself established, but the infrequent letters brought by the wagon trains were a poor substitute for the comforts of a full home life. There were also comments in them about Karl from time to time which raised questions in his mind. Karl had graduated from college some time before, which was gratifying, but because the college was The Citadel, he had been commissioned a captain in the South Carolina Militia. That stirred memories of officers Rhineman had seen in Westphalia in their neat, immaculate uniforms and carrying their heavy swords, berating cowering privates they met on the streets and riding with their ladies in open carriages along the Rhine on Sunday afternoons.

Then another letter informed him that Karl had been engaged in a duel but hadn't been wounded. It was clear that Karl's lifestyle was a radical departure from what Rhineman would have chosen for him, and in Rhineman's mind it came closer to being that of an upper class gentile. Rhineman recalled his deliberations at the time he had started branching out into multiple circuits around Santa Fe and had hired Delgado. He had doubted that Karl would be satisfied to ride a trading circuit, and it appeared that those doubts were amply confirmed.

When the wagon trains began arriving the following spring, the prices were much higher. The number of smaller trains had diminished over the past two or three years as they were absorbed by the larger ones, and the owners of these larger trains were in a position to set their own prices. On some items the prices were exorbitant, and the value they allowed for furs and wool was less than it had been. But there was a steady flow of immigrants traveling to California, and they paid what they had to, as did the people in Santa Fe who had no other source of supply.

The prices went up again the following year, and Rhineman decided to do what he could to break the monopoly the owners of the wagon trains had on trade.

There were several limiting factors on traveling between New Mexico Territory and Missouri before the weather broke. One was the difficulty in crossing the high mountain passes during inclement weather with wagons, an undertaking which would take a heavy toll on wagons, animals, and men, even with the most experienced of teamsters. Indians were more dangerous during winter, swooping down on a wagon train in the midst of a storm while the train was secured to weather the storm, and the frigid cold and blizzards were deadly. The cold sapped the strength of both animals and men, and illnesses were more common during winter. But by far the most serious limiting factor was the lack of fodder for animals. The wagon trains always delayed at Westport until the prairies were green so the mules and oxen would have grass to graze during the trip. Fodder was so bulky to carry that most of the cargo space would be taken up by it if the animals had to be fed from the wagons, making the trip senseless.

But Rhineman didn't even consider taking wagons. The mules he owned weren't the tall, burly mules of the East, which were massively strong but accustomed to their warm stalls and plenty of grain when their day's work was done. Rhineman's were the smaller and more hardy mules of the West, crossed with the burro stock brought by the conquistadors and inured through generations to the burning deserts and frigid mountains. They grew long hair during the winter and ate bark or dug through the snow to find dried grass, and during summer they shed their hair and ate cactus to get moisture, going for days without water. They were frequently balky, intractible, and vicious, but they could endure hardships and constant labor which would kill other animals.

The price of mules went down during the winter, when

no crops were being planted, and Rhineman bought up all he could find at a reasonable price. In late winter he sent out word to Socorro and to the second branch he had established at Silver City to reduce the circuits to essential mules and to send all the extra and spare mules to Santa Fe. The long strings of mules began arriving a week later. The smith's forge glowed constantly and his helpers rushed back and forth as he put new shoes on all the mules. Men worked on packsaddles to put new padding under them and strengthen the straps, and other men made up bales of hay and bags of grain in the fodder barn. In late January Rhineman left with Delgado and twenty five other heavily armed men, leading strings of mules which totaled one hundred and thirty animals, all of them burdened with heavy loads of fodder, supplies for the men, furs, bales of wool, and other trade goods.

There was no trouble with Indians, and they made good time through the mountains because they weren't burdened with wagons. But it was dangerous. Two men and six mules fell to their death in the depths off the edge of icy, snow-clogged trails, and another man was seriously injured when he was kicked by a frightened mule. They carried him in a litter on a mule for three days, and when they unloaded him at the end of the third day they found that he was dead.

A winter storm was still hanging on to the east of the mountains, sweeping the prairies with gusty winds and dry, biting snowflakes which were driven along parallel to the ground. They sheltered in a forest to let the worst of it pass while the mules gnawed the bark from the trees and ate the dry, brittle branches the men cut down for them, then they set out again to the east. The mules became skeletal and weak, but the loads diminished as they consumed the carefully-rationed hay and grain and the men consumed their supplies. The pace was very slow for a time, then the weather warmed and the snow abated, and the men delayed each morning for an hour or two after daybreak to let the mules dig through the snow for the dried grass under it. The mules began regaining their strength, and the pace picked up. The pains in Rhineman's back were a constant torture and his chest congestion was so bad he had difficulty in breathing. Delgado frequentiy suggested stopping and resting for a few days, but Rhineman was driven by a purpose, and they continued onward to the east.

They crossed the Missouri in March, just after the ice had broken. The merchants in Westport were in the process of accumulating their goods to be sold to the wagon trains which would begin forming within a few weeks, and Rhineman found that his trade goods were at a premium. The wagon train owners returning from New Mexico Territory had been charging a high price for them. Rhineman's goods were the first of the season and in high demand. Rhineman had also brought gold with him, and he bought an extra forty mules, heavy loads of trade goods for all the animals and supplies for his men. He recrossed the Missouri and camped to keep his men out of the fleshpots of Westport. When the first tinge of green began showing on the hills, they left for New Mexico Territory.

Rhineman was bedridden for almost a month when they returned. He gradually recuperated and regained his strength, and he was seeing to his affairs again when the first wagon train arrived. The owner of the wagon train found that Rhineman had virtually all of the furs and wool in the area and wouldn't sell them. He couldn't sell his goods because Rhineman had saturated the market and lowered the prices, and he didn't have the money to pay his teamsters their wages for the trip. After a couple of days of bickering with Rhineman and being threatened by his angry teamsters, he sold out to Rhineman, including his wagons and oxen. A local store owner who had been a wagon master and who was weary of dealing with customers offered to captain the wagon train for Rhineman. He seemed honest enough and he had a family he was leaving in Santa Fe, so Rhineman hired him. It took a couple of days to collect up the teamsters from Calle de la Muralla, sober them up, and to load up the wool, furs, and other trade goods Rhineman had in his warehouse, then the wagon train left.

It proved to be a good decision, because the man was honest and much happier dealing with fractious animals and teamsters than he had been in struggling with the frustrations of a business. He returned to Santa Fe punctually, unloaded the wagons into Rhineman's warehouse and spent a week with his family while the wagons were being repaired and the animals were resting. Then he loaded up the goods Rhineman had accumulated and took his lists of goods to be bought, and left again. And Rhineman reassessed his position once more.

With the purchase of the wagon train, he was close to realizing his objectives and ambitions. His business had expanded far beyond his initial expectations. With employees numbering in the hundreds and holdings spread over much of New Mexico Territory, he was one of the most wealthy men in the area. The ancient and honored *rico* families went to great lengths to ingratiate themselves with him, and there were overtures of a social nature from the Territorial Governor and other officials. His network of traders covered much of New Mexico Territory, and every few weeks heavily-guarded couriers arrived from the branches in Socorro and Silver City to bring ounces of gold and bars of silver. He was in a position to bring his wife and son to where he had established himself. All that remained was to build the house that he had envisioned for his wife.

The mountain rose in a smooth slope to a plateau well above and a mile beyond Rhinaldea, to the north and east of his sheep and cattle pasturage. The plateau was covered with a thick stand of pinion and tall, mountain pine. Springs dotted the plateau, running down the mountain and forming into the creek which rushed through the shallow valley adjacent to Rhinaldea. The soil on the plateau was rich and black from the centuries the vegetation had fallen on it and rotted into fertile humus. Near the edge of the plateau the strata of solid rock was near the surface to provide a firm foundation for a massive house. He rode around on the mountain and looked at it, then he bought it.

For some reason it was necessary that he start it with his own hands, unassisted by others. He rode up to the plateau each morning, carrying his lunch, and returned in the evening. At first he worked with a sledge hammer and pickaxe, shaping the lip of the living rock which jutted from the soil near the edge and carving it to form the front of the foundation where the wide, sweeping expanse of the veranda would be; where he and his wife would sit while they looked down at what he had done and where his son's children would sit when they talked about what he had done. When the rock was even, he cleared the brush, cut down a few trees, and used four span of mules and a large scraper to dig away the soil and bare the foundation for the rest of the house.

His back ached constantly and his breath was short, but he worked on. He packed the rich soul he dug up into beds among the trees at the sides of where the house would be. He brought roses, lilacs, and native flowering vines and bushes and planted them where the walks in the park-like gardens would wind among them and where his grandchildren would come on Succoth to build the arbor out of branches and hang fruit from the roof. And the fruit would come from the labor of his hands, because he cleared off an opening in the trees at a distance from the foundation of the house and planted apple, peach, plum, and cherry trees.

Others in forgotten centuries past had come and viewed the plateau as the site commanding the fields and valleys below, because there were stone foundations among the trees where dwellings had stood eons before. They were in a pattern at once the same and dissimilar from the ruins he had seen built in front of massive cliff caves in the more desolate places where his trading circuits reached. He left them undisturbed as he dug channels to bring water from the springs for the plants and trees, and he also left undisturbed a tall pillar of rock set upright in a hole which had been chipped into the center of a wide basin of rock among the stone foundations. It had the look and feel of pagan rites, but it had stood guard for centuries over piles of bones he accidentally uncovered then buried again. Even if it would undoubtedly bring a frown of disapproval from Frau Topol and probably his wife, it had already served or not served its wished-for function and it was no more inconsistent with the house and other things he planned than were the apple, peach, plum, and cherry trees among the pinons and tall pines.

Then when he was through with what he had to do and was ready to start bringing workmen to begin building the house for his wife, the wagon trains and immigrants arriving along the Santa Fe Trail brought news of the growing conflict between the North and the South.

Chapter 5

There had been stories of political conflict over tariffs and slavery, to which Rhineman had given no more attention than he had to political affairs in Westphalia, but he was suddenly involved in the situation. Rhineman wrote a letter to his wife and told her to come with Karl to Westport, where he would meet her with his wagon train and bring her to Santa Fe. He sent off the letter by a courier to take it to Independence. The situation worsened precipitantly, each wagon train bringing stories of the increasing hostilities. It was three months before he received a reply to his letter. It came from one of his brothers-in-law on the same wagon train which brought news of the firing on Fort Sumter and the beginning of the Civil War. The letter informed him that his wife had died and his son Karl was in the Confederate Army, a lieutenant colonel in the 124th South Carolina Cavalry Brigade.

For a time he was oblivious to what went on around him, uncaring because the foundations on which he had built everything had suddenly disappeared. But the means to an objective assumes a purpose of its own when it becomes so difficult it absorbs most of one's attention and energies. Rhineman began devoting himself to his affairs again, at first as a rote, then with an intensity approaching his former dedication.

Opinion on the issues involved was widely divided in New Mexico Territory, no one was interested in states' rights and tariffs because the area was neither a state nor bordering on an ocean. The old *rico* families were somewhat concerned over the slavery issue because of the possible impact on the peons they had on their holdings, but most of the people assumed attitudes according to their region of origin. Many were immigrants like Rhineman and had no particular affiliation, the fighting was far away, and few expressed strong or determined feelings.

But opposing armies were building in Texas and California, there were Union troops stationed in New Mexico Territory, and there was little question that it was a matter of time before the conflict spread to the West. Rhineman knew what war and fighting meant, and he began his preparations to last through the war with whatever property he could retain. He talked over his plans with those who worked closely with him, and he took most of his gold out of the bank and carried it by himself to the mountain in the darkness of night to bury it. Delgado left on a scouting trip to the south to look for an area of which he had heard, leading relief horses so he could cover territory more quickly. Three weeks later he returned, exhausted and having ridden two horses to death, but bringing good news. In the deserts to the south and west there was a place the Indians called Cabizzone, a remote and isolated high mountain valley which was watered by springs and deep in lush grass. It would be a safe hiding place for animals and property.

Delgado picked twenty five of the most trusted men, and they gathered up their families and left after dark to lead pack trains loaded with durable goods to Cabizzone. They left the road south of Las Cruces and obliterated their trail as they crossed the desert. Delgado returned alone. The wagon train returned from Missouri with only a few goods, the channels of supply having closed down, and most of the teamsters left to join one army or the other. Delgado took down more pack trains and goods. He took the wagons a few at a time to be disassembled and packed across the desert by the oxen and mules. Rhineman began closing down the trade circuits, and Delgado escorted the remainder of the animals down as they assembled at Rhinaldea. When the recruiting of soldiers began in Nex Mexico Territory, Rhineman had most of his cattle and sheep driven into the mountains north and east of Santa Fe, breaking them into small groups and sending a drover and two armed men with each group to protect them from Indians, hoping that some of them would make it through the war. He left most of his remaining goods secreted in small caches on the mountain behind Rhinaldea.

The war came to Rhinaldea when a Union major and a company of soldiers arrived to confiscate all the animals. There were thirty sheep, twenty-six cows and steers, and twenty-three mules. The major was furious as he sat on his horse and looked down at Rhineman standing in front of his house.

"Goddamnit, I know you have more animals than that! You have oxen and wagons, because I've seen them."

66

"My oxen and wagons were sent out and have not returned," Rhineman replied quietly.

"Then you were crazy to send them out. Don't you know there's a war going on? But anything for another dollar, right?"

Rhineman lifted his eyebrows and shrugged. "Do you take your money from the paymaster, or do you refuse it? We all make our way however we can."

"We're talking about you, not me," the major barked, glaring down at him. "Where are all of your mules? There are twenty-three there, and I know that you have hundreds of them."

"You see there what I have," Rhineman replied, shrugging again.

"Goddamnit, you have mules all over New Mexico Territory," the major shouted angrily, leaning toward him. "Don't lie to me!"

"Then go all over New Mexico Territory and collect them. You see there what I have here."

The major flushed to a deeper red and started to shout again, then he sat back up in his saddle and snapped his mouth closed with a snort of disgust. He looked at the sergeant sitting on a horse by him. "Give him a receipt," he snapped, then he looked back down at Rhineman with a threatening frown. "When all of this is over, you'll probably crawl back out of your hole and go back to business with all the animals and everything you had. And if you do, then I'm going to come back here and talk to you about it."

Rhineman looked up at him from under the flat brim of his hat, his eyes narrowing and boring into the major's. "Do so," he said quietly. "And when you do, remember to speak politely because New Mexico Territory will no longer be under martial law."

The major's nostrils flared and his face twisted with rage. He started to say something and stopped himself again, then he jerked on his reins and wheeled his horse around, riding away. The sergeant wrote on a scrap of paper, he nudged his horse closer, and leaned down to hand it to Rhineman. Rhineman took the piece of paper and put it in his pocket, nodded as the sergeant touched the brim of his hat in a salute, then he stepped up onto the porch and looked down at the road as the soldiers drove the sheep, cattle, and mules away.

Fort Bliss in El Paso went over to the Confederacy in July 1861, and Lieutenant Colonel John Baylor rode out with a force and took Fort Fillmore and occupied Mesilla, running up the Confederate flag. The Union forces remained in the northern part of the Territory as the Confederate forces spread arcoss Arizona Territory. At Rhinaldea the small contingent remained in a defensive posture, ready to flee, conducting a small trade with people who ventured about, and tried to keep in contact with the groups of animals in the mountains.

The situation remained static until the following year, when Brigadier General Sibley left Fort Bliss and marched north. There was a battle at Fort Craig, it fell, and Sibley continued on to the north. When news of the fall of Fort Craig reached Santa Fe, the Territorial Governor, his staff, and the forces in Fort Marcy overlooking Santa Fe hastily decamped and fled toward Fort Union to the north. The city was still, with everyone huddling in their houses, and Rhineman could hear the uproar of hungry and thirsty animals in the corrals at Fort Marcy the next day. He had several men go to the fort and drive the animals out, leading them in a circuitous route to put them in the pasturage adjacent to Rhinaldea. A few days later a contingent of Union forces came through the city, having been driven out of Albuquerque. They confiscated part of the animals, gave Rhineman a receipt for them, and contiuned on toward Fort Union. A week later Sibley's force occupied Santa Fe without a fight.

A smiling, polite captain with a Southern drawl and a contingent of soldiers in grey uniforms rounded up the rest of the animals, and the captain insisted that he and Rhineman count them together before he made out a receipt. They counted them, the captain asked Rhineman his name, and his mouth dropped open when Rhineman told him.

"Rhineman? Rhineman? Are you any kin to Colonel Rhineman in the South Carolina Cavalry?"

"My son's name is Karl, and he is in the Confederate Army."

"That's right, Colonel Karl Rhineman. Made full colonel not too long ago, and got his own cavalry brigade. Well I'll be ..." The captain looked at the animals his men were driving away. He turned back to Rhineman with a remorseful shrug. "Listen, Mr. Rhineman, I hate to do this, but my colonel told me to collect up all the livestock and he saw them standing right up here on the hill ..."

Rhineman smiled whimsically, looking away. "You must do as your superior orders."

"Well, I sure hate doing it to you, I don't mind telling you that. Do you have anything else to eat on?"

Rhineman nodded slightly. "We will live."

"I'm glad of that, then," the captain said, taking a piece of paper and a pencil from his pocket. He put the paper against his saddle as he began writing on it. "What have you heard from the colonel lately?"

"My son? I have heard nothing since the war began."

"Is that right? That's too bad. Somebody told me he was up in Tennessee now and really giving them a fit. I

69

wouldn't mind being there myself if I could be in his brigade." He finished writing on the paper, signed it with a flourish, and handed it to Rhineman. "There you are, Mr. Rhineman."

Rhineman silently nodded, folded the scrap of paper, and put it in his pocket.

"Like I said, I'm sure sorry about this, Mr. Rhineman," the captain said, stepping into the stirrup and mounting his horse. "I'll talk to my colonel and tell him who you are, and maybe he'll let me bring some of them back."

Rhineman nodded slightly. "Thank you."

"Thank you, Mr. Rhineman," the captain said, saluting as he reined his horse away. "So long, and good luck."

"Goodbye," Rhineman replied.

The captain rode back down the hill, following his men as they drove the animals down to the road. Rhineman walked to the porch in front of his house, stood on the edge of it for a moment and watched them driving the animals away. The captain was back the next day to return twelve of the sheep and six of the cattle. He took back the piece of paper he had given Rhineman, changed the numbers on it and chatted with him for a moment, then rode away again, waving.

General Sibley led his forces north out of Santa Fe in late March, and at Glorieta Pass he met Colonel Chivington commanding the Union forces which had moved to the north, together with a small contingent of New Mexico volunteers, a column of Union forces from Colorado, and a column of Union forces from California. There was a pitched battle, and the Confederate forces were defeated. They streamed back to the south, reassembled south of Santa Fe, and continued on back to Texas. A week later, the Union forces moved back into

70

Santa Fe, and a couple of days later the twelve sheep and six cattle Rhineman had in his pasturage were confiscated and he was given a receipt for them.

The war in New Mexico Territory was over, but an atmosphere of tension and impending doom remained. The soldiers were gone from Fort Marcy, fighting somewhere in Texas, and there was little activity. Those who had mined and trapped were still gone. Virtually every animal in the area had been confiscated. The draft animals had gone to do the labor of war and those which could be eaten had somehow been consumed by not substantially more people than had been there when the flocks had been widespread. The *rico* families were still secure with their peons on their holdings even though the Union had carried the battle, and the Territorial Governor was back in his office and overseeing the sleepy atmosphere of the long, hot afternoons in Santa Fe.

The small landholders conducted a limited subsistence trade with Rhineman, and he began to bring some of his stock back out of the mountains. The Indians had taken some of it, the weather had taken more, and the guards and drovers had disappeared with a few bunches. But others had multiplied, and there was more than he had expected. The ranchers with yellowing receipts instead of animals unearthed small caches of gold or arranged credit with Rhineman for a few sheep, and Rhineman sent Delgado to check on the animals and goods at Cabizzone. Delgado returned three weeks later and reported that everything was safe.

Deserters from both sides began to filter through, some of them enroute to California and others going into the mountains of New Mexico Territory to prospect and trap. A few ounces of gold and a few furs began to come in, and some wool began to collect as the ranchers sheared the sheep they had gotten from Rhineman. Some of the travelers coming through had heard of Karl. A couple of them told Rhineman that Karl had been promoted to brigadier general and was the commander of a regiment. Another told Rhineman that he had heard that Karl had been killed, then another told Rhineman of a pitched battle in which Karl's regiment had fought under his command at a date which seemed to be later than the previous story. Yet another told Rhineman that he had heard that Karl had been taken prisoner.

The seasons wore on and the activity increased, and Rhineman brought out the last of the trade goods he had hidden in the vicinity of Rhinaldea. They lasted for a time, then he was out of goods again. He sent Delgado to Cabizzone to bring back a pack train with part of the people at Cabizzone as guards, and it arrived safely. The people moved into the houses at Rhinaldea and it was less like a ghost town, and the goods brought high prices because of the scarcity of everything. More prospectors and trappers began working in the mountains between Santa Fe and Taos again, and Rhineman began sending out mules on a couple of circuits, accompanied by heavily armed guards.

A wagon train came in with news that the war was over, and it was accompanied by a large group of immigrants, some of whom continued on to California and some of whom remained in New Mexico Territory. Rhineman talked with several people about Karl, ranging from those who were sure he was dead to those who were equally sure he had gone to Europe, with various stories and degrees of certainty in between. The wagon train had brought some trade goods in limited quantities and of inferior quality, and Rhineman bought them. Then he sent Delgado to bring everything back from Cabizzone. A month later the strings of mules were clopping along the streets as they passed through Santa Fe toward Rhinaldea, followed a week later by the heavy, rumbling wagons drawn by the slow oxen. Rhinaldea was more of a seething mass of activity than it had ever been for a time as wagons were repaired, mules were shod, and men were sorted out. The wagon train departed for Missouri, the pack trains left to reestablish the branches in Socorro and Silver City, and the circuits out of Santa Fe began operating again.

The wagon train returned with a fair amount of trade goods and left again, and there was a semblance of normality once more. The news from Socorro and Silver City was good, the circuits around Santa Fe were producing well, and the pasturage had large flocks of sheep and herds of cattle in it once more. The furs and wool were piling up at a gratifying rate, and a few ounces of gold were coming in. But it was less satisfying than it had been to Rhineman before, and he never went to the plateau on the mountain above Rhinaldea again.

He spent much of his time in the general store, because that was where most of the travelers stopped in to buy necessities and that was where he was more likely to hear something about Karl. Some travelers wore bits of blue uniforms and others wore bits of grey uniforms, and there were frequent fights between them in the vicinity of Calle de la Muralla and varying degrees of confrontation in other parts of the city. Not surprisingly, Rhineman found that his questions about Karl occasioned outbursts of cursing among some of those wearing bits of blue uniforms, so he limited his direct questions to those in bits of grey uniforms. But a lot of those who had been in the Union Army made the connection with the name on the sign over the door, and they frequently made grudgingly admiring comments about Karl.

The wagon train returned early one morning in August, and he spent much of the day at Rhinaldea as the wagons were being unloaded, talking with the wagon master about the trip and about the possibilities of making another trip before winter set in. It was early afternoon when he got to the store, and there was a quiet, orderly bustle in it. A number of people who had come in with the wagon train were shopping. Men in worn, heavy clothes, women in long, drab dresses, and wide-eyed children moved through the crowded aisles. The usual crowd of loafers was around the cold stove in the center of the large, dim, cool room, chewing tobacco, laughing and talking, and rattling the stove door as they opened it to spit tobacco juice into it. The clerks were moving around and taking care of the customers, and a couple of them were still working on the inventory Rhineman had ordered in anticipation of the arrival of the wagon train.

The loafers grinned, nodded, and spoke to him congenially as he walked by the stove. Most of them looked forward to picking up a few dollars now and then when heavy work had to be done around the store and none of them wanted to be thrown out. Rhineman nodded to them. He walked to the back of the store, went around behind the counter, and picked up the inventory sheets which had been completed, spreading them out on the counter to look at them. A movement at the edge of the counter caught his eye, and he lifted his eyes from the inventory sheets. A small girl was looking up at him over the edge of the counter, her blue eyes wide and her face browned from exposure to the sun and taut-looking from being scrubbed. Her hair was pulled back and tied tightly with a piece of twine, and her small broadcloth dress was bleached to a nondescript grey from being washed, with patches and sewn tears in several places. Rhineman slowly closed one eye and opened it again, winking at her gravely. She blinked and continued gazing up at him open-mouthed. He glanced around, stepped back to a shelf behind the counter, took a stick of hard candy from a jar, then moved back to the counter and handed it to her. A radiant smile spread across her face as she took it, showing the gaps in her mouth where her permanent teeth were just beginning to grow in.

Her mother and father suddenly came around a rack of clothing, looking around for her. The woman's smile was appreciative toward Rhineman and exasperated toward the child as she pulled at the child's sleeve, and the man thanked Rhineman gratefully. They had two more children with them, and Rhineman gave each of them a piece of candy. They all moved back along the rack of clothes, the man and woman looking at the prices and the children looking over their shoulders at Rhineman and grinning as they crunched the candy. Rhineman looked back down at the inventory.

The conversation of the loafers around the stove suddenly stopped, and Rhineman looked up. A man had come in the door, a tall, powerfully-built man. Others had worn bits and pieces of uniforms, but he was in what amounted to a complete uniform without insignia, a long, grey frock coat, tight grey cavalry breeches, and black cavalry boots up to his knees. The coat was without the sash Rhineman had seen Confederate officers wearing and it was hanging open, showing the edge of the holster of a long Colt Peacemaker riding low on his right thigh. The wide-brimmed grey cavalry hat was without the insignia. but it had a gold tassel around the base of the crown that Rhineman hadn't seen before.

His air of confidence and assurance were almost

provocative. He held a thin cheroot between his front teeth and a thin curl of smoke rose from the tip of it as he looked slowly around the store, his stance erect, his shoulders back, and his chest out. Memories of officers Rhineman had seen years before in Germany stirred in his mind. But not the officers of Westphalia. The rarely-seen but well-remembered elite Prussians, the cavalry which had crushed Napoleon's ranks and had motivated the Russian czars to gaze south rather than west when contemplating expansion of their empire. The mustache was thick and black, and the tanned cheeks were smoothly-shaven, with a silvery line of a scar from the right cheekbone to the point of the jaw, reinforcing the memories of Prussians. The eyes were slightly narrowed as he looked around, and there was something belligerent about the line of his chin. Everything about him indicated an overweening pride, pride which passed over the line of pride into arrogance.

"Well, we got us a johnny reb here, Jake."

The man who spoke had come from an aisle near the front of the store, followed by another man. They were both large, burly men, neither of them as tall as the man in Confederate uniform but both of them heavier. They were both looking at him with sneering grins.

"And a general johnny reb, too. See the braid on his hat, Jake? We got us a general johnny reb here. Where's your army at, general johnny reb?"

The tall man looked at them with a scornful gaze, which somehow seemed to be his neutral expression. He slowly lifted his left hand, took his cheroot between his fingers as the tip of it glowed red, exhaled, then put it back between his teeth and dropped his hand. The smoke rolled through the air toward the two men.

Their grins faded into expressions of rage, and they

moved forward, the one who had spoken snarling angrily. "Goddamn, we'll just see what you're made out of, johnny reb…"

Rhineman was watching closely, his eyes on them, and he still almost missed it. The tall man moved with a speed which was unbelievable for his size. His left fist dug into the first man's stomach and doubled him over, then his right fist slammed into the man's head with a meaty thud. The man spun toward the door, smacked into the solid adobe wall by the door, and careened to the floor, stunned. The second man's mouth dropped open, and he snatched at a knife in his belt. One of the shiny black boots darted upward, and the toe connected with the man's crotch with a force which lifted the man's feet off the floor. The knife fell from his hand and he began collapsing as a scream of agony came from his throat, a penetrating sound which reverberated through the store. He fell to his knees, clutching at his crotch, and the tall man kicked him in the side of the head, rolling him across the floor toward the door.

The shrill, agonized shriek seemed to still hang in the air as a ringing vibration. The two men were floundering on the floor, the one who had been kicked making gagging, gasping sounds as his limbs moved aimlessly, and the other one grunting and breathing heavily as he tried to lift himself and focus his eyes. There was no other sound or movement in the store, the customers, clerks, loafers, and Rhineman stood motionless, watching. The tall man still had the cheroot between his front teeth. He took it between his fingers and inhaled, walked toward the two men and tossed the cheroot through the doorway as he exhaled. He looked down at the two men, prodding the one he had hit with his toe.

"Get up, get out, and take him with you. And get out of

77

Santa Fe. If I ever see either of you again, I'll kill you."

His voice was deep, soft, and emotionless. The accent was Southern, but with a trace of a foreign accent. The threat was at once more and less than a threat, a cold and simple statement of intention, more deadly because of the apparent lack of anger. The one who had been hit pushed himself up to his hands and knees, he got shakily to his feet, and began pulling at the other man, dragging him toward the door. A couple of the customers moved slightly and craned their necks to get a better view. The man who had been kicked was still curled tightly, his body jerking and trembling with spasms of pain as choked sounds came from his throat. The other man pulled him along the floor on his side and through the front door. The tall man turned back around.

It came as a shock to Rhineman when he suddenly realized he was looking at Karl. He wasn't at all what Rhineman had expected. Beyond being a stranger through the passing of the years, he was totally alien in appearance and demeanor to those Rhineman was accustomed to having around him. Despite what his wife had written and what he had heard about his son, the man was too much the epitome of worldly sophistication, too commanding, and by far too arrogant.

But all the evidence was there. The uniform was that of a Confederate Cavalry officer, and the man had said that the gold tassel on the crown of the hat was that of a general officer. More than that, there were his features. He had always had his mother's eyes and something of her attractiveness of features which had been so bewitching on the girl of eighteen in Bingen. The resemblance was still there. But on him the eyes were cold and penetrating where his mother's had been soft and loving. On him the features partook of the predatory handsomeness of the eagle rather than the delicate beauty of his mother.

The eyes stopped on Rhineman. Rhineman's limbs seemed to move of their own accord and without conscious volition as he moved along behind the counter, around the end of it, and across the store toward Karl. He was very tall. From even a short distance away, the width of his shoulders and chest made his height seem less, but he was a very tall man, half a head taller than Rhineman. And he looked very aloof, remote, and withdrawn. Rhineman slowed uncertainly. Then the eyes were suddenly smiling, and the smile spread over his face as he held his arms out and walked toward Rhineman.

Rhineman embraced his son, murmuring something, then he stepped back and looked up at him. There seemed to be so much to say and ask. The multitude of events during the years of their separate lives all crowded together in his mind, and it was difficult to think coherently or to say anything. There were the business affairs to explain, and there was the necessity to make sure he knew that all of it was his. There was the death of his mother to talk about and which could at last be talked about because it was a situation which allowed for mutual sympathy. There was his life with his grandfather to talk about, and his college. There was the war. And so many other things.

But it was impossible to say anything, because there was too much to say. And for the first time in his adult life, Rhineman felt tears filling his eyes. He put his hand over his eyes and began weeping. Karl put his arm around his father's shoulders and led him toward the back of the store.

Chapter 6

Piñole was a cluster of adobe buildings at the junction of a narrow dirt road which ran north and south and a dry creekbed which ran east and west to the low, jagged, rocky mountains which rose on each side of the broad basin of desert. The sun glared down from the brassy, cloudless sky, making dark shadows under the porch overhangs and at the sides of the buildings. The air was stifling and absolutely still, like a weighty, suffocating blanket. A few Mexicans sat in the shade of the porches and at the sides of the buildings with their forearms resting on their knees and their chins resting on their forearms. Their wide sombreros were pulled down as they dozed, and three anglos sat in the shade at the front of the livery stable at the side of the cluster of buildings and conversed listlessly. There was a jangle of a guitar from one of the two cantinas, a rhythmatic squeaking as an old anglo with a white beard rocked back and forth on the porch of one of the dwellings, and a jarring grind of cicadas rising and falling in the sultry air.

A wisp of dust rising on the road far to the north became visible as a lighter color against the sun-baked dun of the desert foliage. It gradually grew larger, and dark specks of mounted riders became visible at the bottom of the cloud, shimmering and dancing from the wavering columns of heat waves rising on the road. The riders disappeared into the glossy surface of the spectacular reflection of the sun off an area of hotter air in a low spot on the road. They reappeared on the other side of it, somewhat larger and distinctly separated into seven riders, one in front and two columns of three following behind. One of the anglos sitting in front of the livery stable looked at the approaching riders sleepily, then curiously, and nudged the man sitting by him. The man turned his head and looked, yawning. The third man also looked, lowering his head to peer along the road between two of the rails in the corral at the side of the livery stable.

The hoofbeats became audible as the horses cantered slowly along at a pace which conserved the horses' strength but covered the miles at a steady pace. As the riders drew closer, the three anglos in front of the livery stable shrugged off this drowsiness and sat up. The squeaking of the rocking chair on the porch across the street stopped as the old, bearded anglo sat still and looked at the approaching riders.

The man in front was a tall, wide-shouldered man, an anglo, riding a large, powerful, solid black gelding. He wore a black hat in the Western style, with a low crown and wide, upswept brim, but the rest of his clothes hinted more of the South, tight black breeches, tall, flat-heeled boots, and a black frock coat. The six following him were all smaller men and all Mexicans, and all dressed in virtually identical clothing—enormous black sombreros studded with silver conchos and embroidery on the edges of the brims, short black jackets with ammunition belts crossed on them, tight black breeches with silver stripes down the seams, and tall black boots with high heels. All six of the men wore heavy pistols on their right side and carried rifles against their chests and cradled on their left arms. They had bandanas tied across their faces under their eyes to protect them from the dust. They rode wiry pintos. The men's clothing was grey with dust, and the horses with lathered and streaked with the dust of many miles.

The hoofbeats became a drumming tattoo as they approached, the cloud of dust swelling up behind them and seeming to sweep them toward the edge of the town. They began reining back as they approached the corral at the side of the livery stable. The gelding in front was a fiery animal, soaked with sweat and lather and breathing heavily but still lively and spirited, prancing and wheeling as he tossed his head and fought the bit. The tall man controlled him with expert pressure on the reins, turning and looking at one of the six and silently motioning toward the corral by the livery stable. The Mexican wheeled his horse out of the line, jabbed with his spurs, and the horse darted over to the side of the corral. The man jerked his bandana down and looked at the animals in the corral, blinking away the thick dust which was caked in his eyebrows and around his eyes. He turned his horse back around, nodding and smiling widely.

"They are here, *Senor General.*"

The man on the gelding nodded, wheeling his horse and waving toward the first cantina. The pintos sprang forward as the six riders jabbed with their heavy spurs, and they spurted toward the cantina. The man on the

82

gelding reined up in front of it, pointing and snapping terse orders. Two of the riders urged their horses forward and plowed through the garbage and wind-blown tumbleweeds at the sides of the cantina, riding around to the rear of it. One of the riders leaped off his horse and ran into the cantina, his spurs ringing and clattering against the porch. The other three riders lined up behind the man on the gelding. The gelding danced and bobbed his head nervously, trying to turn from side to side. The dust the riders had stirred began settling. The man ran back out of the cantina.

"He is not here, *Senor General.*"

The man on the gelding silently motioned toward the other cantina, turning his horse toward it. The two riders came charging back out from behind the cantina and rode toward the other one. The three who had been lined up behind the gelding spurred their horses toward it, and the other man scrambled back onto his horse and urged it toward the cantina. Two of the riders rode around the sides of it to the rear, three waited behind the gelding, and one man dismounted and ran inside. The sound of the guitar playing suddenly stopped. Long seconds of silence passed, and the dust began settling again. Then there was a sound of a commotion in the rear of the cantina. A woman's scream rang out, shrill and penetrating in the hot air, and there was a rumble of heavy furniture being turned over and tossed about. An excited, frightened shout from a man blended with another scream from the woman. The old anglo sitting on the porch rose from his rocking chair and stepped to the edge of the porch to watch. Mexicans dozing in the shade of the buildings rose and moved to the edge of the street to look, murmuring among themselves. A naked, heavyset Mexican woman ran out from behind the building, screaming frantically and trying to cover herself with her hands. She ran across the street and disappeared between two buildings, her flabby breasts and large belly quivering and flopping. A murmur of laughter rose from those watching.

A man ran out after the woman, naked except for the loose, dingy white trousers he held up with both hands. One of the riders pounded after him, foam from the horse's damp lips spattering on his bare shoulders. As he ran out into the street, the rider reined his horse back and to one side, snatching a rope from the side of his saddle and shaking it to build a loop. The man on foot darted from side to side, looking over his shoulder with a terrified expression. The other riders raced around in a wide circle in the street to cut him off. The rope hissed as the loop spun in the air, then the loop darted forward. The man on foot tried to dodge it, but it settled around him. He pulled at it frantically, trying to wriggle out of it, but the rider snapped the reins and the pinto lunged backward and to one side with the coordinated movement of a well-trained roping and cutting horse, snapping the rope tight and jerking the man off his feet. The other riders reined up around the man, dust boiling up as their horses slid to a stop. They all moved toward the gelding in a surging rush, the man at the end of the rope rolling from side to side as he slid through the dust and clawed at his trousers to keep them up.

The rider towing him at the end of the rope wheeled his horse around with a flourish, rolling the man through the dust and bringing him to a stop almost under the gelding's nose. The gelding tried to rear, then wheeled and pranced as the man controlled him. The three anglos in front of the livery stable hitched at their trousers and gunbelts, walking along the street toward the riders. The old anglo stepped down off the porch and walked toward the riders.

Several of the Mexicans moved closer.

"Why did you steal my mules?"

"I was drunk, *Senor General*, and when I awoke I was already many miles away and I was frightened to—"

"It is one thing to get drunk, but it is another to steal mules. A man is fined for being drunk, but he can be hung for stealing mules."

"Do not hang me, *Senor General*. I have a wife and children, and I will do anything if—"

"How much money did you get for the mules?"

"Ten dollars, *Senor General*. It was all that the—"

"Where is the ten dollars?"

"I have six dollars left, *Senor General*, in my shirt. The rest went for tequila, and I paid a dollar for that woman who was with me in—"

"You paid her too much. Your wife is undoubtedly a much more attractive woman, and she is free."

A ripple of laughter ran through the riders. The man looked around at them, grinning anxiously and nodding. He looked back at the man on the gelding. "Please do not hang me, *Senor General*, and please do not tell my wife ..."

His voice faded as the man looked down at him sternly. He was silent for a moment, then he nodded shortly. "I'll give you another chance, but I won't forget this. I won't forget that I had to ride after you and find you and the mules—"

"Thank you, *Senor General*. I will work very hard, and I will do anything you say if you—"

"Listen to me! I'll buy the mules back, and you will lead them back to Socorro. You will not ride, you will lead them. You will be fined twenty dollars from your wages, ten to repay the money I will pay to get the mules back and ten to remind you of what you did. And I will hang you if I

ever have any more trouble with you. Do you understand?"

"*Si, Senor General*," the man replied with relief as he
started pushing himself to his feet. "And I will work hard,
and I will never..."

His voice faded as the man on the gelding reined his
horse away. The other riders backed their horses away
from the man on the ground and followed the gelding.
The rider holding the rope snapped it to loosen it, the man
wriggled out of it and raced toward the cantina. The rider
turned his horse after the others as he coiled the rope. The
on-lookers followed the riders toward the livery stable.

The owner of the livery was standing in the dark shade
of the wide entrance door, yawning, blinking sleepily, and
lifting his hat to comb his fingers through his hair. He
looked at the riders curiously as they approached, then he
stiffened and frowned as two of the men on pintos
crowded their horses up to the gate of the corral and one
of them leaned down to open it.

"Hey, what the hell's going on here?"

"I'm taking my mules back," the man on the gelding
replied, taking a leather purse from his coat pocket. He
opened it, took out a coin, and tossed it. "There's your ten
dollars."

The man caught the coin, looked at it, and flushed
angrily. "Now just a goddamned minute! You can't ride in
here and—"

"You knew those mules were stolen when you bought
them. That's why you paid five dollars each for twenty
dollar mules. This time you get your money back. The
next time you buy mules someone has stolen from me, I'll
burn down your barn and drive your stock off."

The man clenched his fists and opened his mouth to
reply, then closed his mouth with a snap and walked back

into the livery stable, cursing under his breath. The two riders came back out of the corral, leading two mules on halter ropes. The man who had been roped ran out from behind the cantina down the street and trotted toward the riders as he pulled on his wide, straw sombrero, a piece of rope holding up his cotton trousers. He had on a cotton shirt which matched the trousers, and the heavy sandals on his feet stirred up puffs of dust. He trotted to the mules and took the halter ropes from the rider holding them.

"Don't you ever cause me any more trouble."

"No, no, *Senor General.* I will work hard, and I will—"

"Go ahead and get started. You have a long walk ahead of you."

He nodded and grinned anxiously, pulling the mules toward the road. One of the riders commented quietly to another, looking at him, and they chuckled softly. One of the three who had been sitting in front of the livery stable moved closer to the gelding and looked up at the man with a thoughtful frown, then a delighted grin began spreading across his face.

"By God," he said quietly, then repeated it in a louder voice. "By God! You're General Rhineman, ain't you? I knowed I knowed you! You're General Rhineman, ain't you, sir?"

Rhineman looked down at him and nodded. "I'm Rhineman."

"By God, here I am meeting General Rhineman!" the man chortled, grinning widely and stepping closer as he reached up to shake hands. "My name's Henry Bridges, General. I was in McCabe's Georgians at Brook's Hill."

Rhineman smiled slightly and nodded, leaning down to shake the man's hand. "Brook's Hill? That was quite a battle, wasn't it?"

"It was after you got there," the man laughed. "They was giving us a fit until you got there, and ... you was riding a horse just like that one. wasn't you? By God, I'll never forget that day. They was driving us back into the mud until you ..." He turned and looked at the two men with him, laughing and nodding. "I told you all about it, didn't I? They had us whupped fair, then all of a sudden it sounded like old nick had turned loose of every bit of thunder he had, and comes this brigade of cavalry right over and down the hill at full gallop, the general here right at the forefront, bugles blowing, flags flying. They peeled their line back as slick as a knife peeling a apple, then the rest of the general's regiment came over that hill, whopped into them, and mashed them just like pissants." He looked back up at Rhineman, grinning excitedly. "By God, I reckon that was a battle, General. A couple more like that one, and the stars and bars would be flying over Washington today."

Rhineman chuckled and shrugged. "What are you doing here, Bridges?"

"Oh, just roaming around and looking for a job, General. Me and my partners here. You wouldn't have a place where you could put us on at, would you? Looks like you might near got your own army there."

Rhineman chuckled again, then his smile became whimsical. "There are jobs, but you'll have to work."

"Oh, we'll work, General. Won't we, boys? This here is Lew Carrigan and Billy Edwards, General. And we need the money, so we'll work."

"Ride up to Escondito, then, and go out to the copper mine on the west side of the town. The man in charge there is named Kessner. He'll give you a job, and the job will last as long as you'll work."

88

"We'll work, won't we, boys? And we're mighty obliged, General."

Rhineman nodded, reining his horse away. "You're more than welcome. It was good to see you, Bridges."

"It was mighty good for me, General. So long, and good luck."

"Same to you."

Rhineman turned the gelding toward the road. The six riders pulled their bandanas up over their mouths and noses as they spurred their horses and formed two lines behind Rhineman. The horses cantered away along the road, and the man leading the two mules moved to the side of the road and took off his sombrero as they passed. The three men chuckled and exchanged comments as they walked toward their horses tied at the hitching rail in front of the livery stable. The owner of the livery stable emerged from the darkness of the interior of the building and looked at the seven riders moving along the road, muttering to himself under his breath. The rest of the onlookers turned away and scattered.

The three men mounted their horses and turned them toward the road at a plodding walk. The Mexicans went back to the shade where they had been dozing and sat down again, pulling their sombreros down over their eyes and resting their chins on their forearms. The old anglo went back to his rocking chair. The hoofbeats of the cantering horses faded into the distance, and the sound of the three horses walking along the road gradually died away. A guitar jangled in one of the cantinas. The rocking chair squeaked as it rocked back and forth. The sound of the cicadas' shrill clamor rose in the hot, still air.

Chapter 7

His father had died scant months after he arrived in Santa Fe. But before he died, there had been long, quiet conversations while sitting in the cool shade of the modest house above the streets of small houses which comprised the village of Rhinaldea.

"It seems strange that you would fight to preserve slavery, Karl."

"I wouldn't and didn't fight to preserve slavery, and I know of no one who did. It was doomed long ago, because it contains the seeds of its own destruction and would have gone of its own accord. I fought for states' rights and because of selective tariffs designed to limit the trade at Charleston and New Orleans."

"Are such things worth dying for?"

"I know of nothing worth dying for, but a man has to pick where he will stand. If it takes fighting to stand there, then he has to fight. And in fighting he might be killed."

"Did you like being a soldier?"

"Yes. It is orderly and organized, and it is an honorable profession. And war is wine like none other."

"Would you prefer to continue being a soldier?"

"No, my war of that kind is over for me, and I would rather remain here now."

As the days passed, he could see his father becoming visibly weaker. His back pained him almost constantly, he coughed a lot, and neither the doctor in the city nor the one at the fort seemed to be able to do anything to give him relief. But more than his physical infirmities, he had the attitude of one who has achieved a goal and is relinquishing his burden. It occurred to Karl that in coming to Santa Fe he might have brought his father's death with him.

The funeral was in the small synagogue on the south end of Santa Fe, and it was filled to overflowing with the government and business community of the city, with hordes of Rhineman employees filling the streets outside. The burial was in the cemetary plot at Rhinaldea, where an old man named Garcia had been buried a few days after Karl arrived and where others employed by his father had been buried during the past few years.

Living for the few months in the house with his father had brought back memories of life in his grandfather's house before going to The Citadel. The casual attitude toward religion he remembered in his father had been replaced by one more closely approaching his grandfather's attitude. But he found it satisfying, cementing a bond between him and his father and making the years of their separation and the differences brought about through their ways of life diminish into nothing.

His father had talked a lot about the various business affairs, sometimes talking rapidly and moving from one thing to the other as though conscious of a limit on available time and apprehensive that Karl would be without some bit of crucial information. He had covered the way in which each of the separate undertakings had been started and developed, together with the problems and difficulties which had been experienced and resolved, and those which had been foreseen and avoided. He also talked about the employees and about their characteristics, revealing insight into people and a prodigious memory in recalling the names and length of employment of obscure employees at the Socorro and Silver City branches among the hundreds of other employees. Then he wanted Karl to go on a circuit with a trader and to visit the branches, which he did. They discussed Karl's observations and other things his father had thought of to tell him.

The business affairs continued running on their own inertia for a time after his father's death, because everyone knew their job and there were no new undertakings in progress. But his presence gradually began to be felt, and it became clear to everyone that there were distinct differences between him and his father.

In Germany his sphere of activities had been limited to the Jewish community and he had rarely even seen a gentile before the roving gangs began prowling the streets shortly before they left. The jeers and catcalls he had experienced in South Carolina had been a new as well as a painfully humiliating experience, a fulfillment of the stories of persecution he had heard all his life. It was more intense but expressed in less obvious ways at The Citadel, as his grandfather had said it would be, and he disregarded his grandfather's advice about enduring it and searched for other ways of dealing with it. For a time he searched in vain. It caused a deep hurt when the fencing instructor, a French Jew, drove at him with a ruthless ferocity he never showed with the other cadets, berating him for mistakes and slapping his legs with stinging blows of the foil when he slackened his stance or dropped his guard. He responded with an angry, puzzled resentment, and he began practicing with his foil in every spare moment, building the strength and endurance in his right arm, and perfecting his attacks and counterattacks on a dummy. Then his matches with the instructor became heated battles that others came to watch, and it slowly dawned on him that the instructor had motivated him into compacting the learning of months into a few weeks. And the lesson the instructor had been teaching him was learned. He began meeting the cold and supercilious attitudes of the instructors by having his lessons in perfect order, his boots gleaming with a mirror shine, his uniform immaculate, and his conduct and discipline faultless. The ostracism by the other cadets was met by withdrawing behind a wall of indifference and maintaining a constant readiness to retaliate against any overt action or expression. His opponents in the boxing class were always the largest, and his questions in class were already the hardest. He took his beatings and memorized his lessons.

In the second year it had changed. Tradition came into the situation and mandated a change. He was a full cadet and one of the brotherhood of The Citadel. He was captain of the boxing team and fencing team, and he was on the honor roll, and there was a distinct warming of attitudes toward him. When four cadets who had been drinking attacked him, he kept it to himself and resolved to catch each of them alone and return the beating. But a cadet captain found out about it and went to the commandant to prefer court martial charges against the four. Rhineman was called in to be questioned, but he stood on the code of honor and was mute on all questions about the four. Things came full circle. The commandant sentenced him to a tour of marching back and forth on the quadrangle under the blazing sun as punishment for refusing to respond to questions. The commanding cadet colonel posted honor guards on each end of the quadrangle to salute him each time he passed for observing the code. The four were ostracized by the cadet body, and they resigned after enduring a week of what Rhineman had endured for a year. Rhineman was completely accepted by the cadet body.

But the world was wider than The Citadel and had no established and respected code of honor. In its stead, a ready fist served well. And along with his readiness to retaliate, there was a stubborn refusal to have his desires thwarted.

In the days after his father died, the readiness to retaliate was demonstrated when he overheard a muttered disparaging remark between two men in the store, soundly whipped both of them, and threw them out. His reaction to another going against his will was evidenced when he went to a cantina in a morose mood and returned home hours after time for dinner and on the point of being staggering drunk. Frau Topol began loudly packing her belongings and announcing that she was leaving. He ordered her to remain in the house and be quiet about it, and went to bed. When he awoke the next morning, she was gone. He sat in Delgado's house and drank coffee and nursed his headache while Delgado made inquiries. Delgado returned and reported that she had gone to the Nachamson house in the city and Rhineman took a carriage there. The Nachamsons disassociated themselves with the disagreement and disappeared as Rhineman loaded Frau Topol's things into the carriage, then led her out of the house by her arm and put her in the carriage. He took her back to Rhinaldea, unloaded her belongings and took them in, and told her he would thrash her if she tried to leave again. Her uncharacteristically meek demeanor as she settled herself back into the household indicated she at least considered the possibility that he meant it literally. She was silently but nonetheless sternly disapproving about his drinking and the liquor he kept in the house. Each time he drank too much and had a hangover, she radiated triumphant gratification and went about her duties in the house with a boistrous bustle and clatter of noise.

His military training was a large factor in his judgment of what went on around him. Where his father had measured effectiveness almost solely in terms of return, he also measured it in terms of appearance. The haphazard clutter of Rhinaldea irritated him. The casual disposal of garbage, disordered piles of firewood scattered about, clotheslines stretching in all directions, and occasional indifference toward the condition of adobe walls and fences came to an end. Barns, tack rooms, warehouses, and the village became neat and orderly. Some of those who worked as guards for the warehouses and the wagon train and traders in times of trouble with raiders or Indians began to dress more or less the same, in dark sombreros, jackets and breeches. Karl increased their wages to help them pay for the clothes. Within a short time their appearance became quasi-military.

There was a social life of sorts. The Jewish community in Santa Fe was small but growing, and invitations to dinner, small parties, and other situations of a nature to display the domestic and social skills of daughters of marriageable age had begun within days of his arrival in Santa Fe. His father had been acquainted with a number of local *rico* families, from which frequent invitations had also been forthcoming and continued after his father's death. They were more numerous than the Jewish families and were inclined to be larger, with numerically more daughters aged fifteen to twenty. Conversations with the fathers frequently touched on their total acceptance of Judaism as the basis for Christianity and their willingness to encourage this or that attractive daughter in the inclinations she had shown to convert to the Jewish religion. But most of his time and attention were taken up by the business, he had no desire to get married, and he met no one attractive enough to change his mind about marriage or lure his mind away from the business.

The social life broadened to include all of the business leaders and gradually worked into the political leaders in the months after his father's death. His father had isolated himself to a great extent, feeling uncomfortable and awkward in social situations and somewhat too newly risen in wealth to be completely comfortable with the ensuing change in status, and Karl was impatient with many of the artifices and protocols demanded by social situations. But education at The Citadel had included an indoctrination on the necessity for a social life as well as the skills to pursue it, and he was involved in the community at large far more than his father had been. A few of the younger officers at Fort Marcy harbored a degree of resentment toward him for his part in the Civil War, but the older professionals had a more broad-minded attitude as well as considerable respect for his achievements during the War, and he was frequently invited to functions at the fort. That appeared to relieve whatever anxiety the Territorial Governor and his staff had felt about Rhineman's war record, and he was invited to several of the governor's receptions and then to a ball during the spring after he arrived in Santa Fe.

But an extensive social life was precluded by his inclinations and by his involvement in the business. For a time he left everything as it was, watching and learning, until an opportunity developed to buy copper holdings in the south of the Territory. The mining operations had been suspended during the War, and the attempt to revive them had been unsuccessful because of insufficient capital, arguments among the partners in the venture, and other problems. He took Delgado with him when he rode down to Escondito to look at the mine, and they spent several days in examining the situation. It was an undertaking which was risky, because it was only marginally profitable. There was a steady demand for copper, but because of the location the only options lay between buying and installing a smelter at enormous cost and proportional risk or hauling the ore overland to the railhead in Colorado.

Delgado was helpful in finding out things and bringing people to talk to him, but he was carefully noncommittal on the wisdom of investing money in the mine. Even with his lack of knowledge about mining, Rhineman could see why the mine had been losing money. Everything was disorganized, the partners were issuing conflicting orders, the animals and equipment weren't being cared for properly, and there was a lot of time lost because the workers were living in Escondito instead of at the mine. The quality of ore being extracted assayed as good when he took a few pieces chosen at random to the assay office in Albuquerque, and that was the only thing which had kept the operation going for as long as it had been.

When they returned to Santa Fe, Rhineman pondered about it for a time. Several Eastern mining cartels were interested in it, and several entrepreneurs in Santa Fe were trying to put together companies to take over the operation. An engineer named Kessner came to see Rhineman about it. He was from England, where he had been educated and had worked as an engineer in coal and lead mines. He had worked for a couple of mining companies in Colorado, and during their conversation they discovered that their paths had crossed in Virginia, where Rhineman had forced marched his regiment through the night and defended a bridge Kessner had been assigned to destroy.

Kessner's story was that many Jews who worked in corporate structures had their talents employed while benefits and recognition were denied to them. He was a determined, vigorous, and forceful man, and he convinced Rhineman of the wisdom of investing in the mine. Kessner believed that the mine could produce a moderate profit on a short-term basis, but the full potential would be realized at some future time when a smelter was installed or when the railroads were extended and transportation became more economical. Rhineman decided to buy the mine.

He spent a couple of months at Escondito with Kessner to help him reorganize the operation, and he found Kessner to be a tireless and dedicated man who was extremely short-tempered and quick to use his fists. Kessner fired a third of the men on the site, others trickled in, and housing was built on the site. The activity increased sharply, and Kessner went on the first wagon train of ore to the railhead, firing three of the teamsters along the way, driving one of the wagons himself, and impressing two of the guards Rhineman had sent along to drive the other wagons.

Rhineman stayed in touch with Santa Fe through couriers while he was in Escondito, and he remained there until he was satisfied that the operation was smoothly functioning. From his experiences in the Army, he had learned that time spent with the corporals' squads paid rich dividends when battle was joined. He knew the value of making his presence known and in applying his attention to problems he found, regardless of how insignificant they were to the business at large. So he knew the details of the operation at Escondito and the men knew him when he left. When he stopped at the branch at Socorro on the way back to Santa Fe and found that two mules had disappeared, he took the time necessary to locate the thief and mules and return them to Socorro before he continued on to Santa Fe.

Another opportunity developed during the winter. One of the *rico* families with vast holdings south and west of Taos went bankrupt because of gambling debts incurred by the father and a couple of his sons, and the family property went up for sale. A lot of it was in the Rio Grande valley and was excellent pasturage for much of the year. Rhineman looked it over then sent to Escondito for Kessner to find out how difficult it would be to irrigate the land. Some primitive irrigation was already being done, and Kessner came up, looked at the land and at the rude dams, dikes, and channels which were scattered along that area of the river, and told Rhineman that it would be simple.

There was some wheat farming along the Rio Grande, but most of the property was undeveloped and the large holdings devoted to pasturage. The amount of wheat being cultivated had presumably sufficed the needs of the area at one time, but flour had been one of the main items being transported from the East since Karl had arrived in Santa Fe. The cost of flour was high because of the freight charge. It was difficult to transport, the bulky barrels were heavy and hard to handle but also fragile enough so that they could burst as the wagons lurched over rough spots on the trail.

There was no great interest in the land and the price was relatively low, so Rhineman bought two thousand acres of it and sent a courier to St. Louis to place advertisements in the newspapers for experienced wheat farmers and a miller. Most of the peons who had been on the estate were still there, fearfully awaiting their fate. Rhineman enrolled them as employees and had Kessner come back up from Escondito and start them working on an irrigation system. Much of it was completed by the time of the spring flood, and an early wagon train of immigrants brought a large stack of letters in reply to the advertisements for farmers and a miller. Rhineman picked out four of the farmers and a miller from the letters and made arrangements for the wagon train to bring them. They arrived with the wagon train when it returned in April.

The irrigation system was finished and operating when they arrived, and Rhineman went with them to get the undertaking organized. His desire for neatness and order was more paramount than his desire to get the planting started. First he organized all the labor into leveling the existing structures and building a couple of streets of houses to accomodate everyone, forming the nucleus of a town which would eventually be called Wheatland.

After the old houses were destroyed and the new ones built, he put part of the workers with the miller to build the mill and divided the rest of them and the land among the four farmers. The farmers cursed and shouted as they taught the workers the unfamiliar process of plowing straight lines across the fields. Problems and friction developed, but eventually the stretches of black, virgin soil exposed to the sun began to widen and run together as the teams of oxen worked back and forth and pulled the plows along. The wagon train returned from Missouri again and two of the wagons came north along the road to Taos to bring equipment and tools the farmers had wanted, and the planting proceeded as the mill began to take form.

The black of the plowed and harrowed fields was tinged with a pale green for a couple of days, then one morning Rhineman rose and found that the black had disappeared under a coating of pale green shoots of wheat blanketing the fields. On the same morning the miller let water through the flume in the mill, and pronounced it ready to grind wheat. Rhineman had a meeting and appointed the farmer who had shown the most leadership in charge, and he prepared to leave the next morning.

He left just after daybreak with the two guards he had brought with him as couriers to carry messages to Santa Fe. They carried food with them so they could stop briefly at noon to rest their horses and reach Rhinaldea well before dark. They cantered along the road at an easy pace, men stopping work in the small fields adjacent to the road or hesitating as they drove their sheep along to stare at Rhineman and the two men. Women and children in the isolated houses and clusters of two or three adobe houses peered curiously at them. A few loaded burros, small carts, and people carrying firewood, produce, and other burdens moved along the road between the houses and clusters of houses, and occasionally Rhineman and the two men moved to the side of the road and formed into a single file to go through a flock of sheep which flowed around their horses like water, making their bleating noises.

At mid-morning they topped a rise in the road and started down a long, slow incline. Far down the road Rhineman saw two women trudging along on foot. The road had curved away from the river and it was a dry, arid stretch, with no small farms and ranches for a considerable distance, and women rarely traveled for long distances alone. As the horses approached the women, they glanced back then looked ahead again, moving to the edge of the road. One of them was young and the other was old, but they were both dressed poorly in faded, patched clothes with ragged mantillas around their heads and faces. They were carrying bundles which looked like clothing.

Rhineman started to pass them, then reined up and looked down at them. "Where are you going?"

They looked up at him. The younger woman's mantilla covered all of her face except her eyes. They were large, dark, and liquid, looking up at him in apprehension and fright, darting toward the other men, then turning away as she turned her back. The older woman looked at him and at the other two men as she murmured a question in Spanish, her eyes cautious. One of the riders replied, she said something else, and the rider looked at Rhineman.

"They are going to Santa Fe, *Senor General*. They are from Rancho Cadena, and the *patrón* told them to leave because the man of the family died."

Rancho Cadena was only a short distance away, over a ridge of hills to the west and along the river, so they hadn't come far. And there was a danger that the young woman would be raped before they reached Santa Fe. Rhineman nodded and looked down at the young woman again. She was looking at him from the corners of her eyes, and her eyes darted quickly away. He looked back at the rider.

"Tell them they may come to Rhinaldea if they wish. They can wash clothes or carry firewood or something."

The suggestion precipitated a lengthy conversation between the two men and the old woman. Rhineman relaxed in the saddle, taking a cheroot from his coat and

102

lighting it. He could understand isolated words as the men talked, and they explained who Rhineman was, where Rhinaldea was located, and what Rhineman had suggested. Presently the man spoke to Rhineman again.

"They are very grateful, *Senor General*, and they will come to Rhinaldea as quickly as they can."

Rhineman shook his head. "They can't go alone. Tie their bundles to your saddles and let them ride behind the saddles."

The two riders dismounted, explaining, and the old woman smiled widely and heaved a gusty sigh of relief. The young woman glanced up at him again and quickly averted her face, pulling her mantilla tighter over her face. He observed that her lashes were very long and thick. The riders took the bundles from the women, tied them across the front of their saddles, then lifted the women onto their horses' rumps behind their saddles. The rider lifting the old woman had a certain amount of difficulty, but the one lifting the young woman did so easily. She was very small and slender. As the man lifted her, the ragged hem of her faded, voluminous skirt lifted slightly, baring her ankles and part of the calves of her legs. Her legs looked smooth and shapely. Her tiny feet and worn sandals were dusty from the road. Rhineman looked away, controlling his horse and taking deep drags on his cheroot as the men got back onto their saddles, then he relaxed his reins and let his horse move along the road again.

There had been a few casual affairs in South Carolina and during the War when he had remained in one place long enough for them to develop, but the arena in Santa Fe was restricted. The wife of an officer at Fort Marcy had made overtures, but he'd had three duels for whatever purpose they served and wanted no more if they could be avoided. His father had ventured into the edges of the

103

subject behind a wall of euphemisms to warn that the women of Calle de la Muralla were frequently diseased, as he had already presumed. Frau Topol had made her own contributions on the subject, dropping totally irrelevant remarks into a conversation in the form of quotations from the prophets on the efficacy of marriage in quenching the fires of the body. Delgado had made his contribution in its more earthly nature by hinting about unattached women who would be accomodating and undemanding. But everything had its complications. On the other hand, he was in the prime of his manhood. So it was a problem. His mind dwelled on the glimpse of the smooth calves as he rode along the road and listened absently to the conversation between the two men and the old woman behind him.

The sun rose higher and a wind swept along the road, and the conversation behind him died out as the riders wrapped their bandanas around their mouths and noses and the women pulled their mantillas tighter to filter the dust from the air they breathed. At about noon they came to a small creek which splashed down the precipitous hill on the left and watered a thicket of trees and wide glade of grass on the right side of the road. Rhineman turned his horse off the road and into the trees.

The riders dismounted, lifted the women down, and saw to their horses as Rhineman watered his horse, took the bit out of his mouth, and hobbled him so he could graze and rest. The two women moved a few yards away from the men to a pool of water to drink and wash the dust from their faces and hands, and the older woman murmured quietly to the younger one at length. Rhineman sat down under a tree, as the two riders took the food from their saddle bags and built a fire and found a flat rock on which to heat the food.

Rhineman leaned back against the tree, absently watching the men heating the food and thinking about what he had to do when he reached Rhinaldea. The women moved toward the fire. Rhineman glanced at them, then looked harder. The younger woman's mantilla was draped around her shoulders like a shawl, with her hair spreading down over it. She was breathtakingly beautiful. Her face was small and heart-shaped, with a wide forehead, enormous eyes, a small nose and well-defined cheek bones, and full, wide lips, features which were finely-molded and delicate and emphasized her Spanish ancestry. Her hair was thick and long, parted in the center and cascading down over her shoulders and almost to her waist in thick masses, so black it had blue highlights, and it gleamed in the scattered spots of sunlight which pierced through the foliage overhead and shone on it as they walked toward the fire. The dress she was wearing looked as though it might be one of the old woman's or made for someone else much larger than her, because it draped on her. But there were indications of a slender, lithe figure as she walked across to the fire with a naturally graceful, feline stride. The ragged cuffs of her blouse were rolled up, showing her small, delicate wrists and part of her forearms.

She was conscious of his gaze and felt herself on display. She tried and failed to keep an expression of unconcerned insouciance on her face as she walked toward the fire and looked off into the distance as though gazing at something. But she was only seventeen or eighteen, a child of the simple and uncomplicated life in an adobe hut, and her sophistication wasn't up to the task. There was a trace of self consciousness on her face, and a faint blush lay on the smooth, olive cheeks. Rhineman looked at her, reflecting that it had probably been the matron rather than the owner at Rancho Cadena who had insisted they leave.

Both of the men were looking at Rhineman. He glanced at them and looked away. "Share the food with them."

The old woman protested weakly and momentarily, then smiled widely and nodded vigorously to Rhineman in thanks. Rhineman nodded and looked away. The young woman sat down a few feet from him, folding her hands on her lap and looking down at them. The old woman and one of the men went to get something from the bundles on the saddles. The men had brought tamales and fat burritos covered with corn husks to protect them. The man sitting by the fire turned them on the rock to warm them through as he asked the young woman something in a quiet voice. She replied in a soft murmur. It was the first time Rhineman had heard her voice. It had a chiming, melodious quality, retaining something of the clear, ringing timbre of a child's voice but still having a throaty, almost husky undertone of an adult woman's. And she had an utterly charming lisp. She darted a glance toward him as his eyes met hers, and her cheeks turned to a dark crimson as she looked away. The man by the fire cleared his throat softly as he turned the food again.

The old woman and the other man returned from the horses. The old woman was carrying a roll of dry tortillas wrapped in corn husks, the food which had apparently been intended to suffice them for their journey to Santa Fe. They sat down by the fire, and the old woman and two men chatted as they unrolled the husks from the tamales and burritos and scraped part of the filling from the burritos into the tortillas for the women. The young woman ate very little, holding one of the tortillas between her small hands and taking tiny bites from it, looking down as she slowly chewed. Rhineman's usually healthy appetite had deserted him. The old woman ate with a hearty gusto, as did the two men.

Rhineman ordinarily observed the local custom of a nap after eating or in the heat of the day, but the horses had stopped grazing and for some reason he was impatient to reach Rhinaldea. He smoked a cheroot as the old woman and men finished the food, then he stood up and brushed off his coat and breeches, nodding toward the horses. The men put the fire out, and the women walked toward the horses, the old woman talking quietly to the young one.

One of the men's horses favored its left rear foot as they led the horses back onto the road, and Rhineman pointed it out. The man lifted the horse's foot, and found a stone tightly lodged between the inside wall of the hoof and the soft part of the foot. He prised the stone out, and carefully examined the foot. The soft part wasn't cut, but it seemed to be sensitive because the horse jerked his foot when the man pressed the place where the stone had been. He dropped the foot back to the ground and nodded to Rhineman.

"I believe it will be all right, *Senor General*."

Rhineman shook his head. "The young woman will ride behind my saddle. Hold my horse's head so he won't throw her when I put her on."

The man said something to the young woman as he dropped his reins to ground tie his horse. He walked around to the front of Rhineman's horse to hold his head. Rhineman handed him the reins and turned. The young woman was standing at the side of his horse and looking down at the ground. The old woman and the other man were already mounted, and they were looking at him. Rhineman looked back at the man holding his horse.

"What are they called?"

"Cisneros, *Senor General.*"

"Their first names."

"The mother is called Rosa, and the daughter is called Consuela, *Senor General.*"

Spanish had always sounded pleasant, smooth, and flowing when he listened to the men talking to each other in their language, but the liquid ripple of her name in the Spanish pronunciation was no less than beautiful. And it seemed an extremely suitable name for her, the dancing sounds somehow very representative of her. She was still looking down at the ground, her cheeks burning. The other man and old woman were still looking at him. He put his hands on her waist and lifted her onto the horse. His fingers almost met around her tiny waist as he pressed the loose fabric of her dress together. She was very light, and there seemed to be a fresh, heady fragrance about her. Her hands rested on his forearms with a feathery pressure as he lifted her onto the horse, then she clutched the cantle of the saddle as the horse shifted his feet restlessly.

Rhineman put his foot into the stirrup and swung his other leg over the horn of the saddle as he stepped onto the horse. He reached down and took the reins. The horse began prancing, and Rhineman glanced back at Consuela as he tightened the reins and controlled the horse. She had wrapped her mantilla around her face again, and was clutching the cantle of the saddle tightly. He lifted one of her hands and put it on his coat. She grasped his coat with her other hand, moving closer to the saddle. The other man mounted his horse, and Rhineman let his horse out to a slow canter along the road. Consuela's shoulder brushed his back occasionally as she balanced herself and swayed with the horse's movements. He was acutely aware of the light pressure of her hands on his coat.

108

Chapter 8

They arrived at Rhinaldea during late afternoon. Word of
his arrival spread through the village like wildfire, and
women and children darted about to collect up and
dispose of piles of rubbish and stacks of firewood thrown
between the houses as they turned off the road and started
up the hill. There were always empty houses among the
streets of houses which spread down the hill toward the
road, and Rhineman had always found it vaguely
irritating that someone or other was always wanting to
build another house or two even while some stood empty,
adding to the clutter, congestion, and confusion in the
village. He left Consuela and her mother at the nearest
empty house, and turned his horse back along the street.

The affairs of the village were overseen by a council of
elders, fathers of employees who had come to live with
them and a couple of older, retired employees. The old
man who headed the council stopped him on the street.

He felt restless and impatient, but he restrained himself, returned the old man's polite greeting, and listened to him. The council wanted to expand the common area where some small trading was done and where the women washed clothes, and four of the families new to the village wanted to live adjacent to each other, which would require building an extra house at the end of a street where there were three empty houses. Rhineman agreed to expanding the common area, shook his head over building the extra house, and nodded in return to the old man's polite bow as he lifted his reins and rode on along the street.

The affairs of the business ran themselves to a great extent, but during a lengthy absence matters always arose which were beyond the responsibility of those in charge or exceeded the responsibility they wanted to assume. Urgent things were taken care of by courier, and those which could wait accumulated until his return. Delgado met him on the way to the stables, followed closely by Johnson, the warehouseman, and Guitarrez, the smith. The deferred problems were usually the most knotty ones, and Delgado reported that he had a message from Kessner at Escondito that saloons and whorehouses had been set up in tents on property adjacent to the mine property, with a consequent rise in fights, injuries, and absenteeism, and a decline in production. There was also a need for more freight wagons because several had been destroyed in accidents on the Santa Fe Trail and in transporting ore from the copper mine to the railhead. Johnson wanted to build more warehouse space and add a couple more clerks to his crew, and Guitarrez wanted to expand the smithy shops and enlarge the tack room, which was already a building almost as large as one of the warehouses.

While Delgado was talking about the wagons, Guitarrez suggested that it might be feasible to make their own wagons instead of buying them from the East. As Rhineman listened to them, the man in charge of the stables mentioned that he needed more storage space for grain and fodder, and the captain of the guard came in and said that some trouble with the circuits out of Socorro had stretched his crew thin and he needed to hire a few more men if the trouble continued or if something else came up.

There were other things, and Delgado told him there were several letters concerning problems at the branches at Socorro and Silver City which were among the invoices and reports waiting on him at his house. And he had matters concerning the wheat farming to take up with them, but he didn't feel like going into them or trying to make any decisions on the things they had brought up. He told them he would meet with them the next morning and went to his house.

The house was a Germanic island in a surrounding of transplanted Castilian culture because of the furniture and furnishings Frau Topol had wheedled or browbeaten out of his father, and it was quiet, cool, and comfortable. He took a bath and changed into clean clothes, had dinner, and went into the room set aside in the house as an office. There was a thick stack of papers in the center of the old, massive desk in the corner of the room, and he sat down in the chair at the desk and pulled them toward him, idly leafing through them and glancing at them. The light in the room was growing dim, and Frau Topol silently entered with a candlestick, put it on the desk, and left. He thumbed through a few more of the papers, then pushed them away and rose from the chair, and crossed the room to a cabinet to take out a bottle of whiskey and a glass.

The feeble, flickering yellow light of the candle played over a crude, battered packframe in the corner made of heavy sticks or oak and laced together with rawhide, with wide rawhide shoulder straps. It was the packframe his father had used when he had started walking along the road north of Santa Fe and trading with the nearest farms and small ranches, kept by his father as a visible reminder of his beginnings. On the wall above the desk was a cured sheepskin with the fleshed side out. It had a crude map of New Mexico Territory etched into it with a hot iron, showing the locations of the major cities and towns and the branch offices in Socorro and Silver City. Dotted lines represented the trade circuits, and heavy lines represented the major supply routes, with the Santa Fe Trail running off the right edge of the sheepskin. A few months before, he had etched in the mine at Escondito. And now he could etch in Wheatland. He emptied his glass and refilled it.

The rich colors of sunset flooded through the window as he looked up at the map, sipping the whiskey. His father had left him more than a thriving business. Among the papers in front of him were the monthly payroll lists sent by the bank for him to review, and the total amounts were staggering. His father had left him the nucleus of an empire. And he felt a deep responsibility toward it, the need to conserve and expand it. He rocked the chair back and forth, looking up at the map, then looked at the stack of papers again. Strangely, they seemed suddenly trivial in a way while still undiminished in importance. There were problems to be considered and either accepted or resolved, but he felt a brooding restlessness and an impatience toward minutiae. He pushed the chair back and rose, picking up the glass and bottle, and walked back through the house toward the porch.

The sky was crimson with the light of the setting sun,

and the windows in the small houses were beginning to glow yellow as the deep shadows spread. Smoke rose from the chimneys and the pungent odor of woodsmoke blended with the spicy aromas of food cooking. The shrill voices of children laughing and playing echoed through the houses and carried to the porch, and there were shouts from women calling their children home. He sat down in a chair, refilled the glass, and put the bottle on the floor beside the chair.

The sky darkened in the east and the darkness spread toward the west, then the dying rays of the sun lingered on the peaks of the mountains for a moment and faded as the sky became a canopy of velvety black studded with the bright lights of the stars. Frau Topol came out, silhouetted against the light coming through the front door, and asked him in a tone of stern disapproval if he wanted a lamp or candle. He silently shook his head, and she sniffed loudly and went back in. He drained his glass, felt around for the bottle, and refilled the glass.

The sound of guitars and men and women singing came from several of the houses, the different melodies and rhythms conflicting but not clashing, somehow blending into a harmonious whole by virtue of the affinities. To him the songs had a plaintive quality, a characteristically wailing sound of lamentation which seemed at odds with the general optimistic and carefree personalities he had found most Mexicans to have. There were sounds of loud conversation and laughter, and a man and woman argued loudly in one of the houses. Yellow, swinging dots of light moved back and forth as people went from one house to another, carrying lanterns. The squares of light from the windows and dots of light from the lanterns grew brighter as the darkness thickened, broken only by the shadowy haze of glow from the stars.

The massive, glowing disc of the moon rose over the mountains in the east and spread a soft light over the houses, and he could again see their vague outlines and the columns of smoke rising from the chimneys.

His hand brushed the bottle over as he reached for it again. He leaned over, groped for it, and picked it up. None had spilled, because it was empty. He put it and the glass down, pushed himself up from the chair, and went inside for another bottle. Frau Topol was polishing the silver salvers which were displayed on the buffet against the wall in an obvious display of determined industry at an hour when she was usually resting. She glared at him down her nose as he passed through the room.

In a way the whiskey seemed to dull the turbulent restlessness which seethed within him, but in another way it seemed to bring it into sharper focus at a different and more bothersome level. He sipped another glass of whiskey, looking down the hill at the houses in the moonlight and thinking of the events of the day. The wheat farm had prospects of being highly profitable, because the flour could be sold at prices well below the cost of flour transported from the East and still produce a substantial profit. The four farmers had muttered darkly about the weather and about the unfamiliar soil and climate, but the grain had sprouted well before they had expected. He mused about it, then thought about the women. It had been fortunate for them that he and his men had come along to bring them to a place of safety. He refilled his glass, thinking about Consuela.

Normally the village elders saw that newcomers were situated. But others who had come to the village had been family groups, often needy but invariably bringing a few possessions and sticks of furniture on their back or on a bony burro. But Consuela and her mother had only their

114

small bundles of clothing, their only food a stack of dry tortillas. And they undoubtedly had no money. It occurred to him that he had been remiss in not assuring that they had enough money to buy food and other necessities until such time as they began to earn some by washing clothes, carrying firewood and water, and cleaning houses for the unmarried men who lived in the village. As he thought about it, he suddenly found the thought of Consuela doing menial labor very distasteful, particularly cleaning houses for unmarried men.

He felt remorseful that he had overlooked seeing to their welfare. They were undoubtedly in a cold and cheerless house, dusty and littered from being unoccupied and children playing through it, their only food the remainders of the dry tortillas. He emptied his glass and put it on the floor by the chair, and pushed himself to his feet. The world seemed to shift from side to side around him, and he put his hand on the support post on the edge of the porch by the steps, steadying himself. A thin, distant voice in some far recess of his mind murmured chidingly, telling him he had drunk too much and warning him about impaired judgment. He shrugged it off and walked down the steps.

The moon was almost overhead, and its light was deceiving, seeming to be as bright as twilight but only faintly illuminating the rocks and holes in the road down the hill. The thin, high-altitude air had cooled quickly after the sun set, as it always did, and he shivered slightly as the chill penetrated his shirt. There were three or four men standing by the end house on the first street, looking at a burro tethered by the house in the light of a lantern and apparently discussing it. Their conversation died as he approached the houses, and they turned and walked along the street. One of his rules was that animals were to be kept either in the corral or the pasturage rather than among the houses, but the burro standing by the house was doing no harm and he felt tolerant about it.

The street seemed very quiet as he turned onto it. The usual sounds were coming from the other streets, but the one ahead of him seemed almost deserted except for the light coming from the windows and open doors. No one was moving along the street. The sounds from the houses were quiet and muted as he walked along the street, glancing through the open doorways into the houses. Women were doing their chores and men were attending to small tasks, and they were talking softly or not at all. The atmosphere seemed strange. A child came to an open doorway and gaped out into the darkness at him, and a woman's voice rang out, calling the child away from the doorway.

Some of the houses had their doors closed, and he was momentarily confused as to which was the house where he had left Consuela and her mother. He looked back along the street and oriented himself, then turned toward one of the houses, walked to it, and knocked on the door. There was a shuffle of movement in the house, then Consuela's mother opened the door, smiling up at him and opening the door wider for him to enter.

Their situation was far better than he had expected. He remembered that one of the leather hinges on the door had been broken and the door had been hanging at an angle, giving a glimpse of a dirty, littered front room, but both of the hinges on the door looked new and the room was spotless. Moreover, there was a table and chairs, shelves, and a cabinet. Rugs were hanging on the walls and new mats were on the floor, and a small fire was burning in the fireplace. Several of the brightly-painted earthenware pots were against the wall on each side of the

116

fireplace, and a lamp was on the table, spreading its yellow light across the room to meet that coming from the fireplace. Consuela was sitting on the mat in front of the fireplace with a pile of the bits of cotton rags that women briaded into rugs. Instead of the faded, ragged, shapeless dress of before, she was wearing a bright, colorful skirt and a skimpy sleeveless blouse which was cut low in the front. Her hair lay over her shoulders and fell down her back in a thick, heavy, flowing mass which caught gleams of light from the flames in the fireplace.

It suddenly became clear through the confusing muddle of alcohol. Consuela looked both resigned and apprehensive, and her mother's expression was one of relief and pleasure. They had been expecting him. The entire village had been expecting him. The riders who had been with him had detected interest in him for her and had relayed it to the villagers. On the likelihood that he had made a choice, there had been a flurry of preparations, with the villagers helping and bringing things, undoubtedly including the clothes Consuela was wearing. The quietness along the street was also explained. Everyone had been taking pains not to observe him passing along the street, a lack of notice as unostentatious as when he had arrived on a parade field to review his troops to the accompaniment of rolling drums, shouted commands bringing formations to attention, and fluttering guidons dipping in salute.

He suddenly felt like an utter fool. It hadn't even occurred to him that neither of them could speak English, and he didn't have anyone with him to interpret so he could ask them if they needed anything. But they obviously didn't. Consuela's mother closed the door behind him and motioned him toward a chair, rattling something to Consuela. Consuela rose with a smooth,

117

effortless movement and went to the corner of the room and began rooting in a basket. There seemed to be no way that he could immediately leave without being insulting and making even more of a fool of himself, and the fire looked inviting after walking in the chilly night air. He walked over to the fireplace and knelt in front of it, warming his hands. Consuela came back toward the fireplace with a bottle and earthenware cup. She knelt and put the cup on the hearth in front of him, pouring tequila into it from the bottle. Consuela's mother bustled around on the other side of the room, then came and put a small basket of shriveled lemons, a knife, a salt cellar, and a small plate on the hearth. She went back across the room toward a door, saying something which clearly had the intent of excusing herself, and went into another room and slammed the door behind her.

They were suddenly very much alone. Consuela pursed her lips with concentration as she put one of the lemons on the plate and began cutting it into wedges with the knife. Her small hands trembled slightly, and she darted glances at him from the corners of her eyes as the knife sliced through the lemon. He looked at her, revising his estimate of her age downward by a year or two. Her shoulders were slender and delicate to the point of being thin, and her upper arms were almost shapelessly straight, with a fine down on them. She looked almost childlike, despite the rouge on her lips and the dark shadow of cosmetics on her upper eyelids. And her intensity of concentration on what she was doing was also childlike. She cut the lemon into wedges on the plate, put it by the cup of tequila, took the top off the salt cellar and put it by the plate. She looked at everything to make sure she had forgotten nothing, and motioned toward it with a movement of her hand to indicate that it was ready for him.

He didn't like tequila, but it seemed rude to refuse it. He touched his thumbnail to his tongue and dipped it into the salt, picked up one of the lemon wedges and squeezed the juice onto his tongue, put the salt on his thumbnail on his tongue, then picked up the cup and took a drink of the tequila. It burned a trail of fire down to his stomach and the room seemed to shift from one side to the other around him. When he caught his breath, Consuela was looking up at him, her eyes wide and searching. Her eyes immediately dropped from his, and she glanced around in confusion, as though looking for something to do. She reached for the bits of cotton cloth and pulled them closer to her. She began braiding them again with rapid, nimble movements of her small fingers.

The combination of the tequila and the warmth of the fire drove the chill away, and he suddenly felt very weary. He put the cup on the hearth and stretched his legs out, leaning on his elbow and looking at the pile of cotton cloth. Her fingers stopped, then began moving more rapidly. He lifted his eyes to her face. There was a suggestion of soft down on the edges of her cheeks which seemed very attractive for some reason, a tiny flaw which made her beauty more compelling, just as her lisp made her voice more pleasant to hear. Her large eyes darted toward him then away again. The light of the fire played on her face, making shadows in the hollows of her delicate features. A pulse throbbed in her slender throat. His hand seemed to move of its own accord, reaching out and covering both of her hands. Her hands stopped moving, and she jumped slightly as she made a soft sound in her throat. He tightened his hand on hers, pulling her toward him. She pushed the pile of cotton cloth away, and her sandals made a soft sound on the mat as she moved toward him.

The impulse to pull her to him seemed to be the normal

response to the situation. She was there and he was there, they were alone, and he pulled her into his arms in a casual, thoughtless, and unpremeditated reaction. She didn't struggle, even though she appeared to struggle within herself to keep from struggling with him. Tremors of fright raced through her, her small breasts surged as she breathed rapidly, and her lips trembled. But she slid into his arms and lay against him, her eyes avoiding his. He brushed her hair back from her face, looking down at her, and he pulled her closer as he lowered his lips to hers.

Then responses of a different nature stirred, his manhood reacting to her beauty and to her timid submissiveness, her passive acquiescence enough of a willing offer to satisfy the thin and distant voice clamoring in his mind and warning that he was taking advantage of her weak and helpless lack of defense. His hands moved over her to satisfy a hunger which swelled to life within him, giving rise to a deeper and more fiery need which burst to a raging intensity as he crushed her lips under his and held her slender body. He pulled at her clothes and his, his awareness of his surroundings and her tiny whimpers of fright disappearing into a blind and numb rush to satisfy the primitive and demanding need which sprang from the very core of his being. He smothered her body under his, taking her with the driving urgency which had built up within him over the months, accumulating at a level where it was unknown as it waited for its moment to come to life and possess him.

The fire had died down and the room was in darkness except for the weak light from the lamp on the table, its small flame dancing feebly on the wick inside the smoke-blackened glass chimney. Her face was in shadow. The ashes in the fire settled with a soft sound and the flames licked upward for a moment, illuminating the side of her face with a wavering, transient light. Tears had gathered in her eyes and run down her cheeks, and her eyes were open and staring sightlessly at a point somewhere on his chest. Her features were neutral, but reflected a placid satisfaction that it was over, that her pain and terror had not been as devastating as she had imagined. She had been a virgin. In a way she was very young and in another way she was ageless, her enormous and softly liquid eyes contained the wisdom of womanhood which had its origins in the dawn of time. Her skin had a texture which felt almost powdery, dryly soft, and provided a continuing sensual pleasure. Her breasts were small, resilient, olive mounds tipped by large, dark rose nipples, and he was fascinated with them. Her lips were bruised and her cheeks were chaffed from his impassioned kisses, but his desire was only assauged, not satisfied. He held her, felt her, and kissed her.

She stirred in his arms, lifting herself to her elbow, and pointed to a door and murmured something in a shaking whisper. He released her and sat up. She sat up and adjusted her clothes, then pushed herself to her feet and walked to the table to turn the lamp wick down and extinguish the flame. His head swam as he stumbled to his feet, pulling at his clothes. Her sandals whispered in the darkness, and the leather hinges on the door creaked and the bottom of it dragged on the floor as she opened it. He stumbled toward the door. The moonlight came through the window and fell in a pool on the bright colors of the patchwork cover on the small bed. She dropped her sandals to the floor and slipped under the cover. It moved as she took off her clothes and dropped them to the floor. He undressed and dropped his clothes into a pile on the floor, lifted the edge of the cover, and got into bed beside her.

The moonlight shone softly on her small face and gleamed in her large, dark eyes as she lay on her back and stared up at the ceiling. The feel of her naked body by him in the bed made his desire surge to urgent life again, and the corn husks in the mattress rustled as he moved closer to her. Her eyes darted toward him then away again, and she licked her lips and swallowed dryly, moving fractionally closer to him in a mute expression of willingness and invitation. He put his arms around her, kissing her, and she put her arm around his waist and opened her thighs.

Sleep evaded him. Fatigue from the exertions of the day and from the exhaustion of love blended with the remaining effects of the liquor, making a heavy cloud of inviting drowsiness, but he couldn't go to sleep. He lay on his side with his arms around her, looking at her. Her long, thick lashes lay on her cheeks, and she breathed with a slow, deep rhythm. The moonlight made gleaming highlights in her scattered hair. She was warm and soft against him. He moved his hand up her slender body, cupping one of her breasts. Her eyes flew open and she looked at him with a startled, frightened expression for an instant, then with recognition. She blinked, and her eyes moved away, looking up toward the ceiling as she licked her lips and swallowed. He felt her breast, his need returning. Her eyes moved back to his, and she made a small, interrogative sound in her throat. He put his arms around her, kissing her, and she opened her thighs once more.

Chapter 9

The penetrating chill and thick blanket of impenetrable darkness lay over the hill and the silent streets of houses as he went back to his house. A yellow light was glowing in the front windows of his house. When he entered, Frau Topol snapped awake in the chair by the buffet and glared at him in silence in the dim light of the guttering candle on the buffet. He looked back at her in silence as he closed the front door behind him with a solid sound. He walked toward his room, ordering her in a loud voice to make him some coffee.

Dawn came as he sat at his desk and drank the coffee, reading rapidly through the papers on his desk by the light of a candle. He finished the papers and went back outside. He stood on the porch and looked down at the houses. Smoke was rising from the chimneys and there was activity in the village, children running back and forth and shouting, dogs racing about and barking, and people moving about and beginning their day. A thin column of smoke trickled up from the chimney of Consuela's house. He stepped down off the porch. It took an effort of will to walk on up the hill toward the stables, corral, and warehouses rather than down toward Consuela's house.

The weary indifference of the night before was replaced with a driving energy and seething impatience to get things done. He told the captain of the guard to begin a recruitment for new guards and immediately leave and go to Escondito to start a campaign of harrassment of the saloons and whorehouses in the vicinity of the mine until they left. He went through the warehouses to see how much more space was required, looked at the smithy shops and tack room, and sent Delgado for workmen to begin the added construction. He went through the warehouse bills and receipts for the past few weeks and looked over the running inventory, then he got his horse from the stables and rode into Santa Fe to look at the stores.

During the afternoon he rode his horse up the mountain and toward a flat plateau overlooking Rhinaldea, looking at the condition of the flocks of sheep and herds of cattle in the pasturage. As he sat on his horse looking down the mountain, he saw a spot of warmly familiar color in the upper reaches of the creek which provided water for the village. It was the skirt and blouse Consuela had worn the night before. He turned his horse down the mountain.

She was catching crayfish, the rushing water swirling around her smooth calves as she held the hem of her skirt gathered in her left hand and bent over, groping under rocks with her right hand. Occasionally she would find one and walk to a small basket by her sandals on the creekbank and drop the crayfish into it. She had her mind

124

on the crayfish with her usual intensity of concentration on whatever she was doing, and the babbling sound of the water smothered the noises his horse made approaching. When he was a few yards away, the horse's hoofs clattered against some rocks and she looked up at him, her eyes wide and startled. A shy and flushed but wide and radiant smile spread across her face, and she waded out of the creek and stood by her basket, looking up at him.

He dismounted, tied the reins to a sapling, and walked toward her. She became more flushed and confused and began talking rapidly, pointing to the basket and to the water and stones as she rattled in her thin voice and lisped thickly. He put his arm around her and his finger under her chin, and she became silent as she leaned against him and lifted her lips to his. The feel of her body in his arms and the fresh scent of her hair and body in his nostrils brought back memories of the night before yet seemed to suggest the promise of delights he had never before known. He lifted his head and looked down at her, smiling at her as his hand moved on her slender back, feeling her through the thin fabric of her blouse. Her eyes danced and she bit her lower lip between her teeth as she glanced quickly around to see if anyone had seen them, then she giggled and pointed toward a stand of willows. He nodded. She giggled again, moving away and gathering up her sandals and basket. He untied his horse and followed her toward the willows.

There had always been boredom with the partner after the sexual desires were satisfied, but he was unable to satisfy himself sufficiently for his interest in her to wane. And that night she had a guitar. She strummed on it and sang in her chiming, melodious, and lisping voice as he dozed off into the sleep of total exhaustion. The memory of the plaintive, wailing notes of the song remained in his mind as he slept and still seemed to be ringing in his ears when he awoke. He looked at her small, beautiful face in the repose of sleep as the moonlight shone on it, and gently awakened her and pulled her into his arms.

The people who lived in a house at the end of the street nearest his house decided they wanted to move to a house further down the hill. Rhineman had the house refurbished and an extra room and porch built onto it before Consuela and her mother moved into it. He had new furniture made for the house, including a bed of substantial proportions for Consuela's room, and he made arrangements for Consuela's mother to be paid a generous stipend to see to their needs.

It took Frau Topol only a short time to determine the reason behind his nightly absence, and she was appropriately outraged. But she expressed her indignation through indirect means, quoting applicable Biblical passages in a ponderous, stentorian tone at odd and unexpected moments, but she didn't threaten to leave. There seemed to be an element of resignation toward and acceptance of his iniquities, as well as an almost earthly determination to deal with the situation. She had never been in the village before, but she proceeded with Germanic determination and diligence to become acquainted with Consuela and her mother and to teach Consuela English. Consuela had been rapidly picking up a few words so she could talk with Rhineman, and her English began abruptly improving, even though it had an exotic mixture of Spanish and German accents.

When Consuela became pregnant, Frau Topol's despair was of an order which made Rhineman speculate that her interest in establishing communication with Consuela had been for the purpose of making sure Consuela was possessed of the knowledge to prevent such a situation from developing. Frau Topol was distraught for a time, then she summoned reserves of endurance and accepted Consuela's pregnancy as well. Rhineman was remotely bothered by the full implications of fathering a child under such circumstances, but it didn't diminish his interest in Consuela.

Kessner's predictions about the possible returns from the mine proved to have been conservative. The price of copper ore gradually inched upward as some of the large deposits in Colorado played out and a couple of other mines closed for one reason or other, and the operation at Escondito began paying a handsome profit. The first wheat crop began maturing, and Rhineman sent extra employees up to Wheatland to help with the harvest and the replanting of the fields with winter wheat. The yield far exceeded the most optimistic expectations of the farmers. The fertile, virgin soil flooded with irrigation water and the long days of baking in the hot sun producing a dense growth and thick, fat kernels, and there was suddenly an urgent storage problem for wheat and for flour as the mill rumbled through the night and spewed out bag after bag of high quality flour. Rhineman had silos built at Wheatland to store the grain while the mill ground it during the winter and he had a warehouse built at Rhinaldea for the flour, but there was still an excess. The wagon train was in Santa Fe and it was late in the season to send it to Missouri again, so he had it loaded with flour and sent it West. The flour was sold among the mining towns on the eastern slopes of the Sierra Nevada, and the wagon train returned with furs, hides, gold, and silver before the first snow.

The demand for foods preserved in tin cans had grown during the past years since the equipment and techniques had improved to the point that the risk of violent illness or death from eating canned foods had become an acceptable level. They were particularly popular with trappers and miners because the food was precooked and only had to be heated. There was a small canning factory in Santa Fe which went out of business during early winter. Rhineman had hundreds of bags of dried beans and peas in the warehouses which would be worth much more in cans, so he bought out the factory and had all the equipment and supplies moved to Rhinaldea. A couple of people who had worked as foremen in the factory came with the equipment and took jobs with Rhineman. In talking with them, Rhineman found that one of the reasons for the failure of the factory had been the high incidence of swelling and exploding cans because of a lack of care and adequate hygiene among the employees. He resolved that problem by paying the workers part of their wages in cans of food selected at random by the foremen.

The first wagon train in from Missouri brought flour as one of the main items of cargo, as usual, and the owner of the train found the market so depressed that he had to sell the flour to Rhineman at a price below that he had paid for it in Missouri. The loss made the trip only marginally profitable for him and since he had been considering another and a more settled and less hazardous way of making a living, he offered to sell out his wagon train to Rhineman. Rhineman had tried to have wagons made locally, but the skills and hardwoods required for the massive, heavy wagons weren't available, so he bought the wagons. He sent part of them to Escondito to replace some which had been damaged beyond repair in accidents hauling ore, and he filled the remainder with flour and cans of beans and peas and sent them West into the mining towns east of the Sierra Nevada. The wagons returned within three weeks, having sold out.

Rhineman bought vegetables, beans, and peas in the area and kept the canning factory running at full production. He had the next wagon train to the East bring back supplies and equipment to expand the factory. The contents of the cans had been indicated by rough lettering in paint on the sides of the cans, and in order to make them more attractive, he had a printer in Santa Fe print colorful labels and had them glued on the cans. The next wagon loads to the West carried the first of many loads of cans which would become scattered in the compost piles of the mining towns, so that in the following years curiosity seekers prowling the deserted mining towns of the West would come across piles of rusty cans bearing the label of Rhinaldea beans, peas, tomatoes, and other foods.

Consuela gave birth to a brawny, healthy boy. The baby was enormously large for her and she was in labor eighteen hours, but she quickly recovered from the ordeal. She called the baby Carlos, and she collected together sticks and slats for Rhineman to make a cradle with his own hands in what was to him an almost ceremonial procedure of obscure intent. Frau Topol's cautions and admonitions had taken root in Consuela's mind, and at certain times during the following months she denied herself to him. Her difficulty in delivering the baby was only one of the many reasons he didn't want her to have another child, and he never insisted.

The canning factory expanded, and Rhineman had a large building constructed adjacent to it for a factory to make barrels for storing and shipping flour. The trade into the West was highly profitable, and he bought a few more wagons from immigrants who were settling in New Mexico Territory and added them to the trains going east and west. One of the banks in Santa Fe almost collapsed because of overextended credit on a shortage of capital, and Rhineman capitalized it in exchange for fifty one percent of the stock.

Autumn began to approach, and he made his rounds of the business, beginning with the mine at Escondito and the branch offices in Silver City and Socorro. A courier caught up with him at Silver City and gave him a message about trouble at Wheatland because of a boundary dispute with the owner of a large ranch adjacent to the wheat fields. Cattle from the ranch had been straying over and had been driven back, but the owner of the ranch had asserted that part of his land was being used for growing wheat. Rhineman assembled all the extra guards immediately available and sent them north with the four who had accompanied him, carrying a message to the captain of the guard at Santa Fe to go to Wheatland with all available guards to protect the equipment and buildings from possible vandalism, a common tactic when boundaries were in dispute. At the same time, he sent the courier back to Delgado with instructions to go and see the landowner to determine if some peaceful settlement could be worked out.

At Socorro another courier caught up with him, bringing a message from Delgado to the effect that the landowner was negotiating. When Rhineman got back to Santa Fe, Delgado was still at Wheatland and there was a message that he had worked out a price on a large strip of land which went well beyond the boundary under dispute and ended at a long stone escarpment which would provide a visible and indisputable boundary. The price was reasonable enough and included the stock on the land, and when Rhineman went north to Wheatland he sent Delgado back to Santa Fe and talked with the landowner, confirming the arrangement.

There was still a potential for trouble. The peons on the

property had been on adversary terms with the landowner, and they didn't trust anyone. They didn't want to learn to farm wheat, they didn't want to go to Rhinaldea or elsewhere to work, and they didn't want to consider other options. They wanted to remain in their tiny, dingy houses and tend the stock, as their fathers had done before them. Evicting them was a possibility which disregarded humanitarian principles as well as the potential for an extended campaign of vandalism, and the property sloped sharply upward from the river and would require an extensive, complicated, and expensive systems of pumps and aqueducts for irrigation. Rhineman decided to leave the situation as it was for a time, and he designated one of the men on the land to be in charge. He had the captain of the guard designate a large contingent of men to spend the winter at Wheatland to enforce the orders of the man in charge of the peons on the new property, made arrangements for houses to be built for them so they could bring their families up, and went on to the north by himself to check on some of the trade circuits.

The trade circuits had moved, contracted, and expanded in response to the demand for goods. During the past couple of years much of the mining and trapping had moved deeper into the mountains, stretching some of the circuits to distances which took a little over six weeks to travel. He rode along the mountain trails at random, cutting across the circuits traveled by a couple of traders, and talked to miners and trappers. All of them had heard of him, and he knew many of them on sight from their trips into Santa Fe. He spent a couple of nights at their cabins, then he met one of his traders on the trail and traveled with him for a time. The trader was one of the original men who had worked for his father, and in common with most men who spent most of their time alone in the mountains, he had a large store of tales of hardships, Indians, and bears of improbable size and cunning.

The man was entertaining and it was pleasant to ride along the high mountain trails with no problems or concerns weightier than wheedling a miner or trapper out of a few extra grains of gold or an extra fur for what he wanted from the packs on the mules or finding a sheltered place to spend the night. But he was out of contact with the business and things would be accumulating that needed his attention. The season was advanced and the weak sun on the crisp mornings shone down on brilliant splashes of autumn colors. Frau Topol would be disturbed that he hadn't come back in time for Rosh Hashanah and would be difficult for months if he didn't return in time for Yom Kippur. And there was Consuela, more than sufficient allurement to make him think of returning.

On the morning of the third day they rose just before daybreak. As they heated coffee, beans, and tortillas for breakfast, Rhineman told the man he was turning south toward Santa Fe. The man began thinking frantically to remember stories he hadn't told Rhineman so he could tell them before they parted, and they got underway somewhat later than usual. The birds were singing and flying through the trees and the sun was coming up over the mountain when Rhineman's horse was saddled and the packsaddles were on the man's string of mules. They mounted and rode off in different directions.

The trail went back into a fold in the mountain which was a minute wrinkle compared to the massive bulk of the mountain but a distance of miles in the less grand scale of human affairs. It went out and around a bluff where the animals had splashed through water gushing down the bluff and across the trail when Rhineman and the trader had come past the spot the previous afternoon. As the horse cantered slowly along the other side of the fold and back into the breeze blowing across the face of the mountain, Rhineman pulled his coat closer around him. The temperature had been plummeting in the mountains the past few nights, and it had been noon or after before it warmed up to a comfortable level.

The horse started around the bluff, and Rhineman looked out over the hills and valleys below, endless miles of wilderness stretching off into the distance. The horse suddenly stumbled and floundered to get his feet back under him, and Rhineman automatically gathered the reins closer, looking down. There was still ice on the trail from where the water had frozen the night before, and the horse was very close to the edge of the trail. He started to jerk the horse toward the inside of the trail, and he saw that the horse had lost his balance and was falling toward the outside edge of the ledge around the face of the bluff. He started to kick out of the stirrups and leap off the horse. It was too late. The horse fell over the edge with him, its legs flailing as it squealed frantically.

There was a sensation of falling and a blur of the torn earth below the trail rushing past his vision, then there was a crushing blow. He was off the horse, and foliage lashed him as he slid and rolled down the steep slope through clumps of brush and saplings. There was another shattering blow as he struck a large tree, a piercing stab of agony from his right leg, and darkness.

A shrill, ennervating sound pierced his unconsciousness, and the mists slowly receded. Pain returned, and he hesitated and searched for the blankness of unconsciousness again to escape the pain. The sound penetrated again, and a thread of memory returned, a dim recollection of the fall down through the rocks and thin foliage. The instinct for survival surfaced. He struggled back to consciousness. The sound was the horse screaming. The horse was a few yards away and further down the slope, spitted on a small pine which had shattered under him and pierced through his stomach, disemboweling him. His feet scraped at the ground, and he screamed again. Rhineman gathered himself and started to roll away from the tree he was resting against. He almost fainted from the agonizing pain which lanced through his right leg. He drew in deep breaths and fought the unconsciousness, then lifted his head and looked around. The trail was a couple of hundred feet above him, and he was on a steep slope which became a sheer wall directly under the trail. He was lying against a large pine, and his right leg was twisted under him at the impossible angle of broken bones.

The horse came first. He pulled his pistol out of the holster and cocked it, and he held it in both hands as he took careful aim at the horse's head. The sharp boom of the pistol cut through the ragged sound the horse made as he screamed again, and he suddenly went limp as the sound in his throat faded into a wheeze. The pistol almost jumped from Rhineman's hands as it recoiled. He carefully pushed it back into the holster and pulled the safety thong up over the hammer so it couldn't fall out.

He lifted his head and looked around again. There was a small overhang of rock a few yards away with a shallow, cave-like depression under it, an inviting shelter. He grasped at a sapling a few feet away, caught a limb and pulled the sapling down. He gripped it with both hands, pulling himself away from the tree. The pain in his leg seemed to explode, racing through him in waves of seething agony which sapped his strength and brought the cloud of unconsciousness rushing over him again. He closed his eyes and summoned his will to fight off the unconsciousness, holding onto the sapling. It receded again, and he pulled himself a few more inches and had to stop again. Gradually he worked himself into a prone position on the ground away from the tree, with his legs stretched out. He lifted his head and looked at his leg. There was no blood, so the broken bones hadn't pierced through the skin. He dropped his head back to the ground and gathered his strength, then he dug his fingers into the dirt and began inching toward the overhang.

It represented a goal on the scale of a gigantic undertaking, each inch a landmark achieved through pain and toil and at the risk of becoming unbalanced on the steep slope and rolling further down the mountain to certain death. He finally reached it and pulled himself into the depression under the overhang, then he slumped with exhaustion and closed his eyes. There was no conscious-ness of time passing, but the sun was low in the West when he opened his eyes again. He raised himself on his elbow and looked around. There was no wood nearby for a fire, and his bedroll was on the saddle on the dead horse, only yards away but across a vast chasm when measured in pain, effort, and danger. His canteen was also on the saddle, and he was parched with thirst. The situation was perilous. The trader was the only one with even a general idea of where he was, and it would be at least a week before he returned to Santa Fe. The nights were cold, and he was injured and weak. It might have been better if the bones had pierced through the skin, because it would have been quicker.

Spasms of chills were racing through his body when he became conscious again, and his right leg was enveloped in excruciating agony from the constant and involuntary shivering of his body. It was dark and frigidly cold. The pain and cold dulled his senses and diminished his awareness of his surroundings, but after a moment the noises registered and had meaning. There was scuffling in the foliage and a sound of deep growling and gnashing of teeth. It was wolves after the horse. And if the horse didn't satisfy them, they would come for him. The open space below the overhang was bathed in the bright light of the moon, but his vision was blurred and everything looked hazy. There were spots of movement, dark forms rushing back and forth through the moonlight, but they were formless. He felt for his pistol, pushed the thong off the hammer and pulled it from the holster. He pulled the hammer back to full cock and held it ready to fire. His mouth was dry and sticky with thirst.

The pain from his leg became more intense, the seething waves rolling over him, and the darkness returned.

It was daylight, and he was propped up against one side of the depression and holding the cocked pistol on his lap. There was a wolf a few yards from him, silently snarling at him. He slowly lifted the pistol, took careful aim on the wolf's head, and pulled the trigger. The concussion of the shot in the enclosed airspace of the depression brought him into closer contact with reality, and he saw that he had been shooting at a rock. Thirst was a raging torment. He looked down the hill at the horse. Part of it had been eaten, and pieces of skin and bones were scattered about. Small animals were darting back and forth near it and birds were flying down to get their share.

Later it seemed that Frau Topol was standing in front of him. At some level he realized that she was an apparition of his fevered mind, but she seemed very real. She was holding a prayer book open for him to read and prepare himself for death. As he read it, the sound of his voice in his ears seemed to be coming from a long distance away as a weak, hollow echo. Then Consuela was there and holding the child Carlos for him to kiss, and tears were streaming down her cheeks. Still later there was a moment of rational clarity and he realized his strength was ebbing rapidly, and he prayed.

Time became warped, stretching so that a bird resting on a branch in his line of vision with a scrap of the horse's flesh in its beak remained there for an endless time while he examined it, and then contracting so that a day, a night, and another day raced by in quick succession. The periods of awareness became shorter and less frequent.

Chapter 10

There was sound and movement around him, and he contemplated it with a detached lack of concern. Then pain lanced through his leg again after what seemed to have been a long time of being without pain, and the sound and movement came into sharper focus. There were men shouting hoarsely and anxiously as they scrambled about around him. Men in large, black sombreros, black jackets, and black breeches. His men. A trickle of cold water ran into his mouth. His tongue was swollen and his mouth was too dry to swallow. It ran out the side of his mouth. More was poured in. Then his mouth was less dry, and he could move his tongue and swallow a bit. The lip of the canteen rattled against his teeth as he lifted his head and drank greedily.

They lifted him out of the depression and onto a rough stretcher made of sticks and a blanket, shouting back and forth with other men on the trail above. A rifle was firing on the trail repetitively, three shots, a pause, then three more shots, a repeated pattern of fire which sent rolling echoes thundering through the valleys below. Ropes snaked through the air and fell to the ground around the stretcher. The men tied the ropes around their waists and to the stretcher, lifted the stretcher and scrambled along beside it as the ropes were pulled in from the trail. The steep part was difficult, and the stretcher rattled against the stones and brought unconsciousness hovering closer again from the seething agony in his leg as the men struggled frantically to hold the stretcher up and screamed curses back and forth in Spanish.

The stretcher slid over the edge and onto the trail. The trail was a boiling mass of activity, full of men and horses. The sound of the rifle was deafening as it continued firing. There was a small fire on the edge of the trail, and a man ran over from it with a tin cup. He bent over Rhineman and lifted his head, putting the cup to his lips. It was warm chicken broth. The man's dark eyes moved over Rhineman's face worriedly. Rhineman gulped the broth, and the man put his head back down and ran back to the fire. Other men were still shouting, screaming, and cursing, arguing with each other excitedly, and the horses were stamping and moving about. The rifle still fired. Another man lifted Rhineman's head and gave him a drink of water. Then a man gave him a drink of tequila which almost choked him. Other horses approached along the trail at a dead run and slid to a stop, and shouts rang back and forth as the other men ran to him, their spurs clattering. A man's voice cut through the others, authoritative and imperative in tone, giving orders. Rhineman recognized the voice. It was the man in charge of the guards at Socorro. Everyone had been called in for the search.

139

Order formed out of the confusion. Three horsemen raced away along the trail, firing a rifle in the pattern of three shots, and three more raced off in the other direction along the trail, firing a rifle and calling in the searchers in that direction. The man who had given him the warm broth brought another cup, and other men dragged poles and bedrolls about, making a better stretcher. He finished the broth, and they put him on the stretcher and covered him with blankets. They started along the trail with him, four men carrying the stretcher at a trot and the others riding. When the four men became exhausted, four more took the stretcher.

The blankets were piled on him, but he still felt frigidly cold. The jarring of his leg as the men trotted along with the stretcher made the pain come in waves which swelled and ebbed, sometimes soaring to a peak which brought unconsciousness close. More riders came along the trail at a thundering run, reining their panting horses back and joining the group, and some crowded closer to look at him until the man leading the group along the trail snarled at them. Other men took the stretcher, then others. The pain became more intense, and unconsciousness closed in.

The movement had stopped when consciousness returned. A well-known voice was speaking to him quietly and insistently. He opened his eyes. It was Delgado. The men were clustered around and looking down at him, dozens of men, and Delgado was kneeling by the stretcher, speaking to him.

"... hear me, *Senor General*?"

Rhineman tried to reply and couldn't. He licked his lips dryly and nodded. Delgado turned and snapped an order, then turned back around with a canteen a man handed him and carefully poured a few drops between Rhineman's lips. He pushed the cork back into the canteen, handed it back to the man, and leaned over Rhineman again.

"Riders have gone to Taos to bring *un medico* and meet us on the trail, *Senor General.* Do you want to wait for him here, or do you want to go on?"

Rhineman licked his lips and swallowed again, and Delgado leaned lower to hear the whisper. "Go..."

Delgado nodded, standing up and rattling orders. There was a flurry of activity, men mounting horses and other men gathering up the stretcher. The drumming of the hoof beats was loud as they started along the trail again. It was late afternoon, and presently some of the men began searching along the sides of the trail for fallen and rotted pines so they could dig out the resin knots for torches. Darkness fell, and the wavering light of the torches made dark shadows in the trees on each side of the trail. Unconsciousness came slowly and gradually, almost like sleep.

Frigid cold brought him back to consciousness. It was late at night, and they had stopped again at a wide, level spot. Four large fires were roaring, and their leaping flames were filling the glade with light. The blankets had been taken off him, and his bare skin was exposed to the night air. Delgado and an old, grizzled anglo were kneeling by the stretcher, the anglo looking at his leg. There was a black leather bag on the ground by him. His coat was open, he was wearing a flannel nightshirt for a shirt, and his hair was disordered, hanging at odd angles from under a derby hat. He glanced at Rhineman's face, then did a doubletake.

"You back with us?"

Rhineman nodded.

"Well, I goddamned near wasn't a couple of times tonight. Them crazy bastards you got working for you

141

come busting into my house in the middle of the night, scared the shit out of my wife, and stuck a gun in my face and was about to blow my goddamned head off when I told them to just bring you on in. And we killed four goddamned horses getting up here in the middle of these goddamned mountains to you. One fell and broke his leg and had to be shot, and the other three just fell to the ground and died under the men on top of them. I guess them men are still walking this way, which don't no more than serve them right. Still and all, I guess I'd better save you or these sons of bitches will string me up to one of these trees here. That leg's got to come off, son."

Rhineman shook his head.

"No? Well, it's your leg, and I guess it's your say as to what's to be done with it. But that slims your chances down by a bunch." He looked at Delgado. "Did you understand that he wants the leg left on?"

"Yes," Delgado said quietly.

"Then that's what I'm going to do. And I'll do my best for him. But if my best ain't good enough, I don't want no trouble out of this goddamned army of his'n, crazy pack that they are."

"Do your best," Delgado replied. "There will be no trouble."

"It's going to make him smart a little bit. I ain't got no laudanum with me, and that leg's going to have to be straightened out, splinted, and cut open to let drain, else it's going to rot and take him with it right directly. You got any likker?"

"Tequila," Delgado snapped, turning and looking around.

The doctor took off his coat and dropped it to the ground, and began rolling up the sleeves of his nightshirt. A man handed Delgado a bottle of tequila, and Delgado knelt by Rhineman's head and lifted it, putting the bottle to his lips. The fiery liquid burned in his mouth, and he started choking and gagging as the searing trail of fire raced down his throat toward his stomach. He controlled the choking and gagging and drank more. Warmth began spreading out through him from his stomach. The doctor hawked and spat to one side, wiped his mouth with his forearm, and folded his arms and looked down at Rhineman. Rhineman drank more of the tequila, then began gagging again.

"That's all he needs, else he's going to bring it all back up directly," the doctor said. "Let's give it a minute to work on him."

Delgado stood up and handed the bottle to a man. Several of the men passed the bottle around and took drinks. The fires roared and crackled, and sparks leaped up as someone threw more wood onto them. The warmth enveloping Rhineman increased, the pain in his leg diminished, and he became drowsy. The doctor murmured and nodded to Delgado, and Delgado waved to a couple of men and snapped an order. The men knelt by the stretcher and held Rhineman's shoulders and arms. The doctor leaned over Rhineman and put a short stick between Rhineman's teeth, then he moved to the other end of the stretcher.

The pain of before had been mild in comparison. The effects of the tequila were snatched away by the first pangs from the tortured muscles and nerves, then it increased. Rhineman felt his teeth sinking into the stick as his body arched upward off the stretcher. He waited for the unconsciousness, seeking it as an escape, but it wouldn't come. After an eternity of agony, the doctor grunted with satisfaction and looked to one side, pointing. A man handed him a couple of straight sticks, and he laid them on each side of Rhineman's leg and began passing short lengths of cloth under Rhineman's leg and tying the sticks in place. When he was through with the splints, he opened his bag, took out a short knife, wiped it on the sleeve of his nightshirt, and began cutting. There was an instant of unbearable agony, then unconsciousness.

When he returned to consciousness, he was at Wheatland. At first he thought he was at Rhinaldea, because Consuela and Frau Topol were there, but after a few hours his mind had cleared enough to converse and understand what they were saying. On the third day the doctor gave them instructions on keeping the leg open so it would drain and heal from the inside out, and left. After a couple more days, they loaded him carefully into a wagon and traveled slowly along the road to Rhinaldea.

It was a month before he could walk on crutches and another before he could get about on a cane, but it was several months before his full strength returned. The ordeal had left him a skeleton of his former size, and his weight returned slowly. After using the cane a couple of months he discarded it, and he was able to mount and dismount from a horse with no difficulty. But he had a slight limp which was permanent.

The most profound effect of the experience was the reassessment of his life that it forced upon him. He had been hanging onto life by a thread, and the slightest additional adversity would have meant death. In retrospect, he saw that he had been fulfilling his responsibility toward what his father had left in a way, and fulfilling it abundantly, but in another way he had been ignoring his responsibility. If he died, the business would fade into oblivion within a short time, because he had no family to inherit it. His only offspring was the illegitimate child Carlos. Over Frau Topol's strenuous objections, he had acceded to Consuela's wish to rear the child in her own religion. The child was a major part of her life and only a passing consideration in his, when viewed honestly and candidly.

Frau Topol had been irritating but no more than right in her disparaging references to his unmarried state. He was failing his responsibility to himself, to God, and to what his father had left him. As he thought about it, he began to seriously consider the local and immediately available possibilities. There were more than there had been when he had first come to Santa Fe, and despite the fact that it wasn't unknown at large that he had a mistress, he was still considered as a target by every mother with a marriageable daughter. But there were none who were more than average in attractiveness, and a somewhat low average. They all had what he considered a deficiency in education and social talents, and their eagerness made him more cautious and them somehow less desirable. He saw no potential for the development of the mutual love and respect which would come to a compatible married couple in time.

There were a few in Albuquerque but all of them more or less the same, and his ties with Charleston had been severed. Then he thought of a marriage broker. He found it distasteful in principle to have someone act as suitor for him at long distance and to agree to marry someone he had never met, but there were large Jewish communities elsewhere and it was at least a possibility. He looked through the newspapers he received from the East, and saw several addresses of marriage brokers. He picked one at random, an Eleazar Freedman in New York, and wrote a letter to him. It was still a matter of some weeks before he would be sending out the wagon train on its first trip of the season, so he sent the letter by courier to Westport.

A reply arrived on the first incoming wagon train of the season. It was a substantial reply, consisting of a long letter from Eleazar Freedman, letters from several women Freedman had selected as possibilities, small tintypes of three of them, and a marriage contract on each of those Freedman had selected.

The contracts immediately made him wary. It seemed that Freedman had presumed a lot and was trying to rush things at a precipitant pace. But one of the first sentences in Freedman's letter explained that the contracts were being sent in event he found one of the candidates suitable and to avoid the protracted delays involved in corresponding at length between New York and New Mexico Territory. It seemed logical, but the wariness remained.

At first it appeared that the possibilities in New York were little better than those in Santa Fe, at least to the extent that Freedman could call upon them, then the letter became interesting. There was one that Freedman was obviously pointing out as the best choice, because two thirds of his letter was about her. She was Polish, educated by tutors and at a woman's school associated with the university in Warsaw, which was unusual for a Jew. Her father had been in government in Warsaw, which was also unusual for a Jew but it more or less explained her education. She could speak, read, and write French, German, and Russian, and she could converse in Polish and English. It seemed a little strange that what was presumably her native language was one of those in which her qualifications were less, but somewhere he had heard that the situation wasn't unknown among the aristocracy in Slavic countries. She had also studied an impressive list of subjects ranging from geography to philosophy, in addition to languages. There was no dowry, because she was an orphan, but she had brought a

146

substantial amount of belongings to the United States with her. She was twenty two and considered very attractive, blonde and with blue eyes.

As he read on through the letter, he began to wonder why she wasn't already married. Then the reason came near the end of the letter. Her mother had been a gentile. It was immediately followed by assurances that she had been reared in and lived within the Jewish religion, and that she was well educated in matters pertaining to religion. Rhineman didn't find it objectionable, but he knew that some would. Others would view her as too well educated. And still others would balk at the lack of a dowry. But there were still many who would marry her, regarding as assets those things which others would see as drawbacks, because there were others in his position and who would want the same qualities in a wife that he did. He glanced over the letter again. Her name was Rabinowsky. He looked through the tintypes. There was one of her, somewhat faded and blurred, but she appeared attractive enough from what he could see. He looked through the letters from the women and picked out the one from her.

The letter was in French, which he had more or less forgotten after his classes in it at The Citadel, but it was more a note than a letter, formally polite and brief. The handwriting was neat, the lines precisely straight and each letter perfectly formed, the handwriting of an educated woman. There was a formal greeting, an expression of interest in New Mexico Territory, a reference to a couple of things she had read about it, and a formal close. She signed herself as Celise Stephanovna Rabinowsky, in the Russian style.

It was interesting, but he was still cautious. Freedman mentioned in the first sentences of the letter that some of the candidates might be married by the time he received the letter because of the time it took for a letter to get to New Mexico Territory. So there was a likelihood that she was already married, and he was reluctant to make a fool of himself in even his own mind by sending off a contract to marry a woman who was already married. He put all the letters and tintypes back into the heavy envelope, put it away, and went on about his business.

At about the same time, Consuela broached the subject with him in her bizarre German and Spanish accent and heavy lisp. There had been hints that the matter concerned her, which was no more than reasonable, because she obviously considered it highly possible that a wife would demand she be evicted from the village if she found out about her. Consuela had adjusted to the role of mistress and had wisely exerted no pressure toward marriage, as some might have, but she had used her wiles to dissuade him from contemplating marriage in general. Through the occasionally startling intuitive insight that seemed to be a fundamental part of her, she seemed to perceive that marriage was more of an immediate prospect, and she made it clear that her ultimate concern was the child Carlos. When Rhineman assured her that she, her mother, and the boy would be cared for regardless of what happened, she appeared satisfied.

But his caution invited procrastination, and the affairs of the business filled his mind. Marriage began to diminish into a long-range objective again. He was at one of the Santa Fe stores one afternoon when a belligerent drunk came in, and as he started to throw him out the man pulled a derringer and fired it at him at point blank range. The man was drunk, his aim was hasty, and Rhineman managed to partially deflect the man's arm. The ball from the pistol cut a furrow through his hair at the side of his

148

head and took a large chunk from a support post before it embedded itself in the ceiling. Rhineman beat the man's face to a pulp and gave him an hour to get out of Santa Fe, but the incident served to again bring into focus the fragile and uncertain state of mortality.

The Rabinowsky woman was obviously an educated and talented woman who fulfilled everything he desired in a wife. Her European sophistication would be more than a credit to him in the social life in Santa Fe, and she would be an interesting and entertaining companion. And she would give him children. If it turned out that there was anything further needed to make his life complete, there could be a neat and comfortable but not overly ostentatious house not too far from the stores in Santa Fe where Consuela and her mother and the child could live and where he could spend an occasional afternoon.

The Rabinowsky woman's guardian was a cousin, apparently a middle-aged woman from Freedman's references to her, and she wished to be one of the witnesses at the wedding, which was to be expected. Freedman also dropped in the comment that he normally served as a witness at weddings which he arranged, and there were other things which made clear their assumption that he would come to New York. Rhineman had no intention of leaving his business affairs unattended for the length of time such a trip would take, but on the other hand it seemed a little unfair to demand that the cousin make the difficult and hazardous journey overland to Santa Fe and back to witness the marriage.

But there was a compromise solution. They could travel by train to St. Louis and by riverboat to Westport, not a difficult or trying journey by any measure. The wedding could be performed in Westport, where there was a small Jewish community. The compromise was even more attractive in view of a critical need for additional freight wagons, a matter equivalent in urgency to being married in his mind, because he could order the wagons and bring them back from Westport on the same trip. He would pay the travel expenses of the cousin and marriage broker for the trip to Westport and back to New York and give them something extra for their trouble, which should make the compromise completely equitable.

He took Freedman's letter back out, completed and signed the marriage contract with the Rabinowsky woman, and made out a draft negotiable through a New York bank which dealt with his bank in Santa Fe. He had only a vague idea of how much the expenses would be, and he also needed a ring which would fit her and would undoubtedly cost less in New York than in Westport, so he made the amount of the draft far in excess of his maximum estimate. In his letter of instructions on when to meet him at Westport, he included the request to buy a ring which fit and an explicit request to keep an accurate accounting of funds expended and the receipts so the financial matters could be settled at Westport when they met. The wagon train was enroute between Santa Fe and Missouri, and he sent the letter off by courier. Then, in his flush of self-congratulation, he went to a jeweler in Santa Fe and ordered a wedding present for the Rabinowsky woman, a gold Star of David pendant set with diamonds on a heavy gold chain.

He immediately regretted everything he had done. It seemed that it took the jeweler less than an hour to inform every Jewish family in Santa Fe of what was planned, and from there it spread like wildfire. And while he had no desire to be secretive about it, it was his affair and he preferred to introduce a wife to Santa Fe in his own way and at his own leisure.

Frau Topol was ecstatic, and she interpreted an absent-minded grunt over dinner as an affirmative, as she was inclined to do on purchases of furniture and similar matters. As a result, when he returned home the next day he found that Frau Topol had told Delgado that he had ordered an expansion to his house for the woman he was going to marry, and workmen were busily tearing down the back wall to add on extra rooms.

Consuela had an air of grim apprehension and resignation which was a sharp contrast to her usual carefree and cheerful mood that did so much to brighten his moods when he was troubled by something. As he was reflecting on what idiocy had possessed him to sign a marriage contract with some woman he had never seen, he became irritable and snapped at her. She began weeping.

At the same time, while everyone was talking about it and people were stopping him on the street in Santa Fe to give advance notice of invitations for him and his wife, there was a high likelihood that the man racing pellmell through the mountains and across the prairies enroute to Westport was on a wasted trip because he was carrying a marriage contract with a woman who was already married. And the sum total result of all the effort would probably be to provide a hilarious laugh for some people in New York and make an utter fool of him in Santa Fe.

There were other things. The ripping, tearing, and hammering of the workmen on the unneeded addition to an abundantly large house which was being done at great cost and would be better spent on another warehouse he needed made the house uncomfortable to be around.

151

Consuela's cheerfulness had a false, hollow note which was aggravating. The cost of the Star of David pendant and chain from the gossipy jeweler turned out to be astronomical. Frau Topol called a tailor to the house, which was all right because he needed a couple of new frock coats, but she and the tailor seemed to have arrived at a private arrangement between themselves to talk him into buying clothes which would make him look like a drummer, suits with short coats, loose, baggy trousers, and a ridiculous hat. The tailor had the perception to desist, but Frau Topol persisted until he lost his temper and swore at her. Then she retreated into her injured, icy silence, making the house even more uncomfortable.

The courier returned, having almost ruined two horses he took and exhausted himself. Both the rider and the horses had only partially recovered during the more casual pace of the return trip, and the horses had to be stabled for a couple of weeks and the man had to have several days off. But he hadn't lost the letter; it was on its way.

Frau Topol was prominently present and a lot of employees were somehow standing around when the next wagon train came in, and they looked intensely curious when the wagon master handed him the usual stack of correspondence. Rhineman was unable to deny his own curiosity to the extent of glancing through the packets to see where they were from. There was one from the marriage broker. He put the letters in his pocket and talked to the wagon master about his trip, looked through some of the invoices, and looked in some of the wagons. The number of employees in the vicinity kept increasing. He finally began opening and reading the letters, beginning with the one from the wagon factory. The wagons would be delivered on time, accompanied by men from the factory to assemble them ready to roll and assure that everything was satisfactory. Then there was a letter from a manufacturer about supplies which were being sent for the canning factory, and a couple of others. Finally he opened the letter from Freedman. It was short and to the point. He, the Rabinowsky woman, and the woman's cousin would meet him at Westport at the designated time, and he would make arrangements for the wedding. Frau Topol's usually dignified mien dissolved into exhilaration, and the employees began whooping and racing away to spread the word.

But somehow it seemed the worst possible result. If the woman had been married already, the matter would have been ended. There might have been some good-natured jibes about his short-lived marriage plans from friends and associates in Santa Fe, but such an outcome was more or less to be expected in consideration of the delays involved in corresponding at long distance. Consuela's truly carefree and happy disposition would have returned. And there was a possibility that Frau Topol might have become adjusted to having Consuela as a resident of the house, considering that the massive addition which had been built onto the rear of it would be otherwise unused. But none of that would come to pass. He was committed to be married to a woman he had never met. There was no way out of it short of paying a fortune in compensation, unless the marriage broker had misrepresented his client. And in reading back through Freedman's letter, it seemed that he had been deliberately vague in several areas in order to avoid such a charge. The woman unquestionably had positive characteristics, but there were things which weren't mentioned. It could be that she was painfully shy. Or it could be that she had a speech impediment, which was attractive in the case of

Consuela's lisp but could be objectionable in other instances. The tintype was so blurred and faint that it was difficult to really see what the woman looked like. Freedman's letter said she was considered very attractive, but it was another of the statements which were so general they were suspicious. Virtually everyone could be said to be very attractive to someone. And there was no direct, straightforward testimony as to the woman's moral stature, a matter of concern considering the decadence of many East European capitals. On balance, it would have been much more preferable to take some friendly joking about plans which had gone awry than to be in the situation in which he found himself.

Preparations proceeded, and Rhineman's moods became darker. He had made a slight miscalculation on the times involved, and it was going to be a problem to reach Westport by the date he had specified. Delgado suggested limiting the train to six of the best wagons, with each of them pulled by six span of large mules, which was reasonable considering that they would be receiving an additional fifteen wagons on the other end and buying oxen to draw them. Then Rhineman discovered in conversation with Delgado that it had been assumed a large contingent of guards would be accompanying the train. It was usual for ten or a dozen to go along, but Delgado and others had been thinking in terms of thirty or so. The wagon master mentioned some problems which had been experienced with Indians, and since there were no problems anywhere else which required extra guards at any of the branches, Rhineman assented, agreeing that it would be foolish to take unnecessary risks with fifteen new wagons and the herd of oxen it would take to draw them.

The final preparations were made, and they left before

daybreak one morning, Consuela trying to conceal her foreboding, Frau Topol dancing with excitement, and a large crowd of employees and other people gathered around to shout and wave as the wagon train exited from Santa Fe with the traditional noisy rush along the trail. The teamsters shouted and snapped their whips as the wagons rumbled along at a breakneck pace. The large contingent of guards shouted and raced along in front of the wagons, a few of them shooting off their pistols.

After the first turn in the trail, the train settled down to the slow and sensible pace at which it would make the long trek to Westport. And things began going wrong. An axle was broken late in the afternoon and they had to make an early camp and repair it, and some of the mules escaped from their hobbles and had to be chased down the next morning. At shortly after noon the following day, a wagon broke a wheel and caused a delay, then another wheel was broken late in the afternoon.

The gelding Rhineman had bought to replace the one which had been killed was a spirited animal because he liked a good horse, but it was also vicious and tried to bite and kick everyone and every other animal which came near it, and whipping it only angered it to the point of being completely unmanageable. It took constant control over the gelding to keep him in hand as they traveled along, which was tiring and aggravating. The leather on the brakes on the wagons had been replaced only a few days before in Santa Fe, but it was a very poor quality and began burning up and shredding away on the first downgrades, causing another delay while additional leather was put on all the brakes. A lot of the mules cast shoes, and the smith who had been brought along was less than expert. Rhineman's gelding cast a shoe and had to be thrown and tied on his side to replace it. In the process the gelding kicked a couple of men so hard that they had to ride in a wagon for a few days to recuperate.

Other things happened, and Rhineman's mood became more morose as they trudged steadily on toward Westport, across the mountains and then across the sweeping expanses of prairie. He thought about the situation as he rode along in silence with Torres, the man in charge of the guards at his side, and as he sat alone in a wagon or in front of a fire at night and stared into the coals. He gradually became resigned. He had committed himself, and he would marry the woman and make the best of it.

It was unusually rainy and wet for the season, making good graze for the animals and diminishing the possibility of being caught in the open in a prairie fire, but more time was lost in crossing a couple of swollen rivers. A rider was sent ahead with remounts so he could make good time to check on the wagons and alert stock dealers to the need for oxen. He returned in time to meet the wagon train as it neared Westport, and he reported that the wagons were there and that the stock dealers had been notified.

There was a bustle in camp the last night on the trail. The teamsters carried buckets of water to wash their wagons and they curried their mules, and they all shaved and got out their best clothes. The men in the guard chattered and laughed gaily as they carefully brushed their clothes and curried their horses. They shined their boots and saddles and polished their spurs and the conchos on their saddles and bridles until they gleamed. Rhineman shaved and bathed daily as a matter of practice when water was available, and he watched the preparations of the others with a sour expression. They had reason to look forward to arriving in Westport.

An atmosphere of tense anticipation and expectation

hung over the camp as they hurriedly prepared to get underway the following morning, and it intensified as they moved along the trail toward Westport. The animals seemed to sense it, because all the horses in the long lines of guard behind Rhineman were restless, and his gelding was more difficult than usual to control. As they neared Westport, the train closed up, the usual interval between the wagons and the horses diminishing.

Over the sound of the hoofbeats and wagon wheels, Rhineman could hear the teamsters shouting between the wagons at each other, pointing out the landmarks. The excitement mounted, and the men in the guard behind him rattled to each other. There was a tradition of uproarious entry into the destination at the end of the trail, as well as the exhibitionist departure along the trail, and it seemed childish to him. But there was a love of display and fanfare in the West, enjoyed by both those creating the uproar and those witnessing it, perhaps a moment of pandemonium doing something to make the dreary weeks on the trail and the deadly monotony of the towns more bearable.

The train started up a long hill, and the teamsters' shouts became louder. Westport was on the other side of the hill. The talk and laughter among the guards became louder and more excited. Rhineman sighed softly. They were waiting for a signal from him. And while it seemed childish to begin and end the trek in a wild dash, perhaps it was even more childish for him to contemplate denying them their moment of pleasure. Most of the guard had never been to Missouri, and the teamsters had labored hard during the trek. He let his horse out into a trot. Torres grinned at him widely and let his horse trot. The guard behind him broke into a trot. The teamster on the first wagon uttered a shrill whoop, and his twelve foot whip cracked with a loud report. The other teamsters began whooping and cracking their whips.

The train approached the top of the hill, and Rhineman let his horse gallop. Then Westport began to come into sight, a disorderly maze of unpainted warehouses, false fronted buildings along the main street, clapboard shacks, and dusty, ragged tents, with the muddy docks along the river. He let his horse out into a run. The hoofbeats behind him became a rolling thunder as the guards urged their horses into a run. The shouts of the guards and teamsters swelled over the pounding of hoofs and rumbling of wagons, and the whips cracked explosively. On the main street ahead, people began scurrying about to clear the street, and others ran out of the buildings to look. One of the guards fired a pistol, then a ragged volley burst out. They began firing rapidly, emptying their pistols and then firing their rifles into the air. The people along both sides of the street cheered and shouted, waving and jumping up and down. The wagon train thundered into Westport and swept along the main street.

Chapter 11

Rhineman's letter of inquiry about the possibilities of finding a suitable wife was like a heaven-sent gift to Eleazar Freedman, the marriage broker. Freedman was a dedicated man, devoting himself to his profession with a determination and awareness of his awesome responsibilities which was shared by few. The family was the cornerstone of life, and he was the one who set that cornerstone in place. He and his family subsisted from his fees and some small trading he did as a sideline, but beyond the money involved, he was utterly devoted to what he did. Life had given him judgment and a pragmatic insight of sorts into people, and he prided himself that the matches he arranged were as solid as the firmament.

A shy and retiring man needed an assertive wife who would see that the family received due consideration from others, but a man who was accustomed to having his way needed a wife who would be a quiet and obedient helpmate. A person's fundamental characteristics were not always obvious at first, and in fact the face presented to the world was usually the opposite when the characteristics were of an extreme nature. It took several conversations with the individual to gain an insight and accurately evaluate the high and low points of personality so that a matching pattern could be found to fit. And it also took discreet conversations with relatives, friends and associates, questions which seemed innocent and innocuous enough to them but which revealed much to him. Some were more flexible than others and could adjust to slight mismatches in a partner, but for others the pattern had to be a true and smooth fit. Few matters could be broached directly, and frequently what was not said was more meaningful than what was said. An estimation of the approximate degree of sensuality had to be made, a matter which no one could address with a virgin of good family, but it was crucial to the health of a marriage. And due weight had to be given to the allowable degrees of variation according to the sex of the partner. Any good woman would do her duty for her husband, but a man who appeared to live principally on a higher plane required just the right wife in that respect because there was no more acid tongue than the one in the mouth of a woman who felt herself neglected. And intelligence was a factor. In most instances a more or less equal level was good, but when the man was inclined to be dull, it wasn't amiss to have a somewhat keener woman when it was clear that she knew how to be subtle about it. There were many things.

But the personality was only part of it. Some equilibrium had to be established along physical lines.

Again it was a matter of contrasting or matching, depending upon the situation. A small man could frequently find the most happiness with a wife of substantial proportions, but not always. In general there had to be similarity in attractiveness to the opposite sex to keep jealousy from developing. Age wasn't highly important, but if there was a difference it was always better if the man was older. A detracting characteristic in one partner could be offset by a deficiency in another, as when a man of advanced age had been matched with a woman who was young but inclined to corpulence. Bad teeth in one had been offset by large buttocks in another.

And there was also a time to be firm. There were those with an exalted concept of their qualifications, and there were those who had less than a full appreciation of their situation as others perceived it. When it came time to be firm, he knew how to do it.

It was his pride that he had never failed. Everywhere he went, he was hailed and greeted by grateful husbands and wives whom he had brought together and by the parents of his one-time clients. None were turned away. If they were poor, he accepted a pittance and thanks for his services. In each case, a match was found. When a hand was held out to him in a plea for help, it was not ignored.

And that was why the letter from Rhineman had been such a relief. Some months before, a good woman named Adah Rudnicki had immigrated from Poland with two daughters and a distant cousin, and she had come to him for help. The daughters had been the sort of client who made him glow upon meeting them. No pronounced characteristics of any kind, both in their twenties and of average appearance, and both amiable and eager to please. Any one of a dozen male clients would have been fully satisfactory, and the marriages had been arranged within a matter of days. But the cousin had been a problem.

Her name was Celise Rabinowsky, and she had a unique background. Her father had been the son of a gold dealer and artificer in Warsaw and had taken over his father's business at an early age after his father's death. Perhaps as a result of the lack of foresight which would have come with a more mature age, he had been in St. Petersburg collecting a shipment of gold during the Napoleonic invasion of Russia, and in trying to get back to Warsaw, he had been detained by a force of the czar's soldiers. Adah Rudnicki's story of the developments from that point on showed a complete maturity of judgment in Rabinowsky, as well as cunning and something approaching audacity, because he asserted he had come to see if he could assist the czar in some measure in relieving the critical economic situation which existed in Russia. Upon being conducted to some of the czar's ministers, he presented them with the gold which he had picked up at St. Petersburg and which had been disguised as cookware with a thin coating of pewter. Then he had been conducted to the czar, who had conferred Russian citizenship upon him, made him a count, and made him a minister in the government at Warsaw.

Rabinowsky had made a success of his post, apparently winning the confidence and respect necessary to be an effective minister, because he had held the position for many years. In his middle years he had married a gentile, which had been unfortunate, but he had lived in the Jewish religion and had always availed himself of opportunities to assist the Jewish community in Warsaw. The single child from the marriage, Celise, had been reared more or less in a manner consistent with her father's position. The wife had eventually died, and

Rabinowsky's health had apparently started failing as he entered the autumn of his years. In the dark and troubled times following the Revolution of 1863, he had apparently become concerned about his daughter's welfare if death should overtake him, and he had sought means of seeing her settled and safe. Then when his cousin Adah Rudnicki went to him for financial assistance to allow her to emigrate with her daughters after her husband's death, Rabinowsky had agreed to pay the passage and expenses for all involved if Adah would take his daughter with her and see her comfortably settled. A couple of months after their arrival in the United States, word had been received that Rabinowsky had died.

In retrospect, one of the things which had made finding a match for Celise Rabinowsky so difficult was that it had seemed so easy at first. It had appeared that there would be hundreds if not thousands of families eager to match a son with her. But it hadn't turned out that way.

So many of her good characteristics were of such extreme excellence that they went full circle and became deficiencies. Her attractiveness, for example. She wasn't simply attractive, she was dazzling. Her yellow-blonde hair, blue eyes, and slender figure turned eyes everywhere she went, and she had a consciousness of her beauty which made her radiate an aura of confidence. But she wasn't vain. She simply knew how she looked to others. Many young men had been frantically eager, but their families had been adamant. Her beauty was of a quality which would sway a man's mind away from things other than fulfilling his marriage, and his life would be a constant torment of keeping other men away from his wife.

Her command of languages was similarly impressive, and someone had come up with the idea of having her help in meeting incoming immigrants from Russia. She had appeared promptly on time in one of the expensive and eye-catching crinoline dresses and wide hats of which she seemed to have an inexhaustable store. She was always cooperative and cordial enough, but because of her appearance, mien, and what had been found out to be an aristocratic St. Petersburg accent in Russian, the immigrants had been terrified of her, believing the czar's minions had preceeded them across the oceans to the New World. Similarly, Germans and French people were somewhat in awe of her. Freedman had no difficulty in understanding how they felt. He was originally from Birmingham, England, and he occasionally felt self conscious when talking with her because the English she had learned from a tutor was accented somewhat strongly with the haughty overtones of Oxford.

There were a few things which could be considered as faults. The fact that her mother had been a gentile was a problem with some who were rigid about such things, but it wasn't unheard of and was acceptable to others. It was more of a problem that she had been reared to be significantly more assertive and outspoken than most women. But the most serious fault was that she simply didn't fit in with most of the people around her. She had come from a different milieu. It had occurred to him that she might fit in more among one of the wealthy families which had settled in the estates on Long Island, and he had made tentative overtures to find out the possibilities. His overtures had been promptly rejected; such people arranged their own family marriages.

But she seemed to embody just those qualities to which Rhineman referred in his letter. Attractiveness, good education, young and healthy, and the ability to handle social situations. Ordinarily Freedman didn't care to arrange marriages by correspondence, but finding a

164

husband for Celise had become a purpose in life for him. Adah Rudnicki had more than hinted that the money Celise's father had provided was running out, so the letter had come at an opportune time. And Rhineman apparently had no interest in a dowry, because it wasn't mentioned. Everything seemed to fit.

Rhineman's name seemed to be remotely familiar to Freedman, and a friend who was a newspaper editor refreshed his memory. The man had been a general in the Confederate Army and was a highly prosperous business-man in New Mexico Territory. Freedman was delighted until he went to the bank Rhineman had given as a credit reference, then he was exultant. Rhineman owned a bank in Santa Fe, along with other interests and holdings. In addition to resolving the problem of finding a husband for Celise, it appeared that there would be a very substantial fee forthcoming. It was a long distance from the bank to the Lower East Side where the settlement committee had found an apartment for Adah Rudnicki and her charges, and Freedman allowed himself the luxury of a hired carriage.

It was an abundantly large apartment on a moderately quiet street and in a brownstone building only a few years old, but it had been somewhat crowded until Adah's two daughters had married and moved out, because Celise's belongings filled two of the bedrooms. It was also larger than had been planned for them, because they had been scheduled to move into an apartment on the third floor. But when the landlord had seen the long line of carts and wagons bringing Celise's belongings, he had let them move into an apartment on the bottom floor rather than risk overloading the beams in the building.

Adah was a small, thin woman in her late fifties, and she always looked pale and drawn. She had learned enough English for limited conversations, and her smile and greeting were polite and hopeful as she opened the door for him. But there was also a hint of defeatism in her expression, because there had been other prospects which hadn't turned out.

"I have a client to discuss with you and your cousin, Adah."

"Please sit down. I will get her."

The apartment was immaculately clean and had a charming touch of Old World atmosphere, the first undoubtedly through Adah's efforts and the latter because Celise had scattered some of her belongings around in the sitting room, a couple of small tables, an ornamental cabinet, pictures, and ornaments on shelves and tables. He put his hat on the table inside the door and walked to the couch and sat down as Adah went into the hallway. There was a murmur of conversation in Polish, then footsteps coming back along the hallway.

Somehow he had never quite become accustomed to the first glimpse of her, although they had met any number of times, and he rose automatically. She was wearing a light colored muslin dress with puffed shoulders, a wide skirt which swept to the floor, and tight sleeves and bodice. Her hair was piled up on top of her head, as she usually wore it. She was smiling politely, as always. For some reason, he always felt like bowing. And, although he always liked to be on friendly and even personal terms with his clients, it had never occurred to him to address her by her first name.

"Good afternoon, Mr. Freedman."

"Good afternoon, Miss Rabinowsky."

"We were just about to have tea. Will you join us?"

"Yes, thank you very much."

The tea service was Meissen, delicate, fragile, expensive, and undoubtedly from the enormous pile of crates, barrels, boxes, and trunks she had in the two bedrooms. She made a small ceremony of pouring it. There were six small cakes on a plate and they looked good, but he politely declined when she offered them to him because he knew their money was limited.

"I have received a very interesting letter, Miss Rabinowsky. It is from a gentleman in New Mexico Territory who is considering marriage, and it appears that it might be a compatible arrangement for you."

Adah looked blank. "New Mexico...?"

Celise looked at her and talked rapidly in Polish, apparently describing where it was, then looked back at Freedman. "What does the gentleman say about himself?"

Freedman considered opening comments, like first impressions, to be crucial. Even though he had talked with Celise any number of times, he had never penetrated the serene, polite surface, because she never showed emotion. He thought rapidly for something which might stir her interest. From comments she had made and from his limited knowledge of her life in Warsaw, army officers had figured heavily in her social life, much as they did in the better social circles in England. "He was a general in the Army, as a matter of fact. He seems to be a man of many parts."

Her eyebrows lifted. "He was a general in the Army? And he retired? He must be quite old."

"He is forty, and his didn't precisely retire...he was in the Confederate Army. A general in the Confederate Army."

She nodded slowly. "I see."

"The Confederate Army was the one which—"

"I quite understand, Mr. Freedman. Well, what has

this general done other than help lose a war?"

He wasn't sure if it was an unfortunate choice of words, or if there was dry humor in the comment, because her expression hadn't changed. In event there had been an attempt at humor, he pursed his lips and cleared his throat to indicate he considered the matter no subject for levity as he began telling her what Rhineman had written. When he finished, he took the letter from his pocket and let her look at it. She studied it for several minutes, apparently deciphering Rhineman's handwriting and picking out words she recognized. Then she handed it back to him with her unchanging polite expression.

"What is your initial impression, Miss Rabinowsky?"

She lifted her eyebrows and shrugged slightly. "I am very favorably impressed on the basis of what I know. Perhaps when I have met him and known him for a time..."

"Yes, but we must also consider his position, mustn't we? And we must give him adequate reason for making such a long journey to meet you. I would like to suggest that we prepare a contract and send it to him so that—"

"A contract, Mr. Freedman?" Celise murmured. For a moment her large, blue eyes had a sparkle which almost looked like indignation, then she blinked and it was gone. "That would be precipitant, would it not? After all, I haven't even met the man, and I haven't even seen a picture of him."

"That's true, Miss Rabinowsky, you haven't. But please consider the matter from a detached viewpoint, as I must." He tapped the letter with a finger, shaking his head warningly. "On the basis of this right here, he would be a highly desirable match for many women, so I believe some expression of good faith on our part is highly necessary. Consider also the length of time it requires for

168

a letter to get from here to where he lives. It could also be that I am not the only one to whom he has written on this matter, because there are many marriage brokers, you know. And I can say without reservation that he is the most qualified client who has ever contacted me. He is an extremely wealthy man, and most women would be eager to marry him. Now there are several very favorable young women on my list, but I have contacted you first because I have an earnest desire to see you settled in a suitable marriage..."

As he talked, he let a slight tone of admonition creep into his voice, and he emphasized his words appropriately to remind her that other possible arrangements for her hadn't turned out favorably and there were none others presently pending. She looked away, possibly not liking it, but it was impossible to assess her reaction precisely because her expression still didn't change. Adah murmured to her in Polish, looking at her with a pleading smile. There was a momentary silence, then Celise looked back at him.

"Very well."

"And I believe it might be a good idea if you would write him a small letter, if you will. Just a short note to let him see your handwriting..."

"I'm afraid my command of written English isn't the best, Mr. Freedman. I did mention that, I believe."

"Yes, well, I'm sure Mr. Rhineman is a man of parts to the extent that another language would do."

"Russian?"

He hesitated, cleared his throat, and smiled weakly as he shook his head slightly. "Well, Russian isn't a common language here. Let's say French."

"Very well."

"It would also be a good idea to send him a tintype, I

169

believe. I happen to know a photographist who has a shop not far from where I live, and I will bear the expense to show my appreciation for your cooperation, Miss Rabinowsky."

"No, that is quite too much to ask of you, and—"

"Not at all, Miss Rabinowsky," he said in an expansive tone, smiling widely and shaking his head. "I am pleased to do it, because I am quite sure that the money will be well spent. You see . . ." He hesitated, and leaned toward her. "You see, in my profession, one develops a feeling for these things. And I have a very positive feeling about this, Miss Rabinowsky. I am certain that this is going to turn out very favorably for you, if only we can make arrangements to reply to Mr. Rhineman quickly enough."

It was a tactic which almost always produced a more positive and receptive attitude in a client. Celise's reaction was difficult to determine, but Adah nodded and beamed. He rose to leave, thanking them for the tea and talking to Celise about arrangements to have the tintype made as she walked him to the door, and he hurried home to begin work on the letter.

The essential matters to cover in the letter were those which Rhineman had addressed in his letter, and happily they were positive in each instance. Those things about Celise which could be construed as disadvantages had to be referred to in order to be honest, but much of the impact of anything lay in how it was addressed. He worked on the letter until late that night, then had another thought as he was reading through what he had done. The letter concentrated solely on Celise, which might be unwise and certainly represented his very substantial list of female clients very poorly, and he decided to put in a few more clients.

Then as he lay in bed that night, he thought about

Celise's extraordinary beauty. It would proboably be best to minimize it and express the thought that she was above average in attractiveness. He knew little about New Mexico Territory, other than he had heard it was an untamed wilderness. It could be that Rhineman might envision having trouble keeping Indians or wild frontiersmen away from an exceptionally beautiful woman. And it appeared that the tintype wasn't a very good idea on further reflection, but it would take a lot of explaining if he told Celise he had changed his mind. But he knew the photographist, and he could tell him to make it slightly blurred or something so it wouldn't show her face too clearly.

The following day was a rush of activity. He prepared the contract and went to Celise's apartment to get her to sign it and to pick up the letter. He visited several more clients to have them prepare letters, telling them just enough to get them to write a letter but not enough to build up their hopes. Surprisingly, many of them had a cool attitude toward New Mexico Territory, even though he made it clear that Rhineman was wealthy. A couple of them had tintypes, which he collected, and that afternoon he went for Celise and took her to the photographist's shop. He picked up the tintype that evening by himself, and finished the letter that night. The following morning, he mailed it.

There were a number of other arrangements pending, several of which were completed during the following weeks, and other clients came in and were duly put on the list. A shipload of immigrants came in which consisted of families with a high proportion of daughters among them, and he got a lot of them as clients. Then there were a number of men who came in, and the list went back down. Each one received his careful personal attention and it

171

was a period of heavy activity, but Celise was always at the back of his mind and he anxiously awaited some response from Rhineman.

At about the time he began to fear that nothing would come of it, the reply from Rhineman arrived. The draft almost took his breath away, but the letter was something of a disappointment. It wasn't what he had expected and it certainly wasn't what Celise had been anticipating, and he delayed for a day and marshaled his arguments to support Rhineman's viewpoint before he went to see her.

Celise was adamantly against it, refusing to even consider it. Freedman explained that men in the West frequently made all the arrangements for a wife at long distance, sometimes including the actual marriage by the use of a stand-in, then he pointed out the unquestionable press of business affairs which would prevent Rhineman from journeying to New York. Celise remained courteously polite and unwavering. And, unexpectedly, Adah turned out to be a problem. She had heard stories about Indians, and she didn't want to go anywhere near the West.

He let other things go and concentrated on changing Celise's mind. He waited across the street outside the apartment building until Adah left to go shopping. He got Adah alone and talked to her. At first he was congenial and affable, then he gradually became more firm, bluntly reminding Adah that there were no more clients interested in Celise and there might never be any more if Rhineman slipped away. He warned her that it was imperative that she try to sway Celise into agreeing.

Then he visited both of them at the apartment again and talked to them together. It was immediately apparent that Adah had been exerting pressure on Celise, because Celise's composure was less complete than he had ever

172

seen it. He went through all he had covered with her before, then he brought up a final point, which was a telling matter. Celise had signed a marriage contract, and there had been no provision or condition in it that required Rhineman to come to New York. He apoligized for having prepared the contract, admitting that he might have been too hasty, but she and the man who had asked for her had both signed the contract. And it was binding.

It worked. There were indications that maintaining her composure was a struggle for her, but she agreed to do it. He took his leave of them and left to let them work it out between themselves. He hurried home to get off an answer to Rhineman, thinking of how to arrange his business affairs so they would be stable during his absence.

Chapter 12

To Celise, Rhineman's letter represented both the promise of escape from the nightmare which had started a short time before leaving Poland and the possibility of sinking deeper into misfortune. The seeds of the trouble had been sown in the Revolution, although it had scarcely touched her when it started. She had been in finishing school, and there had been talk about it. Some of the other girls' brothers and fathers had been involved because they were in the Army, and there had been stern lectures of obscure meaning in some of the classes. But what happened outside the thick, tall stone walls surrounding the Mariinsky Academy failed to stir the placid calm of centuries which lay over the ancient buildings and the stone walks under the spreading lindens on the inside of the walls. The instructors still stalked ominously along on their way to classes in their black robes and square hats, with their trailing lines of girls in uniform following them, while preparations for classes and the rote of quarrels and reconciliations with other girls had seemed far more important than any revolution.

At seventeen she had graduated and returned home to the towering Georgian brick on the fashionable Marszalkowszka Street, and the effects of the Revolution had been more evident. Before leaving for the Academy, she and her father had gone to a synagogue near the Barbakan, but there had been trouble and it had been closed. When she returned from the Academy, they went to one in the Praga District on the right bank of the Vistula. The route led across the river and through an area of narrow, twisting cobblestone streets lined with old wooden houses which looked like relics of a bygone time, packed tightly together and some of them warped and leaning as though removing one of them would bring streets of them crashing down and dissolving into dry and hoary dust. The street then came out on open roads of cottages where the air smelled fresh with the scent of green and growing things and where there was an aspect of the countryside even though the cottages were tightly spaced.

The dichotomy of origins and alliances and a lack of sense of belonging had begun in early childhood and remained after coming home from the Academy. She was Polish, but tutors teaching her Russian and French from an early age had made them her primary languages. While her mother lived, she communicated with her in French, she spoke with her father in Polish, and with most of her friends she conversed in either French or Russian. But there were exceptions, because she had friends among the wealthy Jewish merchants who had homes near Marszalkowszka, of whom some preferred French and others spoke only Polish. From early childhood, she had often accompanied her father to the Praga District when he visited with his relatives, and they spoke only Polish or yet another language, Yiddish. They had been darkly doubtful and disparaging on the subject of her father sending her to the Academy, creating within her a transitory hope that she wouldn't have to go, but he had sent her and when she returned she found herself able to understand the Yiddish because of its similarity to the German she had learned in the Academy. But her Polish had become heavily accented with Russian, because that was the primary language in the Academy.

The reasons her father's relatives had been discouraging about the Academy had become apparent during the first days. Not even the wealthy Jewish merchants were able to send their daughters there, the most elite school for women in Poland, and the only holidays were Christmas, Easter, and other Christian holidays. When she talked with her father about the Academy, he was interested in some of the things and gruffly impatient with her when she talked about other things, and she finally figured out that there were some things he simply didn't want to hear about. For example, that matins was a required assembly.

But the days had been full when she returned from the Academy, because she still had tutors and studies, and she had found out that she was in competition for the attentions of males in ways other than pulling a tongue at them. There were gowns and parties, and there were handsome young officers. The nurse of childhood had left when her father saw that she was aping the nurse's motion of crossing herself before prayer. Another had come from the Praga District and had refused to remain in the house overnight, and yet another had come from the Praga District and remained, spending most of her time in her room in prayer. She had died and been replaced with a

French governess, Blanche. Blanche had been helpful with clothes and perfumes, but in conflict with her father over conduct, particularly after coming back from the Academy. The changes wrought by the Revolution became more obvious. Her father had been pleased when she had become fast friends with Annya, the daughter of Count Mieroslawski. But Count Mieroslawski had fled with his family to Paris, and Celise's father had been enraged when he found that she was still corresponding with Annya in Paris.

As a child, her religion had caused only mild and passing interest and comment among friends who were gentiles, because it was a matter rarely touched upon in conversation with other girls. After she finished at the Academy, it was of markedly less interest than her appearance among young men at parties, even though it was the occasional subject for acid comment by young women who were less attractive and received less attention. Among the cosmopolitan and sophisticated there was acceptance of differences, and even the laborers and porters who would hurl a curse or a stone at a Jew hurrying along the street would doff their hat to a Jew in a carriage.

She had been almost twenty when the full impact of the reaction to the Revolution began to be felt, a series of measures designed to strengthen the authority of the central government Warsaw, make the government in Warsaw more responsive to the political philosophy of St. Petersburg, and reduce foreign influence in Poland. None of the measures were directed at Jews as a specific class, but many of them were applicable to residents other than ethnic Poles, which included Jews. Limits were set on ownership of property, restrictions were placed on the number of marriages which could be performed, and other prohibitive laws were established to make Poland unattractive to peoples other than ethnic Poles. She became aware that her father was under heavy pressure, visitors arriving and departing at all hours of the day and night with messages and matters to resolve. She had always been remotely conscious of the fact that he was older than the fathers of her friends, but he began to appear very old indeed, with frequent bouts of illness. He had often done things for his relatives and other Jews, and there were indications that there were things they wanted that he couldn't do. And as her consciousness of what went on around her expanded, she noticed that a lot of people were out of work and had no money.

Her father decided to send her and Blanche to St. Petersburg for a time, to stay with relatives of her mother's. The man was her uncle, a government functionary who had lived in St. Petersburg most of his life, his was wife was Russian, and all of his children had been born in St. Petersburg. It was a relief to get out of the ominous atmosphere which lay over Warsaw like a pall, and it was a time of gay parties and balls. The proliferation of religions was even more confusing because the family was Russian Orthodox, but they weren't a religious family. She found that her religion provided her with an exotic touch in the social circles in which she traveled when it caused any comment at all.

There was an abundance of handsome young officers in the elite Horse Guards and Knights Guards regiments in St. Petersburg, and her aunt was delighted over the numbers of them Celise attracted to her home. Several of them began to show serious intentions, which her aunt tried to discourage in order to keep the attraction from being removed, and a couple of them went so far as to talk to her uncle. Then her father summoned her and Blanche back to Warsaw.

And the blow fell. The prohibitions had been tightened in Poland, and the economic situation had worsened. Mobs had prowled the Praga District, and there had been stonings and beatings. Her father had been through a protracted period of illness, and he was very weak and frail. The husband of a cousin of her father's had been stoned to death and she had come to Celise's father to ask for financial assistance in immigrating to the United States with her two daughters. And Celise's father had decided to send Celise with her.

They had never been close. He had always been a source of authority more than anything else, scolding her nurse or governess when he was displeased and occasionally reprimanding her as she became older, and it had always seemed that the Academy and tutors were a way of occupying her so he could devote his undivided attention to his work. He had set standards for her and had shown pleasure in her achievements because they reflected well on him. She had never questioned his authority, but she almost rebelled when she felt her world falling to pieces around her. Warsaw was the focus of her life. But when she examined the situation analytically, she saw she had no alternative to obeying him. There had been overtures of marriage from the time she had been seventeen, but they had all been from gentiles and her father had refused to contemplate them. By law his authority over her was absolute, and she had to do as he commanded.

And the nightmare began. She had known Adah Rudnicki from early childhood, because she had been among those in crowded rooms in Praga District whom her father had gone to see. She had also known Adah's daughters, because they had been among the hordes of children who lurked behind things and peered out at her in withdrawn, unapproachable, and sullen resentment at her bright, frilly dresses and fur capes and boots. As adults they were friendly enough with her, but in many ways they closed her out and became a group of three, isolating her. There were also limitations on what she could take, causing hours of agonizing decisions over clothes, presents she had received at one time or other, and furniture she had selected for her rooms. Finally, there was the sorrow and heartbreak of leaving.

The train journey was hard and difficult enough as far as Dreux, where Blanche remained after tearful farewells, then it became almost unbearable, with Adah and her two daughters on one side of the compartment murmuring to each other in Yiddish or in a Polish dialect she could hardly understand, and her on the other side of the compartment. There was a delay at Brest in cramped, uncomfortable, and unsanitary quarters in the Jewish section of the city. Then Adah had arranged their passage, booking Celise in a first class cabin and her and her daughters in steerage.

New York had much in common with Brest. The apartment was dingy, cramped, and uncomfortable, and almost unbearably noisy from the crowded street outside and the other tenants in the building. And the people were difficult. With the same rational assessment of her situation which had brought her to the point of willingly acceding to her father's command to go with Adah, she had come to the conclusion that marriage was her only path of escape from an unbearable situation. And she tried. Many nights were spent in weeping into her pillow in the solitary misery of her bedroom, and in the mornings she summoned her will and strength to face the day. But the people around her seemed so morose and dull, many of them fanatically religious and all of them apt to take offense at the most innocuous comments. A friendly attempt at conversation was met with hostile silence, and an attempt at humor was regarded with indignation. There was no laughter and no music. She had suffered humiliations, cold and calculating examinations by relatives with attitudes more appropriate to selecting a fat chicken for dinner than a wife for a son, and she had bitten back the barbed comments learned in the slashing repartee of a thousand parties.

And all for nothing. In some strange way, it seemed that the difference between her and the others was exemplified by the way in which Adah Rudnicki had booked first class passage for her and steerage for her daughters, as though it were ordained by some immutable and preordained fact of life. And in the way Adah interpreted it as a slight on the cleanliness of the apartment when she started to do some small task to help.

The situation was unbelievable. Her beauty was a fact of life, and much of her life had been spent in preparing for marriage. Young men reacted as strongly in New York as elsewhere, but their families had been as firmly negative. In some monstrous and shattering way, it was as though she had meticulously prepared herself for a lesson in geography and the class had turned out to be on philosophy.

Then the letter from Rhineman came. In a way it hinted strongly of the attitude of shopping for a pair of boots, but she had almost become inured to that while dealing with Freedman and meeting relatives. And he said all of the right things. There was no mention of cooking, for example, an undertaking of which she knew nothing and had never realized that she might need to know until arriving in New York and sending Adah and her daughters into spasms of horrified consternation by heating herself a glass of milk in a pan reserved for meat. On the other hand, the qualities and characteristics to which he referred reflected common interests and background with her. He could have been an officer of an elite regiment in St. Petersburg from the things he emphasized. The letter was in English, a language which had been difficult for her and in which she was indifferently qualified, and in an impatient hand, many letters only partially formed and a word scratched out here and there. But a bold, masculine hand, in the diction of an educated man. And formerly a general in the Confederate Army. There was something very romantic about the vanquished warrior. She had known a young French officer in Warsaw who had braved innumerable arguments and insults to wear his Napoleonic cockade.

The letter to him was one of the most difficult she had ever written. With the blank paper in front of her, the impulse to express what she felt was almost irresistible. She knew only the most general facts about him, so there was a tendency to cover them and lace them together with a web of attributes she wished him to have. And she wanted to write to that man she saw in her mind, the man who would be able to look at the lines and see into her mind. A kind and gentle man who would forgive moments of foolishness and would be a bulwark against the vicious battering of the world about her. She wanted to beg him to be what he seemed and to come for her. And she wanted to fill pages with assurances of her loyalty and devotion if only he would give her a taste of the laughter and music she had once known.

But the world had shown to her its different faces, and there was no difficulty in remaining in firm contact with reality in the drab apartment, sitting at the table and trying to keep a point on the quill with the knife Adah used for cutting bread. The choice of dresses, whether or not to wear a hat, and how to fix her hair to have the tintype made kept her awake most of the night.

Then it was done, and the dull, grey depression of anticlimax set in. The lesson that hope is the seed of disappointment had been learned but yet not learned sufficiently to deny the insidious allurement hope always holds forth, and it grew despite her best efforts to refuse it sustenance. There was ample time for reflection, as there always had been since coming to New York, because her time was spent rummaging through the boxes of books for something to read which would hold her interest, tossing restlessly in bed through the long nights, and being spurned and ogled at the synagogue. As the weeks passed, disappointment came. And then despair.

She was standing in the window and looking out at the dirty, crowded, noisy street the day Freedman returned, trotting along the street with a letter in his hand. The significance of what it meant came close on the heels of bemusement, exploding in her mind with a fanfare, and she felt faint. Then she rushed to her room and sat on the edge of the bed, her heart pounding and her hands cold and damp. She wrung her handkerchief, listening to Adah answer the door and the murmur of Freedman's voice, then Adah's footsteps came along the hall and she dried her hands on her handkerchief and composed herself.

It was difficult to maintain her composure when she heard what Freedman had to say. The exhilaration and excitement crumbled. The visions of setting the table with her Meissen and silver and receiving a courteous and handsome man who would immediately take charge and make all the problems disappear faded into drab misery. It was so utterly crass. Rather than a human being, she was an item of barter which had been found sufficient for

183

the price, and Freedman kept waving a bank draft around as he repeated the same things over and over. And she rose, went back to her room, and lay down on the bed and burst into tears.

Then Adah came back from shopping the following day, apparently having forgotten her fears of Indians of the previous day. She got out the money that was left and showed it to Celise, then she began begging. Freedman returned. It was the same conversation all over, with one significant change. He reminded her that she had signed a marriage contract. She had committed herself, there was little money left, and there were no alternative courses of action. She almost lost her control in front of him, and she finally gave up and agreed to do it.

There was a flurry of preparations, with Freedman coming two and three times each day to talk to Adah about the arrangements. Freedman found a couple of women to come in and help Adah pack everything. They left early on a grey and rainy morning, with a line of carts and wagons carrying her belongings to the railway station and an interminable wait on the noisy, dirty platform while the things were accounted for and loaded into a freight car. The trip on the train wasn't unlike the trip across Europe some months before, except that the car was larger and the people were different, louder, more boistrous, and more inclined to talk, laugh, and fight with each other. Food was always a problem when traveling, and they subsisted on musty eggs and other things Adah and Freedman had put by.

Freedman had made arrangements ahead, and they were met at St. Louis by a delegation from the Jewish section of the city, with carts and wagons to transport her belongings. There was an uncomfortable night in a small house where she carefully maintained an appreciation for

184

hospitality even though she knew Rhineman's money was paying for it, then early the following morning there was a trek to the docks, with Freedman and a surly gentile counting the boxes, crates, barrels, and trunks and making out a bill as they were loaded onto the boat.

The landscape was more open along the river, small collections of houses and isolated houses mere specks in the wide expanse of miles of forests and fields, with people on the shores and in rowboats waving as the riverboat went by. Men on the deck stared with straightforward insolence, and she and Adah sat in the stuffy cabin and tried to get some benefit from the hot breeze blowing through the open window. The first stop caused momentary consternation as the horn on the riverboat rumbled and she thought for a moment that the collection of rude shanties and rickety docks was her destination, but there was only a moment's delay to load some boxes, unload some others, and for a couple of men to jump off and a couple more to leap on.

Adah's apprehension about Indians increased between the towns and settled regions along the river, and she looked through the window at the thickly forested riverbank with a frightened expression. "I have heard that Indians lose control of themselves when they see a white woman."

Celise knew that problems with Indians were much further to the West. Beyond that, there was the logical deduction that firearms would be much more in evidence if there were any danger of attack, and the riverboat would be armed with cannon. On the other hand, Adah had been largely in her element in New York. And inclined to be smug about it. Her attitude and the attitude of her daughters had reflected something approaching satisfaction that one who had been too fortunate for too long had been brought to heel by life. "I have it on good authority that Indians are not sexually excited by white women."

Adah turned crimson, as Celise had anticipated, but she also looked relieved. "Well..."

"Yes," Celise murmured, letting her eyes wander over the abundant mass of iron-grey hair on Adah's head. "Their only interest in white women is because of the fact that a woman has more hair than a man and their scalp makes a much more handsome trophy."

Adah gasped with horror, her face turning a sickly grey color, and she involuntarily touched her hair with her fingers as she looked back out the window at the riverbank.

There was a layover of two days at Kansas City, and Westport was only a short distance further along the river. It was a disappointment as she looked at it through the window while the horn bellowed and stirred echoes back and forth across the river and the riverboat churned around and edged toward the docks. It looked raw, crude, and unfinished, somewhat larger than most of the small places at which they had stopped, but far less than a city. She had entertained some worries and doubts about the safety of her belongings if they were passed over the rail the way other things had been at short stops along the way, and she felt relieved as she heard the bustle of activity of the boarding ramps being dragged into position to drop them onto the wharf when the boat docked. There was a crowd on the docks, as there had been at other places, people meeting passengers or expecting deliveries, laborers, and onlookers.

The crowd was considerably larger than it had been at other places, and when the boat docked she found that most of them were there to meet her. What appeared to be

186

every adult in the Jewish community in Westport was there, and she experienced a puzzled pleasure over their gracious attitudes. They greeted her with extreme cordiality, the men and women crowding into the cabin and everyone eager to carry things and to assist her. She was escorted along the deck with flattering attention, and the gentile who owned the hotel Rhineman had mentioned in his letter to Freedman was there with porters and a wagon to get her belongings. He appeared to be the kind of man who would openly stare at her in brazen insolence and push Freedman aside with a sneer, a large, burly man with a red face, and there were clear indications that the cordiality between him and the Jews who had met her wasn't common for either of them. But he was fawning and servile, laughing with hearty good nature and sending the porters scurrying about for more wagons when he saw the mound her belongings were making on the dock.

Then the reason for all the attention and courtesy became clear to Celise from the conversation around her. In Westport, the name Rhineman commanded immediate attention and deep respect from everyone.

The owner of the hotel escorted them up a wide dirt street away from the docks, then along another expanse of dirt which ran between the fronts of buildings and served for a street to the hotel, a large structure of unpainted wood. It was almost like a procession, a large cluster of people around her, the hotel owner bellowing at porters, the long line of carts and wagons following behind, and people staring from the sides of the streets. The hotel owner used euphemisms which left the impression he considered Judiasm to be an embarrassing disease which was treated with a special diet in communicating the fact that the hotel dining room cuisine included kosher foods, and there were invitations from all the Jewish families. The crowd filled the large, austere lobby of the hotel, sweeping drummers and old men dozing in chairs aside, and the hotel owner made a couple of ground-floor rooms available to store her belongings, mentioning that the hotel was crowded then sweeping the fact aside as a minor consideration. Celise took her leave of the people who had come to meet her and left Adah chattering with them and Freedman and the hotel owner overseeing the unloading of her belongings as she went up to her room.

The following day was the Sabbath, and there were cordial greetings at the synagogue with no glances or asides which could be construed to reflect opinions that her dress was too bright. Most of the people in the Jewish community were of German origin, and there was the usual problem in comprehending their dialect and the abashed attitudes because of her Berlin accent, the result of countless hours of practice on her part and of painstaking efforts on the part of her tutor. But there was a subtle but significant difference in that they seemed to expect it and even enjoy it, and there was an impression they would have been disappointed in her if she had spoken their dialect. It was a pleasant day, restful after the journey and providing wry amusement in the way Adah basked in the attention and readily emphasized her kinship with Celise, a matter of remote embarrassment to her only days before.

Freedman had been afraid that something might happen to delay them along the way so that they would arrive later than the specified date, and they had arrived early. Celise got out some of her books and built herself a daily routine to fight the growing tension and worry over what Rhineman would be like, taking morning tea in the hotel dining room, reading, walking in a field behind the hotel where a few cattle grazed, and visiting among the Jewish families in the evenings. The boistrous and forward nature of American men was no problem after the first morning, when a drummer in the hotel lobby whistled at her lewdly. He was pounced upon by the enraged hotel owner and thrown bodily through an open window.

Her room had been loudly proclaimed as the best in the hotel by the owner, which stimulated sympathy from her for others who had to do with less in the way of amenities. The floor, walls, and ceiling were bare, unpainted wood which was grimy from the dust of the street, there was a battered dresser with a mirror on it, an iron bedstead, two straight chairs, and a homemade table. The window overlooking the street was covered with a pair of stained and sun-bleached muslin curtains, and she sat in her room during the long, hot afternoons with the curtains pulled back in the hope of more breeze than dust from the street. On the other side of the street there was a row of unpainted slab buildings and shacks, and at the edge of the town a hundred feet away there was a wide area of stock pens, which made the air thick with a suffocating stench when the breeze was from that direction. The muddy river curved around in a deep bend with a wide flood plain which ended only a few yards from the rear of the buildings on the other side of the street, and she could see most of the docks. A couple of days after they arrived, barges pulled up at the edge of the river and unloaded a large stack of crates, a pile of assorted sizes and lengths of timber, and several huge wooden boxes onto the sloped floor plain behind the buildings across the street. During subsequent days, men worked around the stack and the wooden boxes turned into wagon beds as men put axles

189

and wheels on them. Then they began to take the shape of the huge, tall wagons with curved canvas covers on them such as those she had seen in pictures about the West as the men continued working on them.

The tension built despite her best efforts to control it, reaching a climax on the day he was to arrive, then fading into a dull anticlimax when he didn't. Freedman, the hotel owner, and the families she visited talked about the uncertainties of travel across the plains, of how a few days was nothing when considering the vast distances involved. There were many comments which swayed her away from the disappointment she had felt when he had failed to come to New York to meet her, stories about most women having to travel on to the Far West by themselves to meet the men who had sent for them and remarks about how concerned he must be for her safety to be coming to Westport for her. Hostile Indians was a frequent subject of conversation, and most of the stories seemed to endow Indians with superhuman characteristics. Adah took due note of the stories, closing her window and blocking her door with a chair after sunset, and enduring the stifling heat because of her fear of Indians. Celise felt vaguely troubled by worrisome if admittedly ungenerous thoughts of what would happen to her if Rhineman met with some untoward accident on the way to Westport.

The first word of him came four days after the day on which he had been scheduled to arrive. Celise had just returned from her morning walk and was looking through a crate of books in her room for something interesting to read when Freedman called to her from the hallway in an agitated tone and knocked on her door.

"Come."

He opened the door and looked in with an excited

190

smile. "I've just been told by a man downstairs that one of Mr. Rhineman's men has arrived, Miss Rabinowsky."

"One of his men?"

"Yes, to see about some affairs he has arranged. I'll go talk to him and ask him when Mr. Rhineman will be here, but I thought I would tell you first. I'll come back and let you know what he says when I've talked to him."

"Very well, Mr. Freedman. Thank you very much."

He nodded and closed the door, and she could hear his footsteps moving rapidly along the hallway toward the stairs down to the lobby. She went to the window, pulled the curtain to one side, and looked out. There were any number of men moving about on the street and standing in pairs and small groups and talking to each other, as there always were, and none of them looked any different from the others. Then as she started to move away from the windows, a movement by the wagons by the river caught her eye. The man was distinctive because of his hat, and he was dressed in the style she had seen in pictures of Mexicans. His clothes were black, a short jacket and tight breeches which went down into his boots, and he was covered with dust. He was holding the reins on a dusty, sweaty horse, and two more horses were tied by ropes to the saddle on the first one.

The man was talking to two men by the wagons, and he suddenly turned away, leaped on his horse, and began beating and spurring it as he rode at a fast pace behind the buildings on the other side of the street toward the stock pens. The two men with whom he had been talking didn't appear to be satisfied that the conversation was over, because they were joined by two more men as they began trotting after the man on the horse. Freedman came into sight on the street below, stopping a couple of men and speaking with them. One of them shrugged, and the other

191

pointed vaguely in the direction of the wagons. Freedman trotted across the street and went between a couple of buildings. He disappeared from sight for a couple of seconds behind the buildings, then he came into sight again, trotting toward the wagons. He stopped, noticing the man on the horse riding toward the stock pens and the four men chasing after him. He shaded his eyes from the sun with his hand and looked closer, then he began running toward the man on the horse.

It was curious. From the condition of the Mexican's clothes and horses, he had come a long way, but he seemed frantically anxious to be on his way again. He reined up by a couple of men standing by one of the stock pens and dismounted, talking to them. The two men became electrified, and they ran off in different directions, waving and shouting at other men. Within seconds, a crowd of a dozen to fifteen men had collected around the Mexican and his three horses, waving their arms and talking excitedly. The four men from the wagons caught up and tried to push through the crowd to the Mexican. One of the horses bucked and kicked, and a couple of men fell back and pushed forward again. Freedman ran up to the crowd of men and circled around the edge, waving his hand and standing on tiptoe as he tried to catch the Mexican's eye.

The Mexican apparently decided he had talked long enough. He pulled one of the horses on a rope closer and began taking the saddle and bridle off the horse he had been riding and putting it on the other one even as the men continued crowding around, waving their arms, and talking excitedly. He suddenly leaped on the horse in the middle of the crowd. The horse darted forward, pulling the other two behind it. The crowd exploded as men jumped to get out of the way to keep from being trampled.

Freedman was on that side of the crowd at the moment, still circling around it, and he was knocked down as the rider came out of the middle of the crowd, all three horses running.

The rider raced between two of the buildings and came out onto the street with his horses in the pounding run, almost knocking down two men who were walking along in front of the buildings. A horse pulling a surrey along the street reared up in fright as the three horses brushed past it. The two men and the man in the surrey shouted angrily, but the Mexican didn't appear to even notice them as he leaned over the saddle and beat the horse with the ends of the reins. The wind from his wild pace turning back the front of the brim on his large hat. He disappeared along the street. The crowd of men by the stock pens broke up into twos and threes walking away and talking to each other. Freedman walked back toward the street, dusting off his clothes.

He crossed the street, disappeared under the overhang of the porch in front of the hotel, and a moment later his footsteps came back along the hallway and there was a knock at the door.

"Come."

He opened the door and stood in the doorway, looking at her with an embarrassed smile. "Ah . . . he didn't have time to talk to me."

"Yes, I saw him from the window, and he appeared to be in quite a hurry."

"But the other men said Mr. Rhineman will be here either tomorrow or the following day. And they call him General Rhineman, by the way, so I suppose I should as well. And I did find out that all those wagons over there are his. He ordered them to be here when he arrived."

She pursed her lips, glancing out the window at the

wagons by the river then looking back at him. "Do you believe he might have the impression that I have that many things with me? What I have will hardly fill more than two of them, and there are fifteen."

Freedman winced and made a concerned sound in his throat. "I did mention that you had a considerable amount of things with you, but I wasn't specific and it could be that he misunderstood . . ."

She lifted her eyebrows, turning her head to look at the wagons, and she shrugged and clicked her tongue. "They are probably very expensive. But perhaps he can send the rest of them back."

Freedman sighed worriedly and shook his head doubtfully. "I hope he doesn't get angry about it. I had difficulty in understanding what his man was saying to the other men because of his accent, but I got the distinct impression that everyone was anxious to avoid angering him." He cleared his throat and sighed again as he backed through the doorway, closing the door. "Let us hope that everything will turn out all right."

"Yes. Thank you for going to find out, Mr. Freedman."

"You're quite welcome, Miss Rabinowsky."

The door closed quietly, and the boards in the hallway creaked as he walked back toward the stairs. She looked at the wagons again, then shook her head and shrugged as she went back across the room to the crate of books. A few minutes later Adah came in, having heard the news from Freedman and bubbling with excitement. She chattered as she plucked at creases in the dress hanging on the wall that Celise had picked out to wear when meeting Rhineman.

The following day dragged slowly by, hot and uncomfortable as all the other days had been and much the same as the rest of them except that Adah and Freedman were in a state of agitation. Celise's tension had intensified until it was almost unbearable, and there was increased activity around the wagons and the stock pens.

The next day dawned, the sun rising into a cloudless blue sky, and Celise made a concentrated effort to force the matter out of her mind. She put on the dress she had picked out, put out a wide hat with a heavy white veil which tied around the throat, put her gloves by it on the bed, and curtly changed the subject when Adah joined her for morning tea and started talking about Rhineman. She had her tea, went for her walk in the field behind the hotel, then returned to her room, picked up a book, and sat down in a chair, forcing herself to read. Adah's footsteps came back along the hall, she hesitated outside Celise's room, then she went on to her room.

A distant murmur of sound came through the window. Celise lifted her eyes from the book and turned her head to one side, listening. It was the sound of many animals running, blended with a noise like that of heavy wagons jolting swiftly along. It was approaching and becoming louder.

She put the book down and walked toward the window, puzzled. The noise grew louder very rapidly, hoofs pounding and the sound of men's voices shrieking and whooping. There was a bustle on the street, people scurrying about, doors slamming, and shouts ringing back and forth. She moved closer to the window to lean out and look, then there was a sound of gunfire along with the rumble of hoofs and wild yelling. She stepped back from the window in alarm. The uproar became deafening, and the floor began vibrating under her feet. There was a sudden crash as her door flew open, and she wheeled around. Adah darted into the room with a terrified expression, clutching her hair with both hands and screaming at the top of her voice.

"Indians! Indians! Indians!"

For an instant it was almost believable. But there was excitement and exhilaration rather than warning and consternation in the shouts rising from the street. She plucked at the curtain and looked cautiously down at the street as the thunderous rumble rose to a peak and made the hotel tremble on its foundations. She saw him racing along on his horse in front of a large band of Mexicans shouting and shooting off guns, with the wagons pulled by long strings of mules careening along behind. A cloud of choking dust swelled up from the street and billowed through the window, and she couldn't see anything. It wasn't unlike the mental images she had formed from reading historical accounts of the descent of Jenghiz Khan and his savage hordes upon Crakow.

Chapter 13

Rhineman led the riders and wagons around into a circle on the grassy flood plain of the river in front of the three rows of new wagons, and there was a bedlam upon their arrival, with a crowd of on-lookers gathering around. Torres had good control over the guard, assembling them in ranks and calming them down with a couple of angry shouts, and he began appointing men to stand guard over the wagons, pointing out a spot for everyone to stack their saddles and gear, and designating men to take the horses to a stock pen. The teamsters were anxious to get their money and get to the saloons and whorehouses, but the wagon master had good control over them, making them pull the wagons into a tighter circle and then unharness their mules to take them to a stock pen. The man who had come from the factory with the wagons tried to get Rhineman's attention, but looking the wagons over would be a lengthy process he didn't want to rush and there were too many other things going on.

The on-lookers had been prowling around the loaded wagons, and they began giving them a wide berth as the guards took their positions and stood with threatening expressions and rifles across their chests. Rhineman had the remainder of the guard assembled so he could talk to them. They were all adult men, but many of them had never been out of New Mexico Territory and he didn't want to leave anyone in jail when he started back. He warned them about firing their pistols, about getting too drunk, and about whores stealing their money, having Torres translate as he talked to assure everyone understood, then he began giving them ten dollars each.

The teamsters returned from putting their animals in a stock pen and fell into the line to get their money. Rhineman counted out the coins from his pocket book, Torres standing on one side of him as the men filed by and the wagon master standing on the other. He talked with the wagon master about the additional teamsters they would have to hire for the trip back. The last of the men were paid off, and Rhineman folded his pocket book and put it back into his coat pocket, talking to Torres and the wagon master. He had absently noticed a small, thin man with a worried expression and a sniffle as he had circled around the crowd of boistrous, shoving teamsters and chattering guards, trying to get his attention, and as the crowd thinned out he wormed his way through them and pulled at Rhineman's sleeve.

"Ah . . . General Rhineman? General Rhineman?"

Rhineman turned away from Torres and looked down at him. "Yes?"

"Ah . . . I am Eleazar Freedman, General Rhineman . . ."

It took an instant for the name to register. The flurry of activity had to some extent forced the marriage out of his

198

mind, and it returned. Rhineman nodded, extending his hand. "I'm pleased to meet you, Mr. Freedman. Well, is she here?"

"Ah . . . yes, she is," Freedman replied, shaking hands with him. "Yes, indeed. Over at the hotel, and everyone else is there so you can meet them. The rabbi, the witness, Mrs. Rudnicki, and others. And everything is ready. For whenever you would like the ceremony, that is. Everyone is there, and everything is ready . . ."

"All right, I'll be over there in a little while, and . . ." He hesitated, wondering if he was procrastinating, then shrugged. "No, I'll go along with you now." He looked back at Torres. "Make sure all the guards know what will happen to them if they get drunk. And tell them not to kill anyone who tries to get into one of the wagons. They can fire off a rifle to chase them off, or just wing them at the most."

"*Si, Senor General.*"

The man who had come from the factory with the wagons pulled at Rhineman's arm again. "General, wouldn't you just like to take a look and see if everything is—"

"Not right now," Rhineman said, then chuckled dryly. "Hell, I'm about to get married. Torres, you take a look at them and see what you think, and I'll be back after a while to look at them." He looked at the wagon master. "You're going to start looking around for the other teamsters now?"

"Yes sir, General. I'll go down the street and take a look through the saloons."

Rhineman nodded, putting his hand on Freedman's shoulder and turning away with him. "Get men you know, if you can."

"I sure will, General."

Freedman cleared his throat nervously as they began walking toward the street. "I see you have some new wagons..."

"Yes, I ordered them to have them ready for the trip back."

"Well, ah... perhaps I shoud have been more specific about the amount of things Miss Rabinowsky has with her. She did in fact bring a considerable amount of property from Poland, and she—"

"There will be plenty of room for everything."

Freedman looked up at him with a weak smile, trying to keep up with Rhineman's long stride. "Ah... I beg your pardon?"

"There will be room for everything. Did you have a pleasant trip?"

Freedman blinked, glancing over his shoulder and looking at the wagons then looking back up at Rhineman with an uncertain smile. "Trip? Oh yes, it was very pleasant. Very pleasant indeed. Largely because of your very generous allowance for the best of accomodations. Which reminds me..." He dug in his pocket for a handful of folded scraps of paper. "I kept an account of all expenses, and everything has been paid except our stay at the hotel here. And there is, ah... well, considering my fee and transportation back to New York for Mrs. Rudnicki and I, there will be one hundred and forty-six dollars and odd cents left from what you sent. So I will—"

Rhineman stopped, looking down at him with a surprised expression. "A hundred and forty-six dollars?"

Freedman looked up at him with a flustered expression. "I can assure you that I kept very accurate... for example, the train fare was..." He fumbled among the pieces of paper and held one out. "Here is the receipt for that, and I have all the other receipts..."

Rhineman glanced at the paper. The amount seemed astronomical. He suddenly realized that his attitude was too penurious, considering the trouble to which the man had gone, and he chuckled and patted the man's shoulder, pushing the receipt back into his hand. "No, I meant I didn't expect that much to be left. And I appreciate the fact that you and Mrs. Rudnicki went to so much trouble, so why don't you keep what there is left?"

Freedman's mouth dropped open, and he began stuttering. "Well, that is most . . . most generous . . . don't know what to say . . ."

"Not at all," Rhineman chuckled as he started walking toward the street again. "You've gone to a great deal of trouble for me."

"Still, this is quite unexpected, and I can't express how . . . I will give the rabbi and the witnesses a present, then, and I will—"

"Yes, all right. And Celise has been comfortable?"

"Yes, very comfortable, General Rhineman. Very comfortable indeed. And as a result of your very generous allowance for excellent accomodations, I might add. Very comfortable. And looking forward to meeting you. I might also say that I am sure she is going to be delighted. As you are. In my profession, one develops a feeling for these things. And I have a very positive feeling about this, General Rhineman. Very positive indeed. I am certain that this is going to turn out very favorably and you will be a truly happy couple in every respect. . . ."

His voice faded as a couple of men came between two buildings along the street and walked toward them, waving to attract Rhineman's attention. "General Rhineman?"

"Yes, that's right."

"I'm Bill Hunnicut, and this here is my partner Charlie

Givens. And it sure is a pleasure to meet you in person, General Rhineman."

Rhineman nodded and smiled as he shook hands with the two men. "And I'm glad to meet you all. I guess we've done enough business that it's about time we met, haven't we?"

"We sure have," Hunnicut chuckled expansively. "And I hope you've always been satisfied with our trade."

"Well satisfied. You all have given me fair value."

"It pleases me to hear you say that, General, and we'll sure keep her up just the same way. Me and Charlie heard you was in town . . ." He laughed heartily as they began walking toward the street. "Heard you coming, as a matter of fact. And we thought we'd get right on over here and meet you. We have a good bargain you might be interested in, as a matter of fact. We bought out a whole shipment of cast iron stoves of different types and sizes, and we got them at a fair price. Now I don't mind telling you that because I know you're a fair man. A few of them have got a little rusty during shipment and during the time we've had them, but they're all in really dandy shape and we'll give you a good bargain on all or any part of them. The bigger the part, the better the bargain, of course."

Rhineman kept his features neutral as he shrugged slightly. Traditional houses in New Mexico Territory had fireplaces, but there had been a growing demand for stoves as the influx from the East continued. And there was a high demand for stoves west of New Mexico Territory. "I'll take a look at them, but we don't use stoves in New Mexico Territory, you know. We use fireplaces."

"Oh, we know that, General Rhineman, but you've been taking a few on your wagon trains through here we notice, and we'll make you a good deal. And we have a God's plenty of other commodities, of course . . . anything

202

you need. You got much with you to trade this time?"

Rhineman shrugged again as they walked through the smelly, littered alleyway between two buildings to the street. "Not too much, because this was a fast trip. But I have a couple of wagons of furs, three of wool, a big bunch of rugs, and odds and ends of the usual sort."

"That sounds really good, General Rhineman. We'll be glad to take all or any part of it off your hands and make you a good deal . . ."

"You and Charlie got here ahead of me, didn't you Bill?" a man laughed, approaching them as they started to cross the street toward the hotel. He grinned at Rhineman, extending his hand. "You're General Rhineman, ain't you? I'm Frank Albright."

Hunnicut and Givens looked disgruntled over the man's presence as Rhineman shook the man's hand. "Pleased to meet you."

"And I'm mighty glad to meet you, General. Have you been satisfied with my trade?"

"Yes, I have. You've given me fair value."

"Well, I aimed to, and I aim to keep it up. And if there's ever anything that don't set right with you, you let me know and I'll put it right. You think you might be down to my store after a while?"

"Yes, I'll be making the rounds and doing some trading."

Albright nodded, then chuckled as he glanced at Hunnicut and Givens. "Well, don't let old Bill and Charlie here put too many of them stoves they got onto you. They've been trying for months to figure out how to make boat anchors out of them and maybe get back some of the money they got in them."

"General Rhineman's too good a trader for anybody to put anything onto him," Hunnicut replied with a forced laugh. "Like them raw hides you got stuck with to sell for harness leather."

"That's good leather."

"Them is raw hides."

Rhineman laughed and shook his head. "Gents, I'm on my way over to meet the woman I'm about to marry, so now I'm going to have to ask you you excuse me while you discuss each other's stock. And I'll be around to see everyone before I leave."

They laughed and nodded, all of them shaking hands with him again, then they moved away, Albright going in one direction and Hunnicut and Givens going in the other. Freedman looked up at Rhineman as they crossed the street toward the hotel. "You apparently do a substantial amount of trading here, General Rhineman."

"Yes, this and Saint Jo are the main trading points to the West, and almost all of my goods—"

"General Rhineman?" a man said, crossing the hotel porch toward them and extending his hand to Rhineman. "Jim Williamson, the owner of this here hotel. And it's been my pleasure to look after your lady and her people for the past few days. And it's as much of a pleasure to meet you, sir."

"I'm very glad to meet you," Rhineman said, shaking hands with him.

"It's all my pleasure, General. And everybody is right here in the lobby waiting for you, sir. Your lady and everybody else, so if you'll just step right this way..."

Williamson led the way through the door, gesturing grandiosely and almost hitting the rabbi in the face with his hand. Freedman stepped around Rhineman and introduced him as Rabbi Schneider, Rhineman shook hands with him, and the rabbi introduced his wife. The witnesses and a couple of other married couples were

204

standing in a small cluster, and they stepped forward and the rabbi introduced them. The lobby of the hotel was dim after the bright sunlight, and she was standing on the other side of it, a trim, shapely woman of average height in a pink dress with tight sleeves and bodice and a full skirt sweeping to the floor, and a large pink hat with a white veil which hid her face. His reservations about the situation began dissipating. She was exquisitely dainty and feminine-looking, stirring memories of afternoon parties in Charleston. There was an older woman standing by her, and Rhineman and the group started moving toward them as the introductions finished. There was a thump of boots and clatter of spurs on the hotel porch, then they came through the doorway.

"*Senor General?*"

Rhineman turned; it was Torres. "Yes?"

Torres hesitated, glancing at the woman in the group around Rhineman, and swept his hat off and bowed. "Excuse," he murmured to them, then looked at Rhineman again. "The wagon man says he like to take the afternoon boat downriver. And the men bringing the oxen."

Rhineman shook his head irritably. "I told him I'll look at those wagons after a while, and that's what I meant. And tell the men with the oxen to picket them off in a space over by the new wagons. I'll be down there after a while to look at them."

"*Si, Senor General.* And maybe you like to look at wagons good. I think some pine bedboards, and not enough grease on axles."

"Pine bedboards?" Rhineman snapped, stiffening and frowning darkly. He took a step toward Torres, stabbing his finger to emphasize his words. "You go down there and make sure that neither the wagon master nor no one else signs for those wagons, and you tell that man to stay where he is until I get there. And if there are any pine boards in the beds of those wagons, I'll pull them out and ... you tell him to stay where he is."

"*Si, Senor General.*"

"And tell the men with the oxen to picket them far enough away from the loaded wagons that the guards won't shoot one of them accidentally if someone tries to get into one of the wagons and lead starts flying around. We're going to need about seventy span, including spares. Are there that many there?"

"Much more. Eighty span, maybe more, *Senor General.*" He nodded and smiled perfunctorily at the women, putting his hat back on and turning toward the door. "I go see about wagons."

"All right, Torres."

"Sounds like you got a lot going on, General," Williamson observed as Rhineman turned back toward the group. "If you'd like to commence ahead with your marrying, I expect we've got everything ready. Ain't we, gents and ladies? I've had the room right on the other side of the dining room set up with all of your stuff for a couple of days now. So we can go right on through and be done with it, if you want to."

The rabbi looked startled and faintly disapproving, but he nodded hesitantly as Rhineman looked down at him. Freedman smiled quickly and nodded emphatically, and Rhineman nodded absently as he looked back at the door with his brows knitted in a thoughtful frown, thinking about the wagons. The group moved on across the room toward the two women.

It was a long distance from the manufactories of the South and East to New Mexico Territory, and it wasn't at all unusual to be cheated by unscrupulous people who

206

took advantage of that fact. At least some part of the total amount on goods ordered had to be paid in advance, and frequently that would be all they wanted. And what was received wouldn't be worth that much. Barrels of axes or shovels ordered from a factory were much less expensive than those bought from a trader, but a barrel which was supposed to contain axes or shovels might contain junk. Or the handles might be fir or some other inferior wood. When possible, he dealt only with factories with a national reputation or with those with which he had dealt before, but in ordering the wagons such assurances had been impossible. All his previous purchases of wagons had been used wagons, and all wagon factories were small operations. If pine had been used for some of the boards in the beds instead of well-seasoned oak, the wagons wouldn't hold together long enough to get to New Mexico Territory. He mused about it as Freedman introduced him to Celise and the Rudnicki woman, and the crowd gravitated toward the other side of the lobby, through the dining room, and into another room, with Williamson leading the way.

It appeared that his misgivings about the situation had been unwarranted, because Celise seemed everything he could have expected, perhaps somewhat quieter and more retiring than he would have wished, but at least fulfilling everything Freedman had written. He couldn't see her face because of the veil, but she seemed to radiate a kind of attractiveness. Her cologne was a light cloud of fragrance around her, and it smelled like she looked. She untied the bottom of her veil and turned the lower edge of it up as they went into the room, and Freedman scurried around, giving Rhineman the wedding band and the rabbi a copy of the contract for the ceremony. The room had been prepared, as Williamson said, a long table on one side covered with white clothes, and a bottle of wine and two goblets on it. It took only a few minutes, and Celise seemed nervous. He felt a sudden stab of sympathy for her, because it did seem that things were happening with breakneck speed and in an indecorous rush. But there would be time later to assuage any lack of consideration she might feel. Her hand trembled slightly as she took her sips from the goblets, and her hand was cold and damp when he held it to put the band on her finger and repeat the words after the rabbi. Her hand was pale and soft, with long, graceful fingers. She had a quiet, soft voice and a charming accent. Then he broke the glass and bent down to kiss her. He still couldn't see her face properly because the veil was covering most of it, but from what he could see she seemed far more attractive than he had expected. Her lips were in a straight, expressionless line, lifeless as he touched his lips to them. Then everyone crowded around with the traditional wishes of good luck, and Williamson, who had been standing in the doorway and gaping, bellowed at someone over his shoulder to bring in the food and drink.

The weighty atmosphere of solemnity evaporated as a couple of women began bringing in trays. Celise moved away from him and she and the Rudnicki woman began murmuring quietly in Polish. It seemed that there was something he should say to her, because he suddenly felt an intense desire to know her better and to make himself congenial to her. She radiated culture and sophistication to a degree that made the Charleston belles he had known seem lumpish in comparison. As the possible problem with the wagons faded in his mind and he observed her more closely, he found his interest in her growing rapidly. And his satisfaction with how things had turned out grew even more rapidly. He started to move toward her, then the rabbi plucked at his sleeve and said something about the conversation with Torres concerning the wagons. Rhineman began briefly explaining in order to be polite as he edged toward Celise.

The sound of gunfire rolled along the street and carried into the room, and Rhineman looked toward the door with a thoughtful frown. Williamson glanced at him, then crossed the room in a heavy trot which made the wooden floor tremble and crossed the dining room to the windows facing the street. He leaned out of a window and looked along the street, then trotted back across the dining room, shouting.

"Couple of your men headed this way, General! Looks like there's been a shootout or something!"

The Rudnicki woman looked terrified. Celise's lips were still in a straight line, and they barely moved as she turned her head and murmured softly to one of the women in German. The woman replied quietly, her face pale. Freedman looked worried. The rabbi and the other men gave the impression of being more or less accustomed to such incidents.

Rhineman sighed heavily, looking at Celise and glancing around the group. "I'm afraid I'll have to ask you to excuse me for a few minutes."

"I hope it's nothing serious," Freedman said in a concerned tone.

Rhineman chuckled wryly and shook his head. "It's probably nothing at all. I warned my men not to shoot off their pistols, but some of them might have had enough to drink by now that they've forgotten it."

There was an uncomfortable chuckle among the group, and a clatter of spurs and thumping of boots on the hotel porch. Rhineman walked toward the doorway, taking out his pistol and checking the cylinder. It occurred to him that he had forgotten to take off his pistol belt for the ceremony. Williamson followed him across the dining room, and the two men were standing in the lobby and looking around as he went through the doorway from the dining room into the lobby.

"What is it?"

"Raphael Ortega, *Senor General*," one of them replied excitedly. "In whorehouse. Ortega shoot and bouncer shoot with shotgun."

He nodded, walking rapidly toward the door. "All right. You go get Torres and tell him to bring two of the guards. You come with me."

Williamson and a couple of men from the lobby followed him out onto the porch and down the steps to the street. The man he had sent for Torres raced across the street, puffs of dust rising from his boots as his spurs clattered in the dirt and his pistol bounced on his thigh, and Torres suddenly appeared from between two of the buildings. There was a rapid exchange in Spanish, and the man ran on toward the wagons as Torres trotted to catch up with Rhineman. Torres caught up with him and took out his pistol to check it, and a couple of by-standers at the side of the street joined Williamson and the other men following along behind.

The whorehouse was a rickety, two story structure of slabs which was canted sharply to one side, and several people were standing in the street in front of the entrance, peering inside. The dull boom of a shotgun came from the interior of the building, followed by the sharp, penetrating crack of a pistol. The people standing in front scattered, then gathered back together and craned their necks again as they tried to see inside. Two guards from the wagons and the man who had gone for them caught up, all of them puffing breathlessly and their spurs ringing

210

in the dust. They fell in behind Rhineman, and their weapons made sharp, metallic sounds as they checked and readied them. Rhineman pushed through the people standing in front of the door and went inside.

The air was thick with gunsmoke, its acrid odor blending with the foul stench of the place, a combined smell of urine, feces, sweat, and filth. Room doors lined the wall on the right, there was a staircase on the left, and beyond the staircase there was a corridor with room doors on each side and an exit at the far end. A man was crouching at one side of a room door on the right and holding a shotgun poised to shoot again, and the door was splintered with buckshot. He was a heavyset, powerful man, the bouncer, and another man was standing well out of line of fire in the corridor, the owner. They looked as Rhineman came in and his men pushed through the doorway behind him, their spurs dragging on the floor and the guards holding their rifles ready.

Rhineman walked toward the battered door, glancing at Torres. "Tell him to stop shooting and come on out."

Torres shouted in Spanish, and there was a reply from the room. Rhineman stopped by the bouncer, looking at him. "Put the scattergun down."

"Goddamnit, I ain't going to until he comes out!"

Torres seemed to move his shoulder slightly, and the tip of the barrel of his long Colt Peacemaker was suddenly resting against the bouncer's temple at the corner of his eye. The hammer came back with an oily, metallic click. "Down," Torres said softly.

The bouncer's face blanched to a sickly grey, and his head trembled as his eyes swiveled far around to look at the pistol barrel. He slowly and cautiously leaned over, lowering the shotgun, and he put the butt of it on the floor and leaned the barrels against the wall. A man stepped

211

around the bouncer, picked up the shotgun and snapped the breech open, and ejected the rounds onto the floor. Torres put his pistol back in the holster, barking at the door impatiently in Spanish. Ortega's hatbrim came into view around the doorjamb, and he peered cautiously around it and stepped through the doorway, putting his pistol in his holster. He was wearing only his hat and pistol belt, which looked both unusual and humorous, but he was too angry to be self conscious, bursting into a stream of Spanish and gesticulating wildly.

Torres nodded, motioned for him to be quiet, and looked at Rhineman. "Whore take all of his money and jump out window, *Senor General.*"

Rhineman nodded slightly, looking at the owner. "Where is she?"

"He's a goddamned liar," the man said heatedly, stepping out of the corridor and stamping toward Ortega, shaking his fist. "There wasn't none of my girls in that room."

Rhineman looked at him coldly, then took a step toward him, seized his lapels, and jerked him closer as he looked startled and started to pull away. "It's an old trick," Rhineman said quietly. "Where is she?"

"Goddamnit, I don't know what you're talking about, because—"

He broke off into a surprised grunt as Rhineman threw him toward the wall. He slammed against the wall and bounced off it, and Rhineman took a step toward him and drove a heavy right into his midriff. The man doubled over, making a gagging sound as he started to slump, and Rhineman backhanded him across the face, straightening him back up and knocking him back against the wall again. He bounced away from the wall, reeling on his feet, and Rhineman caught his lapels again.

"Where is she?" Rhineman asked quietly.

Blood was streaming from the man's nose and lips, and his eyes were unfocussed. He slumped, Rhineman shook him violently, and his eyes cleared and his face twisted with pain. "Out in the back..."

Rhineman threw him toward the corridor. "Go get her."

The man staggered across the floor to the corridor, caught himself on the side of the door, then shook his head, wiped his nose and mouth on his sleeve, and began weaving along the corridor. Rhineman glanced at Torres and indicated Ortega with his chin. "Tell him to put his clothes on."

Ortega was looking around with a gratified, triumphant expression, and he nodded and turned back into the room as Torres murmured to him. A large knot of people were standing just inside the door and the street outside looked full of people. Four more of Rhineman's men pushed their way through the crowd and came in, and they were followed by two more, all of them with their pistols drawn.

Rhineman glanced at the men coming in, and looked at Torres again. "Send a couple of these men to pass the word around that I meant what I said about shooting. I don't want any trouble with the sheriff here, and the next man who shoots a pistol is going to spend the rest of the time here sitting in a wagon. If they have any trouble, they can come and see one of us."

Torres nodded and turned to a couple of men, and spoke to them quietly. They turned and left, pushing their way through the crowd. One of the men who had come in had a bottle of whiskey, and he moved closer to Rhineman, offering it to him with a wide smile. Rhineman took the bottle, nodding and smiling, and took a long drink and handed it back. Another man offered him a bottle, and he took another drink. The bouncer was standing by the wall with his arms folded, looking uncomfortable. Ortega came back out of the room with his clothes on, and he began talking with some of the men in a rapid flow of Spanish. The spectators around the door murmured to each other, and those outside craned their necks to see inside.

Rhineman took a cheroot from his coat pocket and put it between his front teeth, and took out a match as he looked at the bouncer. "It's all right to wave that scattergun around and keep people in line, but if you shoot any of my men with it, you'd better leave right then for somewhere a long way away. China, for instance."

"I didn't know he was your man, General Rhineman. And I didn't know who you was right away."

Rhineman nodded, striking the match with his thumbnail and lighting the cheroot. "You know what they look like now. And I don't want you shooting any of them."

"Yes sir. No sir. I ain't going to shoot none of your men, General Rhineman."

Another man handed Rhineman a bottle, and he took a drink from it. It was tequila, and it almost took his breath away. He took a deep drag on the cheroot to quench the burning in his throat, then took another drink from the bottle and handed it back. The men chuckled and nodded, passing other bottles around.

The owner came back along the corridor with a thin, haggard-looking woman in a loose, tattered robe. The conversation began dying away. The woman looked around with a frightened expression, and she walked to Ortega and handed him several coins. Ortega counted them, then grunted with satisfaction and put them in his pocket.

"He's on guard duty tonight for firing his pistol when I told him not to," Rhineman said to Torres, indicating Ortega with his cheroot. Torres spat a stream of Spanish at Ortega in a caustic tone, and Ortega nodded and shuffled toward the door, looking chastened. Rhineman looked at the owner, motioning toward the woman. "Get the rest of them in here. I want to talk to them, and I want to talk to you."

The man nodded dully and walked back along the corridor, knocking on some of the doors and calling women out. Two came out of the rooms and along the corridor, and they looked around with curious, apprehensive expressions as they stood in a corner. The other woman joined them. A man shouted angrily when the owner knocked on one door, and he looked around the doorjamb and along the corridor at the crowd as the owner talked to him. The woman came out of the room and along the corridor, the owner following her. The customer came out of the room, naked except for his boots, and walked along the corridor and looked at the crowd curiously. The owner climbed the stairs with slow, heavy footsteps. Presently three more women came down the stairs and joined the group in the corner, and another naked man knelt at the top of the stairs and smoked a cigarette as he looked down at the crowd with a curious expression. The owner came back down the stairs.

The women were about average, most of them old and weary and looking out at the world from behind hard, cynical eyes as they clutched their ragged, dirty robes around them and waited impassively for whatever might happen next. Rhineman took a drink from the bottle in

215

his hand and gave it back to the man who had handed it to him, and looked at the women.

"There's been some trouble here with one of my men, and I don't want any more of it. The next one of you who tries to cheat one of my men or tries to steal his money will be dragged out into the street, stripped, have her head shaven, and then be whipped out of town." He turned his head and looked at the owner. "And this place will be burned to the ground, and you'll be tarred, feathered, and ridden out of town on a rail. You can do your business with my men and they'll pay for it, but if there's any more trouble, I'll end it once and for all. Does everyone understand that?"

They all nodded silently. Rhineman turned toward the door, and his men began pushing through the crowd ahead of him. Someone offered him a bottle, and he took a drink from it and handed it back as he went through the doorway.

Chapter 14

It was something he should have foreseen and forestalled, and it was fortunate that no one had been killed or wounded. There were three more whorehouses further along the street, and he walked on down the street with the men trailing him, going into each of them and talking to the owners and bouncers. Word of what had happened had already spread along the street, and they were all cooperative and courteous. As he and the men came out of the last one, a man wearing a badge met him in the street.

"You must be General Rhineman. I'm Sheriff Gibbons, General."

"Glad to meet you, Sheriff," Rhineman replied as they shook hands.

"Heard there was some trouble down at Fraley's place."

"One of the women took one of my men's money and

jumped out the window with it, and it was working up into a shoot out between my man and the bouncer. But I stopped it, and I'm in the process of keeping it from happening again. I've told my men to keep their pistols in their holsters, and I'm going around to see the people at places where trouble might start."

"That's a good idea. I close up one of these places now and then when I can catch them at something like that, but then another one just like it opens the next day. Most of the time the owner just blames the girl, and she's too scared to open her mouth."

Rhineman smiled wryly and nodded. "That's about the way it happens. I think I'll take a walk through some of the saloons along here and have a word with the bartenders and bouncers."

"That's a good idea too. Well, I'll have to lock up any of your men who get feisty with me, General, but I'll turn them over to you when you're ready to leave unless they've killed somebody or something like that."

"I can't ask for any better than that, and I appreciate it, Sheriff."

"We appreciate your trade, General, because it's business like yours that keeps this town going. And your men are part of it too, I guess. If you need anything from me, my office is right down yonder."

Rhineman nodded, shaking his hand. "Thanks a lot, Sheriff."

"You're more than welcome, General."

Rhineman and his men walked on across the street to a saloon and went in. It was a dark, dingy place, a bar made of rough, unfinished boards on the left with shelves of bottles and glasses behind it and barrels of beer at one end, rickety tables and chairs scattered across the open space down the center and on the right, an old man banging on a jangling clavichord on the opposite end of the place. The bouncer sat on a high stool in a corner with a shotgun across his knees, and several of Rhineman men were in the place, sitting in twos and threes at tables along the wall.

The bartender owned the place, and he and the bouncer were cooperative and agreeable. The men at the tables gravitated toward the bar as Rhineman stood at it and talked to the bartender, and the bartender brought out a bottle of reserve stock and poured Rhineman a couple of drinks. Rhineman bought drinks for the house, then left.

As he left the second saloon, he saw Rabbi Schneider and the other local people who had been at the wedding walking along the street, going home. He stopped them and talked to them for a few minutes, thanking them again and tentatively accepted a couple of invitations to bring Celise and visit the next day. The men shook hands with him, and he lifted his hat to the women as he turned toward the next saloon, Torres and the other men following him.

The wagon master came out of the saloon with a half dozen men as Rhineman approached it. They were men he had recruited to drive the oxen on the new wagons, and Rhineman stopped for a moment and talked to them. A couple of them had bottles and passed them around, and the conversation started Rhineman thinking about the wagons again. If he refused to take the wagons and demanded the money he had paid in advance back, the wagon master would have wasted time and effort in recruiting teamsters. He decided to see about the wagons before he did anything else, and he walked back along the street, went between two of the buildings, and walked down the slope toward the river to the new wagons.

What Torres had thought was pine was yellow oak, which he had never seen before. The canvas on the hoods was somewhat lighter than the Osnabrück linen Rhineman was accustomed to having on his wagons, but it looked durable enough and the hickory bows supporting it were much heavier than usual. The beds were constructed somewhat different than most wagons, the square ends curved up at the front and back and the sides high and narrow as usual, but the boards were bolted to heavy members spaced along the bed and the heavier pieces of wood were bolted together at the bottom, making the wagons heavier but much stronger than usual. The tall wheels had been carefully joined, each piece fitted so precisely that the seams were visible only by looking at the grain of the wood, and there was an extra wheel for each wagon. Torres had thought that the axles hadn't been properly greased because they had used a yellow, almost colorless grease.

"Now, I'll go get some black grease and slap it on over the other, if you want me to, General Rhineman," the man said. "It sure don't make no difference to me."

Rhineman chuckled and shook his head. "Grease is grease, and you can tell your boss that these are good wagons and I'll buy my next ones from him. Let me have your bill, and I'll sign it."

"All righty, here you are, General Rhineman. And the boss'll be glad to hear what you said. He'll appreciate that."

"I appreciate having good wagons. And I'm sorry that I held you up."

"No harm done, because there's plenty of time for me and my men to catch that afternoon boat. And to have a little drink while we're getting our things together. I have a bottle right over here, if you'll have a drink with me."

"I wouldn't mind."

Rhineman had a couple of drinks from a bottle with him as the men he had brought with him to assemble the wagons scurried around and collected their belongings together. The oxen the stock dealers had brought for him to look at were on picket ropes a few yards from the wagons, and the dealers had heard that Rhineman was at the wagons and had drifted over from the stock pens. They gathered around, urging Rhineman to look at the oxen, and Rhineman had a final drink with the man who had brought the wagons, shook hands with him again, and walked over to the oxen.

Each dealer's animals were marked by a different color of paint which had been daubed on the hindquarters of the animals, and there were a few culls among them, animals which were too old, some too young, and some with bad hoofs or galled shoulders. The wagon master came back to see what had been done about the wagons, trailed by a dozen teamsters wanting jobs, and they cheered and whooped when they found that they had jobs. Several of them had bottles, and they passed them around and helped Rhineman and the wagon master look the animals over, examining teeth, hoofs, shoulders, and general condition. Rhineman was bending over and pulling an oxen's lips apart to look at its teeth when there was a tug on his sleeve. It was Freedman.

"Oh, I suppose you thought I got lost," Rhineman chuckled, straightening up. "I'll be back up there in a few minutes."

"No, no, not at all, General Rhineman," Freedman said, shaking his head rapidly. "I more than understand that business affairs frequently won't wait. No, I only wanted to talk to you for a moment and see if you had any objection if . . . that is, Mrs. Rudnicki and I thought we

221

might be able to take the afternoon boat back if you had no objection..."

Rhineman shrugged and shook his head. "No, I don't have any particular objection, but I thought we might have dinner together or something. We haven't had a chance to talk to each other, and I'd like to get better acquainted because I certainly appreciate what you've done for me."

"Certainly, General Rhineman, certainly. If you'd rather we stayed for a few days..."

"I don't want to keep you from leaving if you need to get right back, you understand. I just thought it might be easier for Celise if she had people around her for a couple of days that she knows. And we'll be leaving day after tomorrow or the day after that."

"Day after tommorow or the next day? Hmm, well, I'd have to check the schedule to make sure, but it would probably be another two or three days after that before we could get a boat, then there's the matter of the train connection which could hold us up..."

"Yes, I guess that's right—I didn't think of that."

"In regards to Miss Rabinowsky...I do beg your pardon, Mrs. Rhineman, I should say, you'll find that she is a quite self-sufficient young woman. She isn't antisocial by any means, but she isn't the sort of woman who requires constant attendance, either."

"Yes, I see. Where is she, by the way?"

"She retired to her room. She brought quite a few books with her, and she thoroughly enjoys reading, taking her little walks, and...but if you wouldn't take it amiss, Mrs. Rudnicki and I would save several days if we took the afternoon boat, and..."

"Yes, of course. I wasn't thinking, I'm afraid. Well, it was a pleasure meeting you, Mr. Freedman."

"The pleasure was mine, General Rhineman," Freedman replied, nodding rapidly and grinning up at Rhineman as he shook his hand. "And I have total confidence that this is a day which both you and Miss...ah, Mrs. Rhineman will look back upon with great fondness. In my profession, one develops a feeling for these things. And I have a very positive feeling about your marriage today. I am certain that you will be a truly happy couple in every respect."

"I'm sure we will be. And when you get back to the hotel, you might tell Celise that I'll be along in a little while."

"I certainly will, because I'm sure she is looking forward to...ah, yes, I will. Goodbye, General Rhineman."

Rhineman smiled and nodded, turning back to the ox he had been examining. "Goodbye, Mr. Freedman."

With fifteen wagons, he needed sixty span hooked to the wagons to get them over the mountains, plus spare animals for those which went lame along the way, and he and the wagon master picked out a total of seventy-one span from the herd of animals. Then the bickering began. One of the dealers appeared to have financial problems, because he quickly came down on his price. That set a pattern for the others, and a few minutes later Rhineman had concluded the trading for the animals and was writing drafts on a bank in Independence for the animals. The wagon master and the teamsters took the animals away to put them in a stock pen, and Rhineman walked back toward the street with Torres and a few of the men walking with him.

A man came running along the street toward them, shouting about trouble in one of the saloons. Rhineman and Torres walked rapidly back along the street to the saloons, the men trotting along behind. The trouble was about watered whiskey, and it was still in the shouting stage. Rhineman talked to the bartender, and he found some other whiskey, grinning anxiously and taking a bottle of reserve stock from under the bar to pour a large drink for Rhineman and Torres. Rhineman was already among the saloons and there was a possibility of further trouble, and he began going into the rest of them along the street and talking to the bartenders and bouncers.

Hunnicut met him in the street as he started back toward the hotel after his rounds of the saloons. His store and warehouse were only a few yards further along the street and Rhineman was curious about the stoves, and he and Torres walked on along the street with Hunnicut, Givens meeting them on the way. The stoves were in a large slab addition which had been built onto the rear of the warehouse, and most of them were still in wooden crates, but Hunnicut and Givens had uncrated and assembled one of each of the three types for display. There was a small heating stove, a large one, and a kitchen range, all with grates for wood or coal. They were a little rusty, but it was surface rust which would disappear when they were oiled or polished. Givens produced a bottle, and they passed it around as Rhineman looked at the stoves and discussed the price with them. They offered to sell him an assortment of types at a flat price of twenty dollars each if he would buy as many as a hundred of them, and he thought it over, taking drinks from the bottle and smoking a cheroot. It was a good price for the small heater, a very good one for the large heater, and a substantial savings over the usual wholesale price for the kitchen stove. He agreed, and Givens brought out another bottle as they shook hands on the bargain. The deep, mournful note of the riverboat horn came from the docks as they passed the bottle around.

Albright was walking along the street as Rhineman came back out. Rhineman had traded with Albright a lot from Santa Fe and didn't want him to feel slighted, so he accompanied Albright to his store and looked through some of his goods. He had a number of things which interested Rhineman, a large stock of cotton fabrics in a wide selection of the bright colors which were popular in New Mexico Territory, barrels of machine-made nails in various sizes, and rolls of different types of barbed wire, an item for which a growing demand was developing. Albright brought out a bottle, and they and Torres took drinks from it as Rhineman looked through the things. A local man had started to go into the well-digging business a couple of years before and had ordered a large drill rig and several windmill pumps through Albright, and Albright still had them. Rhineman was interested, and they went out the back of the store and into a long warehouse behind the store where Albright had put them. The sun was setting, and Albright went back to the store to get a couple of lanterns so Rhineman could see the drill and pumps.

It was dark as they walked back along the street, and lanterns on the porches of the saloons and whorehouses cast a dim light out into the street. Whoops and yells in Spanish rang along the street, and men were momentarily visible in the bright windows as they leaped and danced drunkenly about, most of them in the saloons clothed and most of them in the whorehouses unclothed. Torres walked with an unsteady gait, and his spurs made an irregular janging as they dragged in the dust. It was still hot, and Rhineman felt muddled and confused from the whiskey.

Two men came between buildings further along the

street and walked toward the saloons and whorehouses as they laughed and talked and ate fat tortillas stuffed with chili beans. Rhineman hadn't eaten since early morning, and he suddenly realized he was ravenously hungry. He and Torres went between two of the buildings, feeling their way along in the impenetrable dark, then walked down toward the wagons, where a large fire was burning. Several of the men were sitting and kneeling around the fire, and the cook was working over a large pot of beans and a stack of tortillas, ladeling the beans onto them, rolling them, and passing them out.

Rhineman sat down by the fire, exchanging noisy greetings with the men, and the guards around the wagons chuckled softly, their eyes and teeth shining on the edge of the light from the fire. The cook handed tortillas stuffed with beans to Rhineman and Torres, and they ate. After eating, Rhineman was suddenly very weary, fatigue descending on him like a heavy weight. He went to one of the wagons and climbed into it, and lay down on a couple of bales of wool and went to sleep.

Chapter 15

The grey light of false dawn filled the wagon when he woke. He lifted his head, winced, and groaned as the pounding headache throbbed in his temples, and he turned and crawled toward the tailgate of the wagon. A small fire burned in the center of the wide bed of ashes, the wood popping and cracking and the flames casting a faded yellow glow in the dim daylight. He jumped down from the wagon, then leaned against it and held his head. One of the men on guard smiled widely as he picked up a bottle from a ledge on a wagon and held it toward Rhineman, lifting his eyebrows, and Rhineman shook his head and walked toward the fire. The large coffee pot was in the edge of the bed of ashes, and he picked up one of the tin cups from the ground and filled it with coffee. Leaning over made his head swim and his headache throb harder, and he slowly straightened back up, rubbing the back of his neck and sipping the strong, bitter coffee.

The grassy area between the wagons and the rear of the buildings along the street looked like the scene of a pitched battle as the daylight brightened. Men were sprawled about all over it, both the Mexicans and the teamsters, some with their heads pillowed on their forearms and some lying spreadeagled on their backs, snoring loudly. Rhineman went to the wagon where his clothes were and took out clean clothing, then went around behind one of the wagons to the water barrel on it. He stripped and dipped water out of the barrel with a bucket, poured it over himself and scrubbed, then dried off with his dirty shirt and put on the clean clothes. Torres was kneeling by the fire and sipping a cup of coffee when Rhineman went back around the wagon, and he looked wan and pale. He nodded to Rhineman and winced, and Rhineman returned his nod and winced. Rhineman put a pan of water on the fire to heat, then went back to the place where he kept his things to get his razor, strop, soap, and steel mirror.

The sun rose, and smoke came from the chimneys in the town, forming into a long, flat cloud which stretched down the river as a slow current of air moved along in the direction of the water. Some of the men were beginning to stir as Rhineman walked through them toward the street, and he chuckled as he looked at them sitting up and holding their heads. There were two lying in the mud and garbage in the opening between two buildings he walked through, and more lying along the sides of the street in front of the buildings. A few people and horses were moving along the street, skirting around the snoring men, and there were still distant whoops and yells coming from a couple of the saloons down the street. He walked across the street to the hotel.

Williamson was at the registration desk, looking

through a stack of bills, and he looked up and grinned widely, nodding. "Well, you're up and about early this morning, General."

Rhineman smiled thinly and nodded carefully. "Could you tell me what room my wife is in, please?"

There was a long silence. Williamson's mouth dropped open, then he started to smile as though in response to a joke. The smile faded, and he cleared his throat and nodded toward the staris. "Room two ten, General. To the left at the top of the stairs, then about halfway down the hall and on the left."

"Thank you."

Williamson smiled weakly and silently nodded, and his mouth hung open as he watched Rhineman cross the lobby to the stairs and walk up them.

Rhineman walked along the hallway, taking off his hat and running his fingers through his hair. He stopped in front of the door, brushed his coat and tugged it straight, and knocked on the door. There was a rustle of movement on the other side of the door, then light footsteps approaching the door. It opened. He looked down at her, starting to speak, then closed his mouth and blinked, looking again. It was the first time he had seen her properly. And she wasn't attractive. Or even beautiful. She was stunning.

Her hair was a mixture of shades of almost bright yellow to a light, honey brown, and arranged on top of her head in a way which looked both casual and painstaking, with ringlets hanging down in front of her ears. Her eyes were a deep blue which was almost emerald, with tiny flecks of brown in her irises, and her skin was a milky white with a tinge of pink on her cheeks. Her features were delicately etched, her eyes wide apart, her nose with a charming lift in the bridge, and her lips full and wide. Each feature was perfectly molded, and they combined into a breathtaking whole of refined, sophisticated beauty.

She was holding a book under her arm, her finger marking her place, and she looked up at him, turned away from the door and took a few steps, and turned back around and looked at him again. She was wearing a dress different from the one she had worn the day before, a pale blue muslin with a pattern of lace on the bodice and a lace collar which stood up around her neck. He stepped inside the room and closed the door, feeling suddenly awkward and ill at ease, an unusual feeling for him.

"Celise, I am sorry for what I did last night. There were some things which came up and claimed my attention, as you know, but I was disrespectful toward you because I neglected you. And I would like to apologize."

Her expression was neutral, with a hint of polite attentiveness. She pursed her lips slightly, then spoke slowly and distinctly, her pronunciation British and her heavy accent almost French but with overtones of other languages. "Will you speak more slowly, please? I have difficulty in understanding you."

He smiled, making it warm and friendly. "You speak English very well, and it's hard to believe that you have trouble understanding it."

She was looking straight into his eyes, her features still in neutral lines and with no hint of a smile on her lips. "I have no difficulty in understanding standard English, but yours is a dialect with which I am not familiar."

It was in a tone of polite conversation, with no hint of disparagement. But it was also the first time anyone had ever told him he spoke in a dialect. He cleared his throat and nodded. "Very well. What I said is that I was disrespectful toward you and neglected you last evening, and I am sorry."

"What is done is done."

"I realize that, but I would like to beg your pardon for it."

"No."

For an instant he thought there had been a misunderstanding because of a language problem, because her expression still hadn't changed. But it wasn't a language problem. The word had been unemphasized, with the hint of nasal of her accent, but flat and unwavering. It was a direct, straightforward refusal of his apology. The negative and her expression seemed contradictory, but there were other indications which could be an explanation. There was a tiny tremor in her hands and lips and a slight flaring to her nostrils as she breathed that could be interpreted as nervousness. Or the edges of a towering, furious rage showing from behind an impenetrable shield of self control. He suddenly realized that she was far different from anyone he had ever known before.

"Then perhaps I can make amends for it."

"I think not."

The reply came quickly and without hesitation. And her expression still hadn't changed. He looked out the window, drawing in a deep breath and running his fingers through his hair as he sighed, then he looked back at her. She was wearing a cameo pendant on a ribbon around the collar of her dress, and it reminded him of the pendant he had bought for her. He took it out of his coat pocket, walking toward her. "In any event, I will try. And among other things I overlooked yesterday, I forgot to give you this."

She took the box, stepped to a table and put her book down, and opened the box. "It is very lovely. Thank you very much."

"May I put it on you?"

"If you wish."

She walked to him, handed him the pendant, and turned, untying the ribbon holding the cameo in place. He put the pendant around her collar and fastened the chain. The fresh, alluring scent of her cologne wafted around her, and his hands trembled slightly.

"The chain might be just a bit long."

She walked to the mirror, centering the Star of David pendant below her collar, and looked at it. And he noticed that she didn't look at herself in the mirror. The involuntary glance at the features and the subtle shift in the composure of the features wasn't there, which might mean nothing or a lot. "It is a matter of taste, but I am pleased with the length of the chain," she said, turning away from the mirror and walking toward the corner of the room. "And I have a present for you." She picked up a polished wooden case from a wood crate in the corner of the room and came back across the room, handing it to him.

It was a pistol case. He unfastened the catch and lifted the lid, and uttered an involuntary exclamation of pleasure. The case contained a matched pair of dueling pistols, long, thin, and with the long, curved grips of French pistols of the previous century. They were the work of an expert craftsman, with the barrels, locks, forearms, and grips heavily chased with silver. He stepped to the window, taking one of the pistols from the case and balancing it in his hand, aiming it out the window. "These are absolutely beautiful, Celise."

"I am happy that you are pleased."

"I'm more than pleased." He put the pistol back into the case and closed it, and walked to the bureau and put the case on it. "I'll leave them here for now. Would you like to have breakfast with me?"

"If you wish."

"Shall I give you time to prepare?"

"I am ready unless you wish for me to wear something different."

"You look very beautiful as you are."

"I am happy that you are pleased."

The tone and expression were unchanging. There was a key on the bureau, and he picked it up and walked toward the door. She moved toward the door with a soft rustle of her skirt. He put his hand on the doorknob and hesitated, looking down at her.

"I intend to make amends for what I did."

"I think not."

"You don't know me very well."

"Nor you me."

It was both more and less than a challenge, both more and less than a confrontation of wills. In other situations and with other people it would have provoked resentment and anger, but it only stimulated admiration. Her expression still hadn't changed, but shadows in her eyes reflected pride and a will which was perhaps far greater than his. He had a premonition that all the rules and protocols to which he had been accustomed in dealing with women were inapplicable. Before, women had been objects of courtesy, protection and other considerations, but had existed in a world somewhat to one side of and overlapping the real world in places. But there was a feeling that she spanned the world of women and the real world, then went far beyond.

And her beauty was bewitching. His headache was suddenly gone, along with the soreness and fatigue from the restless sleep on the bales of wool, and his smile came naturally without being forced, spreading across his face.

He chuckled softly and nodded. "I am going to, you know," he said quietly.

Her eyes looked straight into his. The color on her cheeks deepened fractionally, and her lips twitched slightly, the corners lifting in the barest suggestion of a smile. Then her eyes moved to the doorknob, and she stood with an attitude of waiting. He opened the door for her and followed her through, then locked the door and put her hand on his arm as they walked along the hallway, still smiling down at her. She glanced up at him, then looked away.

During breakfast he became aware that they were talking about him and what he had done all during their conversation, and in analyzing it he realized that she was a supremely skilled conversationist and had subtly and effortlessly kept the conversation away from her. And he felt like a bumpkin. After breakfast he left her in her room while he went to the wagons to assure that the atmosphere would be suitable for her presence, then he returned to the hotel for her and took her to the wagons. The men were overawed by her, standing and holding their hats as they gaped open-mouthed and stuttered in reply to her pleasantries, which were serenely cordial with no hint of condescension. A lot of women were frightened by large animals, but she was perfectly at ease around them, reaching through the bars to stroke and pat the mules and oxen as he showed her around the stock pens. Her eyes shone with admiration when she saw his gelding, and he was delighted to find that she could ride. She seemed pleased when he promised to buy her a horse in Santa Fe.

The merchants came to the wagons and stock pens while he was showing Celise around, and he introduced her to them and firmly put them off until the next day. She

234

seemed interested in the trading, and he took her back to the wagons and showed her the furs, wool, and other things, explaining the values involved and how the circuits worked in New Mexico Territory. He found that she had a quick, retentive mind which rapidly gathered the facts necessary for an intelligent conversation. During the afternoon they visited with the rabbi and some of the people who had been at the wedding. The women gasped with admiration over Celise's pendant, which gave him a warm feeling of gratification. It was pleasant to visit people with her, partly because he had always felt somewhat out of place with married people and partly because he was proud of her.

They had dinner with one of the families, then returned to the hotel. Williamson had found a couch, an easy chair, and different curtains for the room, making it more liveable. They sat in the room, and he looked at the pistols again as he talked to her. It had occurred to him that the trip would be much easier on her if he bought a carriage for her to ride in, and he mentioned it to her.

"I will be content to ride in a cart."

"Wagon."

"I beg your pardon—wagon."

He shook his head and smiled. "The trip will be hard enough on you without riding in a wagon, Celise."

"I do not intend to be burdensome, Karl."

It was the first time she had used his given name, and it indicated at least a degree of softening. He smiled widely, shaking his head again. "You couldn't be."

A hint of a smile crossed her face, and she looked toward the dark window, where the breeze off the river was blowing the curtains in. Many of the men were around the fire at the wagons, and several of them were singing and playing guitars. "The music sounds very pleasant."

"Would you like to go down to the wagons and listen to them?"

"Do you mind?"

"Of course not," he chuckled, putting the pistols back into the case and closing it, and he crossed the room and put it on the bureau. "Come along."

Williamson got a lantern for him, and they crossed the street, went between two of the buildings, and walked down toward the wagons. He took her hand and held the lantern to light holes and stones along the way. Her hand was warm and soft. Silence fell as they approached the fire, and the men began rising and taking off their hats. Rhineman told them to continue, and a couple of men dragged a bale of wool from a wagon for Celise to sit on as they settled back down around the fire.

Four men were playing guitars and a half dozen were singing, and the flames in the fire leaped up and gleamed on the faces of the other men sitting around the fire as they looked at Celise. She smiled and clapped her hands when the song finished, and they sang another. Rhineman sat on the ground and leaned against the bale, looking up at her as the firelight played over her face. She enjoyed the music, clapping her hands together and smiling as they played a popular song and most of the men around the fire joined in, and the men were entranced with her. Some of them were eating, and the cook filled a tortilla with beans and brought it to her, addressing her as *Doña* Celise. She thanked him politely and took it.

When they went back to the hotel, he gave her a few minutes alone in the room, then he went up and into the room, blew out the lamp, and undressed and got into bed. He put his arm around her and pillowed her head on his shoulder, then relaxed.

"Good night, Celise."

She was silent for a long moment, then she slowly relaxed and lay against him. "Good night, Karl."

They had breakfast the following morning, then he left her in the room and went down to the wagons to have a couple of teams harnessed to two of the wagons and take them down the street to the merchants' stores. He took Celise with him when he went to the stores, which made the conversation more polite and lacking its usual profanity when the pricing of the goods was taking place, but she seemed to enjoy it. She mentioned her belongings a couple of times, and during the afternoon he took a look in the rooms where Williamson had stored her things. The high cost for transportation to Westport was explained, and he revised his estimates on the total amount of trade goods he would be taking back to Santa Fe. The trading continued on into the afternoon, and Rhineman encouraged Celise to look around for anything she might like. She said there was nothing she wanted, but he saw her glance linger on a large, highly-polished cedar chest in Albright's warehouse and he bought it. She looked pleased as the men carried it out to the wagon. That evening they had dinner at the house of one of the couples who had been witnesses at the wedding, and when they returned they went down to the wagons again and sat by the fire as darkness fell and the men played their guitars and sang. *Doña* Celise had become the men's name for her, and she seemed to like it. When they went back to the hotel and he went upstairs and got into bed with her, she moved across the bed to him and lay against him, pillowing her head on his shoulder.

The trading went on into the next day and then the following day, with the teams pulling the wagons of goods to the merchants' stores and taking them back to the edge of the river full of trade goods to go back to Santa Fe. The name the men had given Celise spread rapidly, and the merchants addressed her as *Doña* Celise. The dealer who furnished the yokes and harness for the oxen also had carriages, and Rhineman took Celise to his yard and let her pick out the one she wanted. One of the teamsters was a lanky eighteen-year-old who was bedazzled to the point of being speechiess around Celise, and Rhineman designated him to drive the carriage for her.

The teamsters began selecting their teams of oxen and fitting the yokes and harness to them, and the last of the goods were traded. Celise picked out the things from her belongings that she wanted to take in the carriage with her, and Rhineman had two wagons brought to the rear of the hotel and the rest of her things packed into them for the journey. Rhineman began concluding his trading with cash, buying the drilling rig, windmill pumps, and other things from Albright, and the new wagons were combined into the circle with the old ones as they were loaded, making a large circle on the grassy space at the edge of the river.

The impervious shield of reserved corciality she kept between them began to fray. He spent every possible moment he could with her, talking to her and winning her confidence, and it began to take effect. There were small things at first, a sigh of exasperation while she was fixing her hair in front of the mirror to go to dinner and he was sitting on the couch and looking through some bills. Then there were other things. Occasionally she smiled or laughed at things he said to amuse her, a radiant smile and a bubbling tinkle of laughter that was more than a reward for his effort. And he finally succeeded to a greater extent than he had thought possible at first. She was truly interested in Santa Fe, listening to him raptly and asking questions, and she talked about her life in Warsaw and her experiences in New York. Eventually he realized the degree to which she had been depending upon him and what he would be, the fearful hopes which had built up within her on how their marriage would be. In everything he did and said, he tried to reassure her that her hopes would be realized. The days slipped by, and he delayed the end of the trading and the departure. Before, it had been vitally important to return to Santa Fe as quickly as possible, but he had found something more important to him.

On the eighth night they spent together, she moved toward him and lay against him as she usually did when he got into bed, then she slid her hand up and touched the side of his face with her fingers. "I am ready, Karl."

It was more than he had ever before known, totally fulfilling across a spectrum which he had never suspected of existing, as though desires and needs had arisen in the presence of the means of satisfaction. The scattered rays of the moonlight coming through the window shown on her slender, milky-white body, and the feel of her soft warmth and the scent of her cologne, hair, and body made the torment of accumulated desire from the nights of denial rise to a maddening peak. The conflicting need to be gentle with her virginal body made him hesitant and awkward, but she was more than cooperative and willing, searching to satisfy some need of her own. More than the physical sensation was a sense of blending with her at some deeper level, snatches of memories of her expressions and of how she had looked at different moments flitting through his mind with a feeling that he was partaking of all of them and yet blending with something far deeper and more fundamental, which made her who

239

she was. The fascination outlasted his strength, which returned demandingly more than ever before and found her still eager, and he held her and kissed her as the stars paled with false dawn, looking forward with anticipation to being with her through another day and waiting for the night.

"Never insult me again, Karl."

"I won't, Celise."

Chapter 16

She was a slender, delicate-looking woman, creating an instinctive protective response in all the men, but she had an ability to endure hardships which put the most hardened of teamsters to shame. Her equanimity, poise, and cheerful good humor remained unaffected by the roasting sun of the plains, the dust storms of the deserts, and the drenching rains of the mountains. When a wheel on her carriage collapsed and the carriage turned over, Rhineman raced back along the wagon train to find her climbing through the splintered door of the carriage to see to the boy who drove the carriage, who had been knocked unconscious. But that night he saw the large, purple bruises on her body and knew she had to be in pain. When one of the mules pulling her carriage fell and broke a leg and had to be shot, her features were neutral as she waited for another mule to be hooked into harness. But that night she wept.

The nights on the trail were more cheerful because she was there, enjoying the singing and strumming on the guitars and creating an enjoyment in others. The cook, always the surly and resentful butt of oaths and ribald jokes, was motivated by her compliments to cook food which was edible. Everyone watched out for snakes for her, and on the high mountain passes Rhineman refused to allow her to ride in the carriage around the narrow curves overlooking deep gorges. She was amused by his concern, but he tied his horse to the tailgate of a wagon and walked with her along the dangerous spots until the way was safe again. Eventually his previous dread of such places almost turned into anticipation because of the pleasure he found in walking with her and enjoying her enjoyment of the flowers, birds, and trees.

Everyone in the wagon train was willing to forego the triumphant entry into Santa Fe because Rhineman refused to allow what was left of the carriage to race down the last mile of bumpy road with Celise inside it, but Celise asked him to send the rest of the wagon train on ahead and give the men their reward of excitement and noise after the toil of weeks. Santa Fe was still in an uproar when Rhineman rode through with the battered carriage rumbling along behind him. People waved, called out, and craned their necks to get a glimpse of Celise. Rhinaldea had turned out to meet her, a solid mass of people lining the road from the main road to the house, all of them cheering and waving. The carriage stopped in front of the house at the end of the journey, the trail home lined with grave markers to testify to the grueling hardships. But Celise had the composure of a gracious hostess who has just come from her dressing room as she stepped from the carriage to meet the people in charge of the different parts of the business lined up in front of the porch.

Frau Topol adored her, seeming entranced with the sound of Celise's voice in German almost to the point of missing what she was saying, and she immediately had a fierce, protective dedication toward her. She rushed Celise into the rooms which had been prepared for her and began overseeing the men carrying in Celise's belongings from the wagons, snapping at them irritably when they bumped trunks and boxes together and glaring at Rhineman jealously when he went in to see his wife.

Rhineman had anticipated allowing her at least a few days of rest after the journey, but she laughed it off gaily and they went to dinner at the rabbi's house the following night, to which several more families had been invited. There was a gathering two nights later which included much of the business community, a few officers and their wives from the fort, and a few of the *rico* families, and a couple of nights after that they were invited to a reception at the Territorial Governor's mansion.

As one of the preeminent businessmen in the Territory, Rhineman was well known to the Governor and had been duly invited to social functions. His relationship with the Governor had been less than close and extensive because of the Governor's outspoken support of the Union position during the Civil War and because of Rhineman's instinctive distrust of governmental functionaries. Their attitude had been one of mutual, wary cordiality resulting from the Governor's knowledge that Rhineman exercised heavy influence in the business community and Rhineman's knowledge that government policies exerted an impact on his business affairs, but within minutes after Celise met the Governor and his wife, Rhineman found himself being warmly regarded by the Governor.

Both the Governor and his wife were charmed by Celise's appearance and poise, but after conversing for a moment with her Celise became the most highly regarded guest in the house. The Governor's uncle was the ambassador to Paris, and Celise still corresponded with a friend she had known in Warsaw who was married to a minister of foreign affairs in the French government. The Governor's wife disengaged herself from her other guests and began escorting Celise around to make sure she had met everyone. The Governor got Rhineman a drink and began congratulating him warmly on the success of his irrigation projects and asking him if he could use them as a model to show dignitaries he was inviting from Washington with a view toward requesting federal funding for irrigation of public lands.

The Bishop of the Diocese of Santa Fe was there, a tall, spare man in his sixties who occasionally appeared at social functions in his black cassock with violet piping and violet silk skullcap. He was French, a reserved and ascetic-looking man, and Rhineman respected him for what he had done to pressure *rico* families into better treatment of their peons. He was inclined to be distant, but his aloof detachment faded into delight when Celise was introduced to him and began chatting with him in French. In a way it looked strange, but in another way it seemed very natural for them to be standing together and conversing animatedly in French, the tall man in his robes with a wide smile on his features and the slender woman looking very beautiful as she lifted a hand in a graceful gesture to emphasize a point. The amethyst encircled with small pearls he wore on his hand and the Star of David she wore at her throat representing no barrier to the two European sophisticates.

The following days brought other invitations, and while Rhineman caught up on what had happened while he had been gone, Celise was drawn into the social circles around the Territorial Governor's wife, at the fort, in the Jewish community, and in the business community. The Bishop called on her and brought wine, and she returned his calls and took flowers and fruit. When the next wagon train went out, it took with it a large bundle of letters she had written to friends in London, Paris, Warsaw, St. Petersburg, and a number of places in between.

Rhineman had wanted a wife with social talents, and he found that she spanned the social circles in Santa Fe with a skill that left him befuddled. He overheard a short conversation between her and an officer's wife during a reception at the fort which displayed how adeptly she handled a variety of social situations.

"Somebody told me that your husband just sort of made a deal to marry you while you were in New York. I can tell you that my Bill would never marry somebody he hadn't seen."

"You are fortunate he is so circumspect. Do your children have normal vision?"

The were other instances. For the most part, she was entertaining and serenely cordial and polite, with no hint of snobbery. He had noticed with gratification that she made friends with women as quickly as men, and that she could be amiable with men while leaving no doubt that no suggestion of anything beyond a social relationship would be tolerated. But there was jealousy and spite among some because of the way she had entered Santa Fe and taken it by storm and because of her alluring charm and beauty, and some ventured to be catty. But when they did, they found themselves in the position of a dwarf assaulting a giant. Her tongue and her mind had been honed to a deadly edge in the salons and drawing rooms of Warsaw and St. Petersburg, where slashing repartee from behind a brilliant smile had been practiced as a fine art for centuries. Some he overheard were so subtle that it took him days of puzzling to unravel the meaning buried in the seeming non sequitur, at which time he would burst into laughter and get surprised looks from whoever happened to be around. Others had the immediate, devastating effect of a broadside with cannon, leaving the one who had tried to match wits stuttering in embarrassed confusion and others around choking with contained laughter. And all of them were delivered with the polite smile and attitude of one venturing a comment on the weather. At the same time, she never harbored resentment and she was always willing to accept an adversary of a moment as a friend, and eventually they either shunned her or made peace.

When he took her to fulfill his promise of buying a horse for her, he found that he wasn't immune to her wit when he attempted to skirt around what she believed had been promised. One of the horse dealers had a large, young gelding, but he appeared as vicious as Rhineman's horse and the dealer wanted too much money for him. He was a beautiful animal, in perfect condition and his bulging muscles rippling under his sleek, shining skin, but the price was fifteen hundred dollars.

"I can't go a dime below that, General," the dealer said apologetically. "I've got a bill of sale to show you that I paid thirteen hundred for him in Albuquerque, and I've had him for three months and fed him up some to get him in really top shape before I brought him here. And one of these big ranchers around here will give me the fifteen."

"They might, but I won't. That's too much money, and he's too spirited even if it wasn't. Do you see any other ones you like, Celise?"

"I want that one."

"He's too spirited for you. How about that mare?"

"It would be kind to buy her, wouldn't it? She needs someone to feed her and take care of her. But I would rather wait so we can save up our money and get one I want."

"Save up our money? You talk like I'm a pauper, Celise. I can buy you anything you want."

"I would like that horse, please."

In addition to her other activities, she found time almost every afternoon to go riding on her gelding, and the horse seemed to be docile enough with her, although he bit and kicked a couple of men in the stables. When Rhineman was around the warehouses or the corral, he frequently saw Celise riding on the mountain above Rhinaldea, expertly controlling the large gelding with the reins and her crop. He found that her venturing around the plateau on the mountain above Rhinaldea had taken on a purpose beyond exploring and exercise when the subject of the house was discussed over dinner. Her belongings had congested what he had considered the wastefully large addition which had been made to the house before he had gone to Westport for her, and he was contemplating another addition to give her more room.

"Do you plan to have it made of mud like the rest of the house?" she asked. "The people here are very clever, are they not? Who would have thought someone could build a house of mud."

"It isn't mud, it's adobe."

"Is that the Spanish word for mud?"

"I don't know what it's the Spanish word for, but you need more room and I'll have some workmen come up and see about enlarging the house."

"Workmen? I would have thought the children in the village could make mud blocks."

"Celise, do you consider this house inadequate for you?"

"Of course not, Karl. It is a magnificent house. For one made of mud."

"What would you rather have a house made of? Adobe is the most practical material for construction here."

"Saint Francis is made of stone."

"The Catholic cathedral? That's a cathedral, Celise."

"Made of stone."

"I don't intend to undertake construction on the scale that the Catholic Church does, Celise. And I believe this house is adequate and comfortable."

"Then there is no more to be said, is there?"

The preliminary work on the stone house began about a week later, and Rhineman immediately discovered that his concept of the scale of the proposed house was miniscule compared to Celise's. As were the costs and the length of time required to build it. He had envisioned a house to live in. She had envisioned a house to endure for centuries. They walked together over the plateau on the mountain overlooking Rhinaldea, and she pointed out the dimensions she wanted to have in the house and where the gardens she proposed would extend out behind it and incorporate flowers, bushes, and fruit trees someone had planted on the plateau. There was a tall spire of stone which had been set into a large dish of stone, a somewhat repellant object to him, but she also wanted it left in place and she wanted to use the living stone on the mountain as a foundation for the house. She explained.

"It will take time and money. But we have both, because we are young and you are wealthy. But it is very necessary to spend the time and money, Karl, because of what it will be. This will be the house of Rhineman. From here, the house of Rhineman will overlook Santa Fe. And New Mexico Territory. So we must spend time and money in amounts consistent with what is involved."

There was a volcanic deposit of stone some fifteen miles away, the hard, grey stone from which the cathedral had been built, and Rhineman sent to Colorado for masons to begin quarrying the stone. Workmen cut a road up the mountain and laid a heavy bed in the road to support the sturdy oxen-drawn carts which would bring the stone to the site, and Celise wrote to a friend in Frankfurt, Germany, whose cousin was an architect, giving the dimensions of the plateau and proposed house and asking that plans be drawn up.

Rhineman found that his life had developed dimensions and character which made his life before he married her fade into dull shadows in his mind in comparison, and his pleasure in being around her and conversing with her seemed to constantly grow. Her personality was sparkling, an endless source of enjoyment to him. She was a deeply religious woman, without ostentation but with a sincere depth of commitment. Along with it, she had a sophisticated acceptance of other religions which exceeded his.

"A chapel? A Catholic chapel? In Rhinaldea?"

"Yes, that's right. The Bishop and I were discussing it, and we agreed that it would be a good idea. It is a not inconsiderable distance to the cathedral for people who are ill, and he agreed to send out a priest to conduct services. It would be only a small one, of course. An unused house could be converted."

"The use of the word converted makes me uncomfortable, considering what we are discussing. I think rebuilt would be a better word. And I am more inclined to put money into a synagogue than into a Catholic chapel."

"Come, come, Karl. There are seven Jews in Rhinaldea and some three hundred Catholics."

"I'm talking about the one in Santa Fe."

"If everyone matches our contribution toward the new synagogue in proportion to their means, we will have a magnificent synagogue. But on the subject of the chapel, do you forbid me from proceeding?"

"I will think about it."

"And how long did you have to think about it before you established a saloon and a house of prostitution in Rhinaldea?"

An empty house was being used for a small retail trade in liquor, and some of the unmarried men were using an isolated, empty house to occasionally quarter a couple of women from Calle de la Muralla, which fell short of his definition of a saloon and a house of prostitution. He shook his head. "I have established nothing like that in Rhinaldea, Celise. I am only letting some people use a couple of empty houses for entertainment to keep them out of Santa Fe and out of trouble. And I've ordered them to keep the level of activity in those houses down, and it's small enough that there's no reason for anyone to be offended by it."

"Then I will also let some people use an empty house. If they wish to put a cross on the peak of the roof in the process of their use of it, I will order them to make it small enough to keep it from being offense to anyone."

The discussion about the chapel was only one of several discussions which indicated her strong interest in the welfare of the inhabitants of the village, and the villagers quickly found that she was considerably more severe than Rhineman had been about cleanliness and sanitation. But they also found that they had an immediate and effective source of assistance for any emergency at any time of the day or night, as well as specific and continuing help for mothers and children. She had some of the villagers build a tiny corral at one side of the village and bought cows and goats to put in it so expectant mothers and children would have all the milk they could drink, and she did other things.

Most of what she did in the village was at long range because of the multitude of demands on her time, but she did occasionally get into the village to look around. And Rhineman worried about her finding out about Consuela. He talked to Consuela a couple of times to make sure she and her mother were still getting everything they needed, and he pondered about what to do. The boy obviously hadn't been fathered by a Mexican, he was large and brawny for his age, and a distinct facial resemblance to Rhineman had developed as he began walking and lost the chubby build and face of a baby. At first he had been afraid that Frau Topol might say something, but it became evident that she intended to remain out of the situation, possibly because she was afraid that Celise might leave. Rhineman worried about the same thing. Consuela kept the boy out of sight when Celise was in the village, but it was a constant danger and the situation seemed more hazardous and complicated than what he had envisioned before going to Westport for Celise. If he moved Consuela to Santa Fe, which seemed prudent, it would seem a continuing, secretive affair if Celise happened to find out about it. But if he left Consuela in the village, Celise might consider it only evidence of a passing moral frailty and eventually forgive him if she happened to find out.

While he was contemplating the situation, she found out. He had anticipated perhaps a cold and hostile silence

251

over dinner one evening then an outburst of scathing recriminations, but she was totally consistent in that she invariably dealt with a situation in a way he was unable to even imagine in advance, much less predict. He walked into the house, smiling as he saw Celise sitting in the chair by the buffet and reading a book, then his smile became an expression of consternation as he saw Consuela sitting in a chair in the corner of the room, the boy on her lap and a frightened expression on her face. Frau Topol was rearranging some ornaments on display on a shelf. She looked at Rhineman with triumphant disgust as she crossed the room toward the hallway, and she stalked along the hallway and into the kitchen. Celise glanced at him, her features in neutral lines. She took a book marker off the edge of the buffet, marked her place in the book, and put the book on the buffet. Rhineman took off his hat and combed his fingers through his hair as he looked out the window and sighed heavily.

"I have need of a personal maid," Celise said in a soft, even tone, staring into space in front of her. "Do you have an objection to my engaging a personal maid?"

"Of course not, Celise. I would like to—"

"Thank you. I am engaging this woman you see here as my personal maid. She is young and attractive, and she appears to be highly intelligent. In most areas. She will be able to assist me with my clothes and hair, and she will also be able to assist me in learning Spanish so I will be able to converse freely with everyone here and determine if there are things I should know and of which I am unaware. I have assured her that she will be well paid and well treated, and in no respect will she suffer from misfortunes brought on by the previous mistreatment of those with authority over her."

"Celise, I would like to—"

"You will observe that she has a child. Her child will be brought up in this household as a member of this household. He will be cared for, educated, and treated in other ways as though he were my child, with the exception that he will be reared in the Catholic faith rather than in the Jewish religion."

"Celise, I would like to—"

"In assuming the responsibility for this child, I have discussed his name with his mother. She has agreed that he should have a name which is appropriate with his parentage." She moved her eyes slightly, and they bored into his. "I had contemplated naming my first son Karl, but that wish has been overcome by events, it would appear. This child will be known as Karl Herzen."

He knew enough German that the reference to the heart in the last name wasn't lost on him. It was difficult to face the stony glare in her eyes. He sighed again, looking away and combing his fingers through his hair.

Celise's eyes moved to Consuela, and her expression softened. "Go to my rooms, Consuela," she said quietly.

Conseula rose from the chair and clutched the boy to her as she crossed the room rapidly to the hallway, her sandals slapping on the floor. She disappeared into a doorway. Rhineman looked along the hallway, wondering what was going to happen. Frau Topol stuck her head out of the kitchen doorway and looked at him with the same expression of triumphant disgust, tossed her head and sniffed loudly, then her head disappeared.

"Why didn't you tell me?"

There was no anger in her voice, and her features didn't reflect the dreaded impersonal withdrawal he had overcome in Westport. She was simply asking a question. He thought about what to say to explain, then decided to reply briefly and truthfully. "I was afraid to."

Her lips lifted in a slight smile, and she rose from the chair and picked up her book. "You had reason to be. If I had seen you within the hour after I first saw that child, I might have been a widow." She turned toward the hallway, then turned back, her eyes boring into his again. "Are there any more?"

"No."

She looked into his eyes for a long second and nodded, then her smile returned, a slow, thoughtful smile. "I realize it was lonely for you here, Karl. This is the one thing a woman should never be asked to accept or understand, but I believe I understand in some measure in spite of myself. I understand because I have at least some grasp of how it was here for you. And because I want to understand. I love you, and I want to understand. From a completely detached viewpoint, I suppose it would be difficult to blame you. She is very beautiful." She turned toward the hallway again and turned back once more, her smile widening. "Nor can I blame her."

He watched her walking along the hallway, her book tucked under her arm. He breathed a long, deep sigh, and his shoulders slumped with relief. It was over. There had been a dark and threatening cloud hanging over him, and it was suddenly gone. He hadn't even wanted to contemplate the possibility that he would lose any part of what he had found with Celise, and even as he had been forced into considering it, the danger was past. She looked very beautiful as she moved gracefully along the hallway. And proud, her shoulders and back straight and her long skirt moving slightly as she took firm, even steps. The men's name for her had spread. Throughout Santa Fe she was known as *Doña* Celise. And the name seemed very appropriate.

The first cart came from the quarry, a squat vehicle

built of massive timbers which crushed stones in the road under its low, wide wheels as four span of powerful oxen leaned into their yokes and trudged along the road through Rhinaldea and then up the mountain to the site with a single large slab of grey stone. Within a week after the first one came, four and five were passing slowly along the road each day, and the piles of the stone slabs began to accumulate on the plateau. When Celise was outside the house and glimpsed one passing, she always looked at it with a thoughtful half-smile and watched it until it disappeared up the mountain. Eventually spots of grey on the plateau were visible from Rhinaldea as the piles of stone grew larger, and the carts still continued to move up and down the mountain. The weight of the carts eventually eroded the roadbed, and workmen worked feverishly to sink more stone and repair it to support the carts even as the carts continued moving back and forth and passing among them as they worked on the road, as though the patient strength of the oxen in moving the ponderous slabs of stone were a process with a meaning of its own and an inertia which could not be stopped once begun.

Then the plans arrived from Germany. The design was German Gothic, a breath of the Rhine to be transplanted to the sunny mountains of New Mexico Territory in heroic scale. The main section was to be three storys high with towers capped with steep slate roofs at each corner, with wide wings stretching out on each side. The front entrance was to be huge, spanned with double doors which curved into a dome at the top and then rose to a peak in the center, with flanking windows in the main section which repeated the design and rows of similar but more narrow windows along the front of both wings. Rhineman looked at the ambitious undertaking in silence, allowing Celise to proceed, and he continued to remain silent even when she began modifying the plans of the interior to suit her own tastes.

The business continued to thrive. He expanded his land holdings in the Rio Grande valley, and with the well-digging equipment he had bought in Westport, he bought vast stretches of arid desert in the southeastern part of the Territory and turned it into lush pastures for cattle by pumping the underground water to the surface. While he was absent from home overseeing the fencing and construction of homes on the ranch lands, Celise started her first labor and a courier from Santa Fe brought him racing back in time for the birth of his son Josef.

Saint Michael's College had been established in Santa Fe some years before, but the public school system was of uneven effectiveness and there was a concerted effort to improve it. Celise served on a committee of wives which worked out of the Governor's office and arranged fund-raising drives, and Rhineman made a substantial contribution to the cause. They had more than a passing interest in the matter, because Karl Herzen entered public school that year.

Rhineman started a brewery, locating it in a large building adjacent to the canning factory, and he expanded the canning factory when the processes and equipment were perfected to the point that meat products could be preserved in tins with what was to him an acceptable level of risk of spoilage. There was a period during which the brewery was marginally profitable, then the saloons from Taos to Albuquerque began to buy from him and it started producing a substantial profit.

Each weekend there was a steady flow of sight-seers from Santa Fe to the plateau overlooking Rhinaldea to see what had been done on the house the previous week. It gradually took shape, dozens of workmen laboring around it as the massive walls reared into the sky and became visible from miles away. The stonework of the front entrance was completed, and the doors were shipped from the East, solid panels of seasoned oak three inches thick which were covered with bronze. The upper panes of all the windows were stained glass, and the lower panes were clear glass. The entrance hall took shape, a vaulted cathedral ceiling with staircases on each side leading up to a mezzanine, which opened into corridors on each end. Celise had blended touches of Western decor smoothly into the structure, with wood paneling and places for colorful rugs to hang on the walls. The main sitting room had a massive stone fireplace and hearth, and it was paneled with wood. Rhineman walked around and looked through the place as it began to take its final shape, thinking that the cost of the structure might have been a minor expenditure in comparison to what it would cost to furnish it.

The furnishings and decorations Celise had ordered began arriving, but the first thing which went into the house was the primitive packframe which Karl's father had carried on his first ventures on foot to do trading north of Santa Fe. Celise took it up to the house and hung it over the fireplace in the main sitting room. Then the furnishing and decorating was completed, and the rabbi came and conducted a prayer service. They moved into the house in time to observe passover in it that year, and in time for Eliahu to be born in it.

There were joys and sorrows, successes and failures. Celise had always been quietly observant of the fast days and annual calendar of rituals, and Rhineman became more observant of them to set an example for the children as they became older. Celise delivered a stillborn girl, then the next year a stillborn boy. Rhineman tried to sell a stock issue to capitalize a power and light company for Santa Fe and failed, then he capitalized it himself. It was a poor investment, struggling along with losses each year, but it was of great benefit to Santa Fe and the Rhineman family kept it viable in succeeding years by putting more money into it and taking a loss. In later years, there would be those who raised their voices against people who reaped profits from selling the essentials of life. The Rhineman family would relinquish the power and light company to the control of a public-owned utility structure, and the rates would quadruple within the year.

When Celise was pregnant with Adam, word came to Santa Fe in the middle of winter that an epidemic had struck Shawnee Wells, a town on the eastern slopes of the Sangre de Christo Range. Epidemics of cholera and influenza had wiped out a couple of towns during the past year, and it was a severe winter, with many of the high mountain passes closed. The news was received and absorbed in silence by Santa Fe at large. Rhineman was in San Francisco and Karl Herzen was in training at the Socorro Branch, so Celise sent a courier to Socorro to bring Karl Herzen back while she made her preparations. When he arrived, she left him in general charge of the business and set out across the mountains with a train of thirty mules carrying food, medical supplies, two employees from the hundreds who had volunteered, a medical officer from the fort, a priest, and eight whores she had recruited from Calle de la Muralla to be nurses. They reached the town after struggling through the snow drifts and frigid wind for eight days, and found that it was influenza. Several had died and were unburied, most were too ill to move about, and many had fled into the mountains. A hospital was set up in a saloon, and Celise

258

helped the medical officer and whores care for the ill while the priest conducted funeral services and the employees dug graves. Within a week the crisis was past, and when the whores began practicing their primary profession with their erstwhile patients, Celise gathered together the rest of the party and set out back across the mountains. She was met in a high mountain pass by Rhineman, who had returned from San Francisco and set out after her.

The story of *Doña* Celise's perilous journey through the mountains on her errand of mercy spread like wildfire and exploded into the newspapers across the country. Reporters flocked into Santa Fe to interview her and were refused admittance to the massive house overlooking Rhinaldea, and the one who confused her name with that of one of the whores in the story he filed from the telegraph office in Santa Fe was horsewhipped out of Santa Fe by an enraged Karl Herzen while Rhineman was searching in another part of Santa Fe for the man to kill him. Someone wrote a song about it, and it was popular for a time. Then the story gradually passed into oblivion everywhere except in Santa Fe, where it was incorporated into the legends which had accumulated during the centuries since the conquistadores had ventured north along the Rio Grande.

The arrival of the railroad in Santa Fe sounded the death knell for the Santa Fe Trail and brought the end of an era. The wagons which had traveled east and west from Santa Fe were no longer needed on the overland trails, but they became urgently needed to carry copper ore to the railhead in Santa Fe as the true value of the mine developed. The activity at the brewery mushroomed as the cost of freight from Santa Fe to nearby points over the mountains to the east and west declined and new markets opened up, and in one of the expansions a bottling plant was set up to service outlets other than saloons.

The area expanded, and along with everything else, the graveyard on the slope below the massive stone house grew. By common practice it was in two general sections, a smaller one for the Rhineman family graveyard and a much larger one as a graveyard for employees and retainers. For the most part, stone crosses marked the graves in the larger graveyard and Stars of David marked those in the smaller one, but there were exceptions. Frau Topol became ill and died, and she was buried in the large graveyard, as were other Jewish employees. When Consuela was bitten by a rattlesnake and died, Celise had her buried in the family graveyard to the left of Jacob Rhineman's grave. When her husband died after a lengthy illness, Celise had him buried by Consuela and reserved the space on the other side of him for herself so that in death she would lie on his right side and Consuela on his left.

Chapter 17

The sun beamed down on the marketplace, hot and glaring, and the sonorous voice of B. Franklin Calhoun, candidate for the United States Senate, filled the marketplace and seemed to make the stifling air more thick and suffocating. An adobe church filled one side of the square, its sides spotted with places where the whitewash and part of the adobe had crumbled away and the wooden cross on its peak canted to one side, and along the other sides there were a couple of cantinas, a feed and seed, a hardware, a couple of cafes, and the local Rhineman store in long, low adobe buildings with dark porches behind the hitching rails. The marketplace was where the two streets of the town crossed at right angles. Further along the streets there were small adobe houses where burros dozed in the patches of shade, scraggly chickens clucked and scratched the ground busily, and faded clothes hung limply on clotheslines made of unraveled strands of barbed wire. A local entrepreneur had built a rickety platform which stood a couple of feet off the ground on the side of the marketplace facing the church, and it was used for the musicians at local fiestas and other occasions. The speaker stood on the edge of it and exhorted the fifty or so Mexicans scattered around the marketplace, most of them gathered in front of the platform and a few leaning against the hitching rails and the Model A parked at the corner, all of them silent and listening to the speaker.

Adam Rhineman sat on the wooden bench which had been built along the rear of the platform with two of the men in B. Franklin Calhoun's entourage, listening and waiting. The past weeks had been grueling, he was tired with a weariness which seemed to be a heavy weight dragging him down and which would take long, cool days of quiet solitude to dissipate. And he was beginning to wonder if it was worth it. It was perhaps the sixth or seventh time his path had crossed that of B. Franklin Calhoun while working back and forth across the state, and there had been a nagging, growing conviction that he was in a contest in which he was at a disadvantage. He hadn't known the rules at first, and he hadn't known that how things appear means more than how they are. It had seemed a clear, straightforward matter of issues, of presenting his standpoint on matters and letting voters choose between his standpoint and that of others, but that naive concept had quickly died when the visits from the professionals who had offices near the courthouse in Santa Fe had started. So he had made concessions to get party support, but they had also made concessions because the name of Rhineman automatically drew widespread support in New Mexico and he would have split the party wide open as an independent.

But Calhoun also had the support of his party, and he was good. A large, portly, white-haired and florid-faced man originally from Ohio, and a thoroughly professional politician. He even looked like a Senator. As impersonal as a doctor working on a patient, he knew what had to be done and he did it. Adam had talked to him a few times in more or less private situations, and he hadn't been unfriendly. Almost congenial but keeping his cards close to his chest and not giving anything away, a little condescending toward an amateur taking the field against a professional, but a touch of camaraderie because they had the contest in common. In the Little Texas district south of Tucumcari to Carlsbad, where there was a high proportion of anglo ranchers and laborers, a lot of his speeches had consisted basically of subtle derision toward anyone who would even contemplate sending a Jew to the United States Senate.

While prejudice was common enough, there was a firm conviction that Calhoun had no prejudice against Jews. It was simply a handle. There were others. The degree from Harvard Law School was a highfalutin, fancy, and yankeefied education, and the family fortune had brought dark hints that no one who controlled the pocket books of the people should be entrusted to pass laws over them which would enable him to dip deeper into their pocket books. Karl Herzen had even come into it for a time through references to mixed blood within the family, but that had stopped quickly enough some weeks before. Of all the brothers, Karl had turned out to be more like their father in size and disposition, and when he had heard about it he had almost demolished a Model A getting to Roswell to confront Calhoun while he was making a speech—to the utter delight of the crowd, which had been more eager to see a fight than listen to a speech.

263

But Calhoun was also smart, and he learned rapidly. His people had warned him, and each time their paths had crossed his speech had contained no hints or references to Adam. Mexicans were courteous people, and his advisors had warned him that seeing someone insulted to their face would automatically put them on the side of the injured party. So the speech was on general matters, how the newest state in the Union was also the greatest, and how it had to be capably represented in Washington. The deep, booming voice was very impressive, but it lost some of its effect in the more modest tones of the interpreter, as well as something of the intent.

Calhoun finished, whipping out a large handkerchief and wiping his brow as he beamed around the marketplace. There was polite applause, and some of the people murmured to each other. Adam gathered himself, summoning his energies for one more try, and he made his smile wide and friendly as he stood up, looking at Calhoun. Calhoun hesitated for an instant as Adam stepped toward him, smiling widely and extending his hand, then he quickly put his hand out. It had happened each time they had met in front of a crowd, and the first two times Calhoun had lost the crowd to Adam. The people watching were Adam's, not Calhoun's, and it was Adam's instinctive knowledge that to these people a gesture of friendliness meant total confidence and no fear of the opponent. In Calhoun's terms of reference and in his experience it meant the opposite, so he had miscalculated and lost two crowds. But his advisors had apparently told him about his mistake, and after the second time his smile had been as wide and his handshake as enthusiastic as Adam's. They pumped each other's hand and patted each other's arm, nodding and smiling widely at each other, then Adam moved toward the edge of the platform and Calhoun sat down on the bench. That was something else his advisors had apparently told him about. He had lost the third crowd to Adam through the snub implicit in leaving and not listening to what Adam had to say.

Adam didn't use an interpreter because he didn't need one. He was truly bilingual, his rhythm of speech in English reflecting the Spanish he had spoken from childhood and his vowels in Spanish reflecting that he spoke English most of the time. And he didn't talk about how great New Mexico was. He talked about how poor it was. About what it needed. The irrigation projects to grow more food and make pasture for more cattle, and industry to make more jobs for people. He didn't call the place Lordsburg, because he knew they called it Cactus in their own language, and he pointed out why it was an appropriate name for it and how it might be called Corn if there were sufficient water to grow anything except cactus. He talked quietly and slowly, his eyes moving from face to face as he phrased the sentences in the figures of speech used by those who wore cotton pants and sandals. The men leaning against the hitching rails and the Model A moved slowly across to join the rest of the crowd, the sombreros clustering together as they looked up at him.

It wasn't a speech, because he didn't know how to make a speech. He only knew how to talk to people and explain a standpoint or series of facts, as he had talked to juries and judges. He explained to them what he wanted to do about the things they needed. He talked about voting, telling them that the time when they could point to the east and curse the *tejanos* for their problems were past, that the means to deal with their problems now lay in their own hands. It was voting. New Mexico was a state and they were citizens, and they had to vote. If they voted for his opponent, if they voted for him, or if they wrote in their own name on the ballot was of secondary importance to the fact of voting. They had to vote. New Mexico was a state and they were citizens, but none of it meant anything if they failed to vote. Then he thanked them.

There was polite applause, Calhoun pumped his hand again, and they stepped down from the platform as the people murmured to each other and began moving away. The man who owned the platform weaved through the people toward Adam and Calhoun to collect his fifteen cents from each of them for using the platform. Adam took change from his pocket and gave the man a dime and five pennies, and he tightened his lips to keep his smile from forming as he glanced at Calhoun and walked across the street to where his horse was tethered to a hitching rail. Calhoun had pulled a thick roll of bills from his pocket and peeled off a bill, and the owner of the platform had turned away to go to a store and get change. The man didn't know the people. All during the time he had been campaigning, Adam had kept a couple of dollars in change in his pockets so when he paid for something he could count out the coins. As they did.

Adam mounted his horse and turned it along the street to the east. A few of the people waved, and Adam nodded to them and lifted his hand. Calhoun and his people were walking to the corner where they had left their Model A, and Calhoun waved. Adam waved to him and let his horse out to a slow canter. Within a hundred feet of passing the last house, there was only a dirt road ahead and the untouched desert on both sides. A moment later he heard Calhoun's Model A rattling and popping along behind him, and he reined his horse to one side of the road. The

266

Model A roared past in a cloud of dust, bouncing and clattering along the rough road. It was obscured by the dust as soon as it passed. The dust was thick for a few minutes, then it began settling as the noise of the automobile diminished. Presently the automobile was only a spot of dust in the distance.

On the face of it, Adam had a clear advantage. He was a native New Mexican, he spoke the language, and his name automatically drew a lot of support. But it wasn't that simple. Calhoun's stronghold was Little Texas, and he had canvassed the area so thoroughly and sounded such dire warnings that they would all vote. In addition, Calhoun had strong support from many of the large *rico* families. The Rhineman family had a cordial social relationship with virtually every *rico* family in the state, but over the years the peons on the *rico* estates had become more restless and demanding because of the visible example represented by the progressive employment practices in the Rhineman business activities. So most of the *rico* families wouldn't want a Rhineman in Washington. Both they and the anglo owners of large holdings exercised a heavy influence over the people who worked for them.

The next town was Deming, referred to as Encino by most of the Spanish speaking people, and the local Rhineman store was operated by a man named Alvarado. The town was small, a half dozen businesses and perhaps twice that many houses stretched along the road. Alvarado put Adam's horse in the stable adjacent to his house behind the store. Adam shared their dinner of beans and tortillas and slept in a leanto at the back of the house which had been vacated by an older son who was working at the store in Grants. The following morning Adam walked through the town and shook hands and

267

talked to a few of the people. Most of the people in the area worked on a large ranch north of the town owned by a *rico* family, and he had been through the town several times on weekends and had talked to most of them while they were in town drinking or shopping. At about ten he saddled his horse and thanked Alvarez and his wife for their hospitality, and he rode on toward the east.

The Model A had broken down while driving from Almagordo to Las Cruces four days before. He had walked the remaining fifteen miles into Las Cruces to the company yard, told them to go and pick up the automobile, and had taken the horse from the stables and rode on. At the time it had seemed almost a disaster because there had been no available trucks in the yard and he had wanted to circle on north through Silver City once more. But in retrospect it seemed much less important. He had been to Silver City several times, and there was nothing he could say that he hadn't said before. The ride on the horse had given him time to think instead of worrying about every rock and rut in the road ahead. To think and wonder if it had been worth it.

The business had changed over the years. The miners and trappers had disappeared, and the original trading circuits had collapsed and faded into legend and the faulty memories of retired oldsters who limped around the yards on their canes and tried to find those patient enough to listen to their stories. The original structure of the business had changed into a network of distribution centers which delivered to the Rhineman stores, one of which was located in virtually every town in New Mexico. The Los Cruces office had been established fairly recently in comparison with most of the offices, about fifteen years before, and it more or less fit the standard pattern that had been developed for the main distribution centers. The long, low adobe buildings formed three sides of a large rectangle, and they contained warehousing space, stables, a smithy, and a repair shop for trucks. The third side was filled in by a tail adobe wall with gates in it, and a retail store was located at the side of the road and in front of the wall. The open space in the rectangle was used for outside storage of durable goods, lumber, fencing, sheet metal roofing, and similar items, and it was also used for parking the trucks and wagons which were in.

The place reflected a transition. There were two of the tall, massive, old-fashioned freight wagons which were drawn with oxen, and oxen in the stables to pull them. There were six smaller and lighter wagons which were drawn by teams of mules, with mules in the stables for them. There were also trucks. There were strong divisions of viewpoint on whether or not it was progress, as was abundantly evidenced by the bloody noses exchanged by teamsters and drivers, but it was unquestionably a period of transition. The freight wagons were used for transporting bulky, heavy loads when there was no urgency involved, and the smaller wagons were used for lighter loads which had to be in place within a specified time. The trucks were used when things were urgently needed or when the cargo was perishable. But as more trucks were being bought, the freight wagons were gradually being sold off or scrapped, and the trucks were being used more routinely.

As luck would have it, there were two trucks in the yard, one being loaded out of a warehouse. Four days before, the sight of the trucks would have brought a sigh of relief. But after the reflection of the past four days, it seemed just as well that they had been employed for some useful purpose rather than in transporting him to Silver City.

The Model A was repaired, and the repairman bustled around and found the broken axle he had replaced and went into a long explanation of what that had involved. Adam wanted to be on his way, but he contained his impatience and nodded and listened to the incomprehensible explanation in a mixture of Spanish and English. The repairman appeared to be well qualified, but many weren't. There was a story making the rounds of two repairmen in Portales who had dispaired with a truck which wouldn't run and had towed it with a team of mules to a church to have it blessed by a priest. Whether true or not, it aptly represented the difficulty in maintaining the trucks. The original group of men who had been sent to Detroit had come back with stories of the frigid cold, how people jeered at sombreros and boots, how tequila wasn't available, and how whiskey cost three dollars and a whore five. But a few more had gone, a few master mechanics had been found and hired, and an active journeyman training program was in being at several of the distribution centers. So it was less than satisfactory, but it was improving.

The general manager came out and Adam spent a few minutes talking to him, then he left, rattling along the road to the north with two five gallon kerosene cans filled with gasoline in the back. The noise and dust gave a feeling of separation from the terrain, as though it were a kinetoscope scene moving past, and driving an automobile was tiring, a constant jolting motion and a necessity to constantly watch the road ahead. But it was much faster. And an automobile didn't eat fodder when it was parked.

Josef controlled the land holdings, farming, and ranching, and he was headquartered at Socorro, where he was more or less centrally located among the widespread holdings. Adam arrived in Socorro just before dark. He drove to Josef's home, a large, quiet adobe mansion behind high adobe walls not far from the Socorro distribution center yards. Josef was in Clovis on some problem with one of the ranches, and a servant showed Adam to a room. He cleaned up, then he went back downstairs and joined Ruth, Josef's wife. He had met her in Charleston while visiting with some of their grandmother's relatives, and she had remained very much a Southern belle, a soft drawl and a bland exterior concealing a mind like quicksilver.

She perceived that he didn't want to discuss the campaign, and she talked about her children off at school and asked how Martha, Adam's daughter, was doing at Radcliffe. Martha had wanted to come home for the election, and it was more or less typical of her that he had received her telegram that she was on her way within an hour of dispatching a telegram telling her to stay in Cambridge. Ruth laughed softly and told an anecdote about one of her eldest son's children, then she began talking about some woman whose husband had died of a ruptured appendix a few weeks before. Since his wife's death five years before, it seemed to Adam that the entire family had been working in concert to get him married again, including his daughter Martha. Ruth was more subtle than some of the others, but she still managed to communicate that the woman was attractive, only thirty, and had two well-behaved young children. Then she perceived that he didn't want to hear about it, and she changed the subject again. Josef was a lucky man. She was a good woman, intuitive, entertaining, and a good conversationist. And her voice filled a void of silence for him and kept him from thinking about the election until he was tired enough to go to bed and go to sleep.

271

He left early the following morning and drove on north to Albuquerque. It had been expanding rapidly during the past few years. When the costs of rebuilding some of the buildings at the distribution centers had escalated some time before, a large team of workmen had been formed to make the rounds and repair or rebuild the buildings at all of them. At about the time that finished, there had been a boom in real estate in Albuquerque because of a large influx of people, and instead of disbanding the construction team they had been put to building houses on a family land holding just south of the main part of Albuquerque and north of Isleta. The profits had been astronomical, more land had been bought up, and Rhineman Construction had come into being.

Eliahu, who controlled financial matters and the banking interests, was headquartered in Albuquerque in the family bank. It was in a new building on Central and Fourth, a tall, modern brick building which had surprised everyone but Eliahu by quickly amortizing the costs of its construction by revenues from leasing office space on the upper floors. The inside of the bank was modestly luxurious, with an atmosphere of quiet efficiency, and Eliahu came out of a meeting to spend a few minutes talking with Adam. The conversation was mostly anecdotes about Eliahu's function as the overseer of a dormitory for the family children attending the university, as he referred to his house located on East Central. Then Eliahu perceived Adam's discouraged attitude about the election, and he thought it hilarious. He clearly believed Adam's chances of winning the election were good, and if it turned out otherwise he viewed losing the election as less than a defeat in meaningful terms. And Adam thought differently in both instances. They talked for a few minutes, then Adam left and drove on north.

He stopped for a few minutes at his office before driving on through to the Rhinaldea District, and Martha was there. She squealed with delight, her warm brown eyes flashing and her teeth sparkling as she raced across the outer office and threw herself at him.

"Dad!"

He hugged her and kissed her, then stood back from her with his hands on her shoulders and looked down at her, trying to get a stern expression on his face. "Martha, you are supposed to be at Radcliffe, and you are—"

"I knew it, I knew it, what did I tell you?" she chattered, looking at the receptionist with an exaggerated expression of distress. "Didn't I say that would be the first thing he said?" She turned back to him, pushing out her lower lip in a mock pout. "Now do you think I'd miss this? My own dad maybe being a Senator? And anyway I have permission. It's right over here in my purse, and I'll show you—"

"From whom? You don't have permission from me, because I sent—"

"From the dean, that's who! Do you think I'd just twenty three skiddoo from college? After all the lucre you've spread out for me to—"

"All right, all right," he chuckled, shaking her slightly. He started to say something else, then looked down at her, studying her face. She was very beautiful. And very much like her mother had been. And he loved her very much. He put his arm around her shoulders and turned her toward his office, looking at the receptionist. "Hello, Miss Fowler. Is Mr. Ortega in?"

"Hello, Mr. Rhineman, and welcome home. No sir, he's in court, but he's due back just any moment."

He paused, lifting his eyebrows. Ortega was in charge of the office in Adam's absence, and the normal office

273

routine left little time for courtroom work. "In court? It must be a big one."

"It's a hearing on the Rancho Murieta case, sir."

Adam nodded, walking toward his office with Martha again. "That's a big one. Would you ask him to come in when he returns?"

"Yes sir. Was it a pleasant trip?"

"It's more pleasant to be back."

She chuckled politely in response to the humorous tone in his voice as he opened the door of his office and led Martha in. He closed the door, atuomatically started to look at his desk to see what was on it, then firmly turned away from it and looked down at Martha.

"Is it going any better for you now, baby?"

She grinned and started to reply with an emphatic affirmative, then hesitated and nodded, her grin fading to a thoughtful smile. "It's all right, Dad. And you were right—I'm learning. Some stand around and hate at me, none stand around and love at me, but I haven't walled myself off. So I've made a few friends, and it's all right."

He nodded and sighed heavily, walking over to his desk and sitting down in his swivel chair. "I hope I did the right thing in sending you there."

"You bet you did," she said firmly, following him and perching on the edge of his desk. "Because this is going to prepare me to do a few things. And I mean real things. I'd never be satisfied with squirting out a few babies and calling that a life's work, and this will—"

"Martha!" he exclaimed, frowning darkly. "What are they teaching you there?"

She leaned toward him, her eyes large in a comically exaggerated expression of consternation. "You mean I'm not supposed to know yet?" she intoned in a hoarse voice.

He tried to maintain a concerned, fatherly expression,

but the laughter burst through and he leaned back in his chair and began laughing. She wrinkled her nose at him and giggled, leaning over to punch him in the ribs, and he pushed her hands away, shaking his head and laughing harder.

She sat back on the edge of the desk, looking at him with a fond smile. "All right, Dad, I've got just one really important thing to talk to you about, and then I'll get out of the hair you used to have."

He chuckled and nodded, leaning forward and reaching for his wallet. "How much?"

"No, it isn't . . . well, you can let me have ten, and then I'll tell you about the important thing."

"I have to pay you to tell me what you want from me?"

"Come on, Dad. Mr. Ortega will be here in a minute, then you two will be muttering about torts and briefs and I won't be able to make myself heard."

He chuckled again, taking out his wallet and giving her ten dollars, then he put his wallet back in his pocket and sat back. "All right, what is it? And if it's having an automobile at Radcliffe, you can—"

"No, it's more important than that," she said, tucking the money into her pocket. "It's this. Mrs. Kaplan told me that there's to be a state-wide Hadassah meeting in Albuquerque next Tuesday, and I told her I'd see if I could get you to be one of the speakers. Now this is—"

"Tuesday? I'm not sure, baby, because I—"

"Now this is important to me, Dad," Martha said in a firm tone, pointing her finger at him and looking at him narrowly. "I intend to have a national office in Hadassah by the time I'm out of Radcliffe, and I'll never make it if my home chapter doesn't support me. And they won't support me if I can't deliver on a little thing like this."

He drew in a deep breath and sighed, nodding his head.

"I'll try. And it isn't a little thing, Martha. I haven't been in this office a full day for weeks, not to mention what all I'll have to do if lightening strikes and I win that election. So all I can say is that I'll try."

She started to say something, hesitated, then nodded and slipped off the edge of the desk. "All right, I'll leave it at that. For now. But you'll hear more about this."

"I don't doubt that for a moment," he murmured wryly. "Go on up to the house, and I'll see you up there."

She nodded and smiled, leaning over and kissing him, then she hesitated as she started to walk toward the door. "What are you driving?"

"A Model A."

"Wonderful!" she chortled, taking a key from her pocket and dropping it on his desk. "Let me have the key to it, and you can take the truck."

He frowned, taking the key from his pocket and handing it to her. "Those trucks are for deliveries, Martha, not for gadding about around Santa Fe."

She wrinkled her nose and giggled, shaking the key in her hand as she walked toward the door. "Then you should hurry and get it back to the yard, shouldn't you? I'll see you at the house."

He laughed wryly and shook his head as she opened the door and went out, winking at him over her shoulder. He took the stack of papers out of the tray on the corner of the desk and placed them in front of him. They were summaries of cases which had been through the office, mixed in with some correspondence which Ortega had determined he should see. He closed his eyes, collecting himself, then sighed heavily and began reading through the papers.

When he had come home from Harvard, it had been with the idea of managing the ever-increasing complexity of the legal affairs of the family business. He had, and his office continued to do so, but from the beginning there had been a sideline activity in land claims. The old original Spanish land grants had been based on faulty surveys, with boundaries established at creeks and arroyos which sometimes changed over the years, and they had frequently overlapped. Parcels of land bought from the original owners had also frequently overlapped and sometimes hadn't been properly registered, and a fire shortly after the area became New Mexico Territory had destroyed many records. As the population grew and land in some areas began to be measured in yards rather than in miles, the disputes multiplied. Over the years his office had expanded to twelve attorneys, several of them specialists in dealing with litigation on land claims, and most of the summaries in the pile of papers were on the status of various land claim cases.

Ortega came in and they talked for a few minutes, then Adam left. Over the years the rising land values had edged the main center of the business further north, and eight years before it had been completely rebuilt two miles north of the city and consisted of a large yard and a sprawling complex of warehouses adjacent to a railroad siding. Adam went to the yard and found a driver to drive him to the house and return the truck to the yard, and they went back along the road toward Santa Fe and turned off into the Rhinaldea District. It was a sea of houses in neat, orderly rows which extended over the hill adjacent to the road and up the side of the mountain toward the family home.

There was always a sense of homecoming when he saw the huge house in its majestic, isolated splendor among the towering trees, and there was a quiet and restful atmosphere of ancient gentility about it. A maid told him that his mother was sitting in the back garden, and he went to his rooms, cleaned up and changed clothes, and went back downstairs and out into the back gardens to talk to her.

It was her favorite place to sit, at the end of a long stone walk which led back through the luxuriantly thick growth of shrubbery, flower beds, and trees. There was a stone bench near a tall, thick spire of rock embedded in a flat dish of stone, which Martha had identified as a phallic symbol with an expression of smug worldly wisdom while at home on vacation the summer before, and part of the foliage had been trimmed away to give a view of the valley from the bench. She was sitting on the bench with her cane leaning against the end of it, the flowing skirt of the old-fashioned dress with a tight bodice and long, tight sleeves tucked around her ankles. Her hair was snowy, thick and long and piled up on her head, her face was deeply lined and wrinkled but somehow didn't look it, and the large, blue eyes looked like those of a twenty-year-old. He bent over her and kissed her.

"Hello, *Doña* Celise."

"Good afternoon, Adam. It is pleasant to have you home again."

He smiled as he sat down. "Well, it's all over now. The voting is tomorrow."

"Tomorrow? Then it is hardly over. Tomorrow is when it begins."

He chuckled and nodded, and his smile faded as he looked at her. Her voice was clear, without the tremor of most old people. Her accent was strong, basically British pronunciation with an overtone of a Southern accent she had picked up from her husband, in addition to a heavy accent which sounded almost French. Her back and shoulders were straight, not touching the backrest on the bench, and she was a slender woman. And a giant. He felt guilty over the fact that his wife had never become the central female figure in his life, but his guilt was tempered by the fact that his mother towered over other people like the grey stone mansion overlooked Santa Fe.

"I'm afraid I'm going to lose."

"That is impossible. You will be either be elected a Senator or you will have gained knowledge which will be invaluable the next time."

Her sympathy had always been predicated on the assumption that the recipient had an iron will and unending endurance and determination, which hardly qualified as sympathy. He nodded glumly. They sat in silence for a few minutes, then she reached for her cane and gathered herself to rise. At fifty a horse had fallen with her and rolled over her, breaking her hip and leg, and she had been using a cane since. But she had continued to ride until she reached sixty. He rose, making an abortive movement to reach for her arm.

"May I help you, *Doña* Celise?"

"Help yourself, Adam," she replied crisply.

Her steps were careful and slow as she crossed the grassy space by the tall spire and wide dish of stone, then they became firm and sure on the walk, her cane tapping against the stones as he walked beside her.

"We should have paving stones put around your bench for you."

"No. I started to have that paved a long time ago, and the workmen found bones of people buried there. So it should be left as it is. I can manage if they can."

He looked over his shoulder at the grassy area around the bench, and he nodded as he turned back and walked beside her toward the house.

Martha chattered gaily as the three of them ate dinner.

279

Celise enjoyed listening to her, smiling quietly and looking at her as she slowly ate. Adam expected Martha to bring up the Hadassah meeting over dinner, but she didn't. She talked about events at Radcliffe and other things as they sat at one end of the massive table, and her voice seemed to be lost in the far reaches of the distant corners of the large dining room. Returning home seemed to have brought the accumulated fatigue of weeks crashing down on Adam, and he went to bed early and slept soundly.

The following morning he went to the courthouse in Santa Fe to vote, and most of the candidates for the various offices were there, making pontifical statements to reporters and posing for photographers. It seemed very tiresome and futile, but he went through the motions for a time and then went to his office.

Josef, Eliahu, and Karl began arriving during the afternoon and were all there in time for dinner, ostensibly to pay a call on Celise because they happened to be in the area and reflecting surprise that everyone was there, but they had all come prepared to spend the night. Martha was having dinner with a family in Santa Fe, and the four of them had dinner with Celise, discussing a few business matters of general interest and their families. Celise went to her rooms, and they went into the main sitting room and sat in the chairs around the fireplace. Ortega telephoned from the office of the Secretary of State in the Capitol Building to let Adam know that he was watching the returns as they were counted in the districts and the results were telephoned in. Scattered returns were starting to come in from the Little Texas district, and Calhoun was well ahead.

Martha returned home at nine, her arrival announced by the slamming of the front door and a giggling comment to a maid, and she came into the sitting room. "Hello, Dad. Hello, Uncle Josef, Uncle Eliahu, and Uncle Karl. May I fix anyone a drink?"

"May I fix anyone a drink," Adam repeated, chuckling wryly and glancing around at the others. "I keep wondering what they're teaching her at Radcliffe, but I'm afraid to ask."

They laughed, and Martha giggled. "How is it going, Martha?" Eliahu asked.

"It couldn't be better, Uncle Eliahu, thank you," she replied, smiling at him, then looked around again. "No one for a drink? Well, I'll go on up to my room so you can tell dirty jokes, then. Say, Dad, there was a piece in the newspaper today about a fortune teller who said you were going to win the election. But she's the same one who predicted that earthquake last year that didn't happen."

They laughed again, and she walked toward the doorway, wrinking her nose and winking at her father as he laughed and nodded. She went through the doorway, and her smile faded as she walked toward the staircase and glanced at a large clock against the wall in the entry hall. It was still too early for a meaningful number of ballots to have been counted. She trotted up the stairs and walked along the corridor to her room, passing her grandmother's rooms. There was a light showing under the door to her grandmother's sitting room. She hesitated, then continued walking on along the corridor and went into her room.

She glanced disinterested through some books she had brought with her, then pushed them aside with a grimace and walked toward the bed, yawning and stretching. She kicked off her shoes and lay down on the bed, staring up at the ceiling, then she yawned again and closed her eyes. Presently her breathing became deep and regular.

Her eyes popped open and she glanced quickly around the room, orienting herself, then she looked at a clock on a shelf. It was just after eleven. She sat up, yawning and stretching, worked her feet into her shoes, and crossed the room and went out into the corridor, closing the door quietly behind her. As she walked along the corridor, she noticed that the light was still showing under the door to her grandmother's sitting room. She knocked on the door hesitantly, then opened it and looked inside. The door to the bedchamber was open on the other side of the room, and she could see her grandmother sitting up in bed and reading. She entered and closed the door quietly behind her, and walked across the room.

"Gran? I saw your light on, and I wondered if you were all right."

"Yes, I felt like reading for a bit, Martha."

"But it's way past your bedtime, and I thought..." Her voice faded as she moved closer to the bed, looking at the book. "Gah! Heine! And in the original! And in script, yet!"

Celise chuckled softly, shaking her head. "The enjoyment is well worth the effort of learning, Martha."

"I'll take your word for it. Can I get you anything, Gran?"

"Yes, I think I would like a small glass of wine, Martha."

Martha nodded, turning back toward the doorway, then hesitated and turned back. "Gran, there's something I've been thinking of talking to you about..."

"What is that, Martha?"

"There's this state-wide Hadassah meeting in Albuquerque next Tuesday, and they asked me to ask Dad to speak at it. I talked to him, and he said he would if he could. But I was thinking that if you would mention it to

282

him, then there would be no question..."

Her voice faded as Celise shook her head, smiling slightly. "No, I can't presume to allocate your father's time for him, Martha."

"But this is important, Gran."

"I agree. It is highly important. But he has other important matters as well, and only he can decide which takes precedence among them."

"But how could anything else he might have to do even begin to compare in importance with this, Gran?"

"You ask me to give you a measure for comparing matters of religion against those of the world? Very well. Jesus of Nazareth said, 'Render unto Caesar the things that are Caesar's, and unto God the things that are God's.' That is the only measure I know, and it is the one I have used all of my life. And it is up to each person and that person alone to decide which is which."

Martha looked at her for a moment in silence, frowning thoughtfully and thinking, then she smiled slightly and nodded as she turned toward the doorway again. "Thank you, Gran. I'll go get your wine for you." She stopped in the doorway and looked back at her grandmother with a timid smile. "And could you not tell Dad that I asked you to talk to him about the meeting?"

"I won't unless he asks me specifically, and if he does happen to ask me I'll see that he doesn't become angry at you."

Martha grinned and wrinkled her nose at her grandmother, nodding, and walked across the sitting room to the corridor door. As she opened the door, she could hear the distant murmur of masculine voices laughing and talking in excited tones. She frowned slightly and cocked her head to one side, listening, then her eyes widened and she raced through the doorway, leaving the door open and running along the corridor toward the mezzanine. A moment later her footsteps came back along the corridor, and she skidded into the sitting room, shouting.

"Gran! He won! Dad won! He won the election!"

Celise smiled calmly and nodded. "I am very pleased, my dear. Go down and congratulate him, and ask him to come up and see me so I may."

Martha nodded rapidly as she wheeled and darted back across the sitting room, and she slammed the door behind her with a loud boom as she ran out into the corridor. Celise put her book to one side and closed her eyes, drawing in a deep breath and releasing it in a long sigh. Her lips began trembling, and she pressed them tightly together, controlling herself. She opened her eyes, and they were swimming in tears. She searched blindly around for her handkerchief on the coverlet, found it, and wiped her eyes. Then she turned her head and looked at the picture on the nightstand by her bed, her lips trembling as she smiled.

"Our son Adam is a United States Senator, Karl," she murmured softly.

PRIME TIME
James Kearney

LB499-2 $1.95
Novel

The book that picks up where *Network* left off . . . The explosive novel of violent power struggles inside a giant television network. The United Television Network. Outside an austere glass facade . . . inside a seething hot bed of ambitious men and women whose motto was "show your rivals no mercy" . . . men and women who would get what they wanted at any cost. (Foil cover)

FLAME IN A HIGH WIND
Jacqueline Kidd

LB500-X $1.50
Adventure

A Powerful novel of romance and adventure on the high seas. The War of 1812 ended for all but Capt. Denny Poynter. Branded pirate, pursued by British and Americans alike, he fought and plundered his way around the world. But his reckless freedom would be soon jeopardized as his first lady, the sea, gave way to the fiery Renee.

THAT COLLISION WOMAN
Deidre Stiles

LB501-8 $1.95
Novel

Fleur Collison was known as the most beautiful and wilful woman in all England. The young English-woman would return to her ancestral home of Ravensweir despite the fact that it was inhabited by her former lover, now brother-in-law. She was determined to take what she wanted from the world . . . and her sister.

ELENA
Emily Francis

LB502-6 $1.50
Mystery

The commune on this small Greek island lived a placid life among ancient monuments and clear blue sea until Elena came. They gave her friendship and love. She brought them death.

HOW TO DIVORCE YOUR WIFE
Forden Athearn

LB503-4 $1.95
Nonfiction

Practical advice for men from an experienced divorce lawyer, Forden Athearn on what to do before you tell your wife, how to tell your wife, family, boss, how to select a lawyer, and more!

DAY OF THE COMANCHEROS
Steven C. Lawrence

LB504-2 $1.50
Western

Slattery had witnessed the rape, murder, and pillage by the savage Comancheros but it wasn't personal until they put him on the end of a rope. No one dared stop them. Someone had to.

KILLER SEE, KILLER DO
Jonathan Wolfe

LB505-0 $1.50
Mystery

It started out as an innocent Halloween party. But innocent soon turned to bizarre when the treats stopped and a trick involving voodoo brought death to the scene. Someone was jailed and Indian detective Ben Club meant to set him free.

GUNSMOKE
Wade Hamilton

LB506-9 $1.50
Western

Ben Corcoran had become boss of Sageville range by killing anyone who tried to settle. When the quiet gambler came to town no one took notice . . . until he led the farmers in bloody revolt. First Time in Paperback.

DEATH IN FIVE BOXES
Carter Dickson

BT51203 $1.50
Novel

All four had been drugged. One had been killed, a sword umbrella through his back. Had it been a meeting of a crime cartel? Had it been a ruse for murder? Sir Henry Merrivale had to find the answer.

"If you want ingenuity of plot, airtight development, and good pungent writing, this is your meat."
—New Haven Journal Courier

THE SECOND LADY CAMERON
Frieda Thomsen

BT51204 $1.50
Gothic

No sooner had Barbara married Lord Cameron of Glen Tor than she discovered the strange and terrible curse that plaugued all Cameron women. Now that she too was a Cameron, Lady Barbara was in jeopardy. It took all her courage to enter the gloomy castle, and all her strength to resist death who was waiting to come for her. A BT Original.

BAD GUY
Nicholas Brady

BT51202 $1.50
Adventure

In the tradition of Gator McCloskey, Jake Colby, Southern stock car racer cum hillbilly hoodlum runs a dope ring for a big city mobster. When Colby double crosses his boss in a Vegas heist both the cops and hoodlums are after his hide. Teaming with a wild Creole girl he sets out on a one way ride through the all night glare of Las Vegas and into hell. A BT Original.

SEND TO: LEISURE BOOK
P.O. Box 270
Norwalk, Connecticut 06852

Please send me the following titles:

Quantity	Book Number	Price
_____	_____	_____
_____	_____	_____
_____	_____	_____
_____	_____	_____
_____	_____	_____

**In the event we are out of stock on any of your
selections, please list alternate titles below.**

_____	_____	_____
_____	_____	_____
_____	_____	_____
_____	_____	_____

Postage/Handling _____

I enclose . . . . . . _____

FOR U.S. ORDERS, add 35¢ per book to cover cost of postage
and handling. Buy five or more copies and we will pay for
shipping. Sorry no C.O.D.'s.

FOR ORDERS SENT OUTSIDE THE U.S.A.
Add $1.00 for the first book and 25¢ for each additional
book. PAY BY foreign draft or money order drawn on a
U.S. bank, payable in U.S. ($) dollars.
☐ Please send me a free catalog.

NAME_____

(Please print)

ADDRESS_____

CITY _____ STATE _____ ZIP _____

Allow Four Weeks for Delivery